Her
Immortal Soul

a Novel

Julien Longo

LOST
COAST
PRESS

Lost Coast Press
155 Cypress Street
Fort Bragg, CA 95437
(800) 773-7782
www.cypresshouse.com

Cover and book Design: Michael Brechner / Cypress House
Cover illustration: after *Astarte Syriaca* by Dante Gabriel Rosetti

Library of Congress Cataloging-in-Publication Data

Longo, Julien, 1966-
    Her immortal soul : a novel / Julien Longo.--1st ed.
       p. cm.
    ISBN 1-882897-83-8 (pbk. : alk. paper)
    1. Heretics, Christian--Fiction. 2. Immortalism--Fiction.
3. Middle Ages--Fiction. 4. Nobility--Fiction. I. Title.
    PS3612.O535H47 2004
    813'.6--dc22   2003024757

PRINTED IN CANADA

2 4 6 8 9 7 5 3 1

*For my mother Diana
Because you are precious in my eyes,
and honored, and I love you.*

AND THE LORD SAID TO THE ARCHANGEL MICHAEL, *Go, and extract Enoch from his earthly clothing. And anoint him with my delightful oil, and put him into the clothes of my glory.* And so Michael did, just as the Lord had said to him. He anointed me and he clothed me. And the appearance of that oil is greater than the greatest light, and its ointment is like sweet dew, and its fragrance myrrh. And it is like the rays of the glittering sun. And I looked at myself, and I had become like one of his glorious ones, and there was no observable difference.

(2 Enoch 22:8–10.)

Prologue

BELOVED,

I have ached for you to return to me. Decades have passed since you held me in your arms, your soft heat falling over me like a velvet cloak. How I have missed you, the tender brush of your lips, your hands on my body, searching in the intimate curves for my eternal soul.

Night comes as I write this. I watch her spreading black wings across the horizon. And then the squall, white wind pulling clouds and rain across the sea to bang on this old tin roof. The sound of the waves rolls up over the cliffs and through the field to meet me here.

Ah, I long for you tonight.

I write this from our little house that faces the sea, still standing against the jungle after all these years. You lived with me here once. It was long ago and you cannot remember it, but you were here with me, my Hawaiian love. Those were long days, ripe and swollen, when we were all that existed. As it has always been, our only enemy was time.

After a thousand glorious days, treasured above all else, you died. Alone, I lived on for too long without you, because I was immortal. I could not die. I could not pass through the veils of unconsciousness to follow you.

Is it possible for you to believe me? To grasp what it is that I say now, the majesty of it and the horror? Immortal. And you once were, too.

Can you imagine how it has been for me all these years, left behind? Remembering your touch, your smell, the soft caring in your voice — it has haunted me. I remember in the end when your body had defeated you and you lay here, on this porch, listening to the wind. Reaching out to me with only your voice. "Dear Heart," you said, "listen to the wind in the bamboo. Do you hear it?"

"Yes, my love."

"That is how I will speak to you soon." Your voice coming softer, "I will be in the wind running through the field, blowing plumeria into your hair the way I like it…." Minutes of pain as you struggled to breathe. "Wear your hair down for me. Let it loose so that I can sweep through it and remember…."

Silence.

I did not have to use my immortal gifts to know that these were our last minutes together. Moving from my useless vigil at the side of your bed, I pulled back the soft patchwork spread and crawled up against your withered frame. All bones where flesh had once been ripe and beautiful. Age had scoured your body as you fought against it, trying so hard for so long to stay with me. Gently pressing my warm, young body against you, a body that has not aged in six hundred years, I touched your flesh for the last time. Laying your head against my breast, I stroked your cheek. Emotion pressed hard on my chest, and my hand shook as I stroked you, unable to speak.

"Justine," you whispered my name.

Then you were gone.

I have stayed sequestered here since then. I have spent all these years letting the wind blow plumeria in my hair, listening for your voice whispering in the bamboo. Many times I have reached out into the world with my immortal vision, searching again and again for your soul's return. I have always known you would come back, but when and how would I find you? More difficult, even if I found you, would you recognize me? I should have known you would come back now, at the dawn of a new millennium, with so much to say and do. I should have realized that you would recognize me, for how can a soul forget its mate?

I have pulled out this old leather book, pages crisp, for me to spill my heart upon. Before you died you gave me this book in this very house, telling me to write it all down, my story, the birth of my immortality. But how could I? You were soon gone and my broken heart could not bear to look back. So it is that I will write it for you now, and perhaps explain for you the magic between us, easing the confusion I see in your eyes. For although you are drawn to me now, I see that you do not understand why. You do not understand who I am and how it is that you feel already an unending love. The mortal you are now cannot remember. I understand. So many mortals have forgotten how to listen to what they know. It is only the persistent voice of your soul speaking through your heart that reveals me.

But I tell you now, you have known me before, and your longing for me is as natural as the sun and the moon and the stars above. I will try to answer your questions by telling it all from the very beginning, from before the day when the holy oil was laid upon me, and my mortality was lost. Perhaps from my tale you will understand. Perhaps, when I have told all, you will even remember.

Part One
Justine

One

IT WAS A HOT SUMMER DAY late in the fourteenth century when they condemned my mother to burn.

A mob took her, men in holy robes leading the villagers from our town. Superstition and ignorance had turned them against her, the countess who had led them through twenty years of peace and prosperity. Fear swelled within their hearts, and a heavy web of injustice spurred them on. They dragged her through the streets, while those who were our friends stood in silence. Gathering in the shadows of the walls, they watched as my mother fought against her persecution, calling out the names of the men who held her to the ground, men she had helped, from families she had saved. But they only turned their heads, or spat on her, shrieking "heretic!" and "witch!" She had tried to reason with them at first, the countess who should be safe in her own streets. Her small body was poised and dignified, hair falling in dark ringlets about her face. But the priest urged them on, thrusting his long finger at her, shaking dramatically beneath his black robes.

"Heretic!" he screamed. "Enchantress!" He seized her by the hair. "Shut your ears to her!" he cried, pulling roughly on her embroidered cloak, pushing her to her knees. "It is the voice of the devil taunting you, trying to reason with your souls!" The men, frenzied and afraid, began to drag her through the dust, toward the great stone bridge and the church, which loomed on the other side.

I would have killed every one of them. Or at least I would have tried. But I was not there. I watched this scene in the calm waters of the goddess pool, miles away in the blue hills.

Two

I HAD ALWAYS HAD THE GIFT OF SIGHT, and surely that is part of what marked me for the events that were to come. Looking back now, I realize that the voices and the presence of immortals had always been with me, only I had not yet recognized them as such. It had always seemed natural to me that I could see the fate of a love affair, the birth of a child, the outcome of spring crops. These were commonly asked questions in my youth, and the answers came easily to my lips. I assumed that this gift had come to me from my mother, to whom the town outside our castle gates turned for help and healing. She was a visionary, my mother, known as a "seer". There was no need to hide this fact in the early years, for we were country folk from South Wales, surrounded by rolling hills and deep valleys where cattle and sheep grazed on hot summer days. Our ancestral lands held a great oak forest that rose into the high uplands where winter's white cloak would settle and wolves ran in wild packs. Our castle and the village beyond the walls lay at the mouth of an estuary that opened to the sea. The river ran deep and calm around the edge of our town, which sat high on the north bank.

When my mother had come here from Italy to marry my father, the count, the town had been little more than a few dozen cottages scattered around a tavern and a smithy. The peasants had been treated badly by my father's family and the knights who served him. The nobility believed that they were divined to be the ruling class and that the peasantry was literally of a different race. It was their understanding that they were to protect the peasantry, in return for which the peasants would provide for the nobles' every need and comfort. Thus, most nobility could not understand the needs or the cares of the common folk. But this was not so with my mother. She had lost her own mother when she was young, and was raised as the only woman in a very wealthy merchant household, and so learned early in life how to lead. She pleaded with her father to educate her, for she shared his great love of books. These she had brought with her from Italy.

Ah, yes, she loved her books. We had a library filled with them, leather-bound and scrolls, even parchment her father had purchased in Egypt and Turkey. There were things written in languages that I could not understand, though my mother had seen to it that I could read Latin and Greek. She could allow me an education only because my father was killed in battle, shortly after my brother Nicholas and I, twins, were born. Upon my father's death, all was left in her keeping until Nicholas would come of age and claim his title and our ancestral lands. So my mother took a position of power that was remarkable in the high Middle Ages, a time when women were considered chattel, owned by the men they served in marriage. She took her position seriously, keeping to the very old and outdated notion that our responsibility as nobles was to *serve* our people, making our territory prosperous and safe. She built up the village, creating a proper market and mill that brought merchants and miners and money. Nicer houses were built, walls were repaired, festivals were held with every change of season, and this brought more people, swelling the populace of our town.

Although we were a remote community, we were linked inland to the east by an ancient road built by the Romans, leading to Cardiff and Bristol. The ruins of their stone barracks and fortress lay on the other side of the river across a good stone bridge under which boats passed with the rising tide. On top of these ruins the small priory was now built where a group of old monks tended gardens and a herd of cattle and sheep. Not an active sect, they did not increase their wealth as would most churches in a burgeoning community. They were simple monks, holding services for the town in the stone chapel, living an austere life in their plain wooden dormitory, which was worn down from years of neglect. I would not have you believe that my family were good and devout Christians, but in those days Christianity was a sort of omnipresent law that was the very foundation of our lives. Church doctrine did not lend itself, any more than it does today, to the notion of intuition or immortality being inherent human potentials. No, the Church thrived on our belief in its canon: that life was just a temporary exile on the way to God. The Church offered us salvation, which could only be reached through its rituals and through the hands and mouths of its ordained priests. So you must understand that gifts such as those that ran in my family were not favored in our culture at large. It was only the circumstance of our country estate, secluded from London society and the high courts where the Church's elite held power and privilege, that allowed my talents to develop unchecked, as they did. And it was the simplicity of our people, and the hard country life they led that accustomed them to my mother's matriarchal rule.

Our manor was set among vast orchards right beside the river. My brother and I were set free on a rich and well-organized estate. I was quiet then, always in the shadow of my brother. Nicholas was all charm and valor, leading the way to adventure, and always restless. He was the dreamer, the leader, ever yearning for something beyond our country universe. Everyone loved him. He was the perfect young lord, sociable, with an elegant grace that set him apart from our country surroundings. For me, it was different. I was sensitive and shy, preferring the vast, lonely sea to the bustle and noise of gatherings. Nicholas did not seem to have my sensitivities, the intuitive waves that would overcome me, filling my sight with visions, and my senses with the awareness of people's feelings. No, Nicholas was not sensitive in that way at all. Yet, I could tell him everything, the visions that weighed on my heart, the pictures that would accost me when visitors came, and he would listen quietly, steadily, to these things, and bear with me their weight.

I dearly loved my brother. We did everything together. I was not aware at the time how unusual this was, but, as there were very few children on the estate, and manor life consumed my mother's attention,

I shared in many games and lessons that most girls did not. I listened to tales of war and played with swords made of wood. On hot summer days we would escape our lessons to hide in the orchards, picking apples and lazing under the trees by the river. It was a lovely time, when I was innocent still, unaffected by the gift that would transform my life forever.

I WAS ONLY ELEVEN WHEN IT ALL BEGAN TO CHANGE. It was the day my older cousin, Sir Rhodri, who had been newly made a knight, came to pay his respects to Nicholas. Rhodri had enrolled in the service of Edward the III of England, but his true obligation would one day be to my brother, the count.

I remember well our first meeting: a tall young man with blue eyes and fiery red hair, he came to the castle near sunset of an August evening, with a small troop of men. Having finished our lessons early, my brother and I sat on the floor of the study room, playing knucklebones, while Clara, our nurse, was openly asleep on her stool by the window. The sun fell softly through the window, casting small pools of gold on the splintered mosaics of the floor; bees droned lazily outside in the roses, and the steady rhythm of the wood-chopper's ax lulled us from a distance. When the sound of hooves pounded into the courtyard, and the servants began to shout, the wood chopping stopped abruptly, and Clara came awake with a snort. Nicholas was halfway to the window before Clara caught him up, pulling sharply at his tunic and smoothing his hair, so we understood immediately that the visitor was someone of importance.

"Justine!" Clara had finished with my brother and was now ready to fuss with me. "Child, look at you!" Her plump hands dusted off my dress. "Sitting on the floor in all this mess! What kind of a Lady will you make?" I ignored the comment, as I was used to hearing it frequently enough. Never mind that it was Clara's job to keep me from the folly

7

of knucklebones; I was happy that she was old and easily distracted. There was a sound on the stair, and the door pushed open.

I broke from Clara and ran to my mother, but Nicholas reached her first.

"Who's here?" he asked eagerly.

"It's your father's nephew, your cousin Rhodri." Her voice had a soft Italian accent that sounded majestic.

"He's come from London?" Nicholas was excited.

"Yes, he's been with the king."

"And the war with France," Nicholas went on, "has he been fighting yet?"

She tried to suppress a smile.

"I don't think so, Nicholas. He has only just been knighted. It is customary that he should present himself to you, as you will be the next count, and he will serve under your banner one day. He is your closest relative and holds a reasonably high station, so restrain yourself from childish behavior." With a stern look in my direction, "You are a lord and lady and I will expect you to behave as such. Do you understand me?"

"Yes, mother." We understood very well. We were accustomed to our mother's expectations, and in her presence games like knucklebones were far from our reach.

My mother turned abruptly and headed down the corridor to the small, elegant chamber where we received our important guests. Nicholas and I followed closely, sharing excited looks. Just as we reached the room, she suddenly stopped, so that Nicholas and I stumbled into each other trying not to bump her. Scrambling back into place, I was surprised to see she had not noticed. Before I could think, I blurted, "Mother, what's wrong?"

She answered, with a thin tension that made her look all at once older, almost as old as Clara, "There is *something*…" Her voice trailed off at the last and she stood up very straight, as if gathering some strength to her. A shiver went up my spine, but Nicholas did not seem to notice.

"Come, mother, let's meet him!" he urged.

At length, she pushed aside the thick curtain at the doorway.

A man stood at the mantel, gazing at the tapestry on the wall above. His red head almost touched the beams. He wore all black and his fingers were covered with jewels. Standing before my mother, who wore a simple house-robe of white linen and a soft blue mantle, he looked young, but smart, like a wolf.

"Sir Rhodri," my mother said as he stepped forward, extending his hand.

"My Lady," he bowed low, graceful and courteous. "And this must be my cousin Nicholas!" Again he bent low. There was a broad smile on his face as he rose.

"This is my daughter, Justine," my mother presented me.

He gave me an appraising look and then an obligatory nod of his head. Then his attention was with Nicholas. My brother was at once taken with him. He ushered Rhodri to a chair before the fire, as if he were already a man himself.

"You come from London, cousin?" Nicholas began.

"Yes," Rhodri relaxed into the chair. My mother and I took our usual place by the fire. As I came near him, I noticed that his eyes, though narrow, were a striking blue, as clear as my brother's. His soft doeskin boots were splattered with mud, and the smell of horses and sweat came from him. I was surprised to see he had come to meet Nicholas before even removing the muck of travel.

Rhodri talked easily enough, of London and the society of kings. My brother had pulled up a stool and sat at his feet, staring up at our cousin with admiration as he answered, in precise and often gory detail, every question Nicholas put to him. He talked on as the sun set and the servants lit the castle with rushlights. Even when we went to supper, Nicholas begged for more, until I was grateful when my mother signaled that it was time to retire.

It had been a very warm summer, and there was a truce that year between England and France, so Rhodri had been inclined to idle as our guest for several weeks. Nicholas had been following Rhodri around the entire time, and our cousin, to my surprise, tolerated it. I would even say he encouraged it, as if every man of eighteen would welcome a puppy trotting at his heels. Grudgingly, I followed when I could, keeping close to Nicholas' side, silent and alert. I had never had to share my brother's attention or affections, and clearly, Rhodri had taken both. He would take Nicholas out with his men, riding through the harvest fields, hunting, and fishing. Then they would spend all of supper sharing their tales of adventure. From the size of the stories they told, all the fish they caught were as big as sea monsters, and the deer were ferocious stags! I seemed the only one who did not find the stories entertaining. I grew quiet and withdrawn, furious that I was cast out of such escapades. At first I went to my mother to complain, but she only bade me let him be.

"He's becoming a man, Justine," she said. "This is what men do, and you should be at your loom!" she scolded.

I was discouraged by this, and wholly uninterested in the ominous loom my mother wished me to master.

"Yes, mother," I replied, returning to the old-fashioned room where the women gathered to do their weaving and chatter. But I could not concentrate. A sense of dread began to lay itself upon me. I avoided Rhodri, keeping to my rooms and my studies. It was not difficult to stay out of his way, as my father's palace was still large, having stood for hundreds of years, surviving Roman occupation and a disastrous fire. Time and war had badly disfigured parts of it, but the main house still stood, richly decorated with my mother's things from Italy. I noticed that these fine things did not escape our cousin's attention. He seemed to linger in each room, his eyes valuing all they beheld. I was nervous when I came upon him at such moments, for he would set his eyes upon me as if I were one of those fine things.

The back half of the main portion of our manor was surrounded by what had once been Roman slaves' quarters, which wrapped around a small courtyard where the cooks and servants labored. Just through the courtyard, on the other side of the buildings, were my mother's vast rose gardens. Farther, behind the gardens and very close to the eastern wall, was a small Roman-style chapel, with long columns at the front. Beside the chapel was our family's burial ground, complete with ten generations of gravestones and two mausoleums, elaborately carved and gilded. Ours was a very old and war-honored nobility, and in the cemetery one was reminded of it. This was the place that Nicholas and I had chosen as our own. When we could escape Clara's grasp, or Demetri's lessons in Greek or Latin, this was where we would come, out of the way, where no one could hear us in our rebellion.

One day, several weeks into Rhodri's visit, I slipped away from Clara, letting her assume I was in the care of the ladies at the loom, and went out through the courtyard, disappearing into the maze of roses, toward the chapel. I went quickly, pulling my skirts close so as not to catch them on the thorns. As I came down the path I began to hear voices, and finally, my brother's boyish laugh. I stopped abruptly.

"You are lucky when it comes to this subject, cousin! Most men must marry for money, not love. It's very expensive to be a knight, to travel and fight wars. Why, your own family had emptied its coffers on such things, until your father married your mother."

"I didn't know." Nicholas' voice was timid.

"Well, you should, and if you had a father he would tell you such things. You see, Nicholas, your mother had no title, but a great amount of wealth. Your father had a title and no currency. They were, therefore, the perfect match. It's happening all over Europe this way, wealthy merchants marrying their daughters to impoverished noblemen so their grandchildren will have titles. Its just how things are done!" His tone was casual, as if he were talking with an intimate friend, rather than his count.

"I see," Nicholas replied.

"Oh, don't look so serious, cousin. You won't have to marry for money. Look around you. This estate and all the land for miles up the river are yours. You will be a very wealthy man, with power besides. An enviable station you have been born into, indeed." A chill pressed against my neck.

"And what about your sister?" Rhodri was saying, "What does she think of me?" There was a brief silence.

"I'm not sure," Nicholas hesitated. "Justine is not fond of newcomers. It takes her awhile to get to know people. Just give her some time—"

Rhodri was laughing now. "You mean she doesn't find me charming and handsome?" Nicholas began to laugh, too. "She's not interested in such things!"

"Nonsense, all females are interested. Besides, if something were to happen to you, dear cousin, before you beget an heir, she will have to marry to secure your family's title."

"I'll have plenty of sons!" Nicholas replied confidently. I imagined him thrusting out his chest as he said it.

"Yes, of course. But tell me, has anyone come yet to make an offer for her hand?"

"No!" A pause, then, "I don't think so. Besides, Justine isn't interested in that sort of thing."

"I think you're wrong again, cousin. I tell you, the only thing women are interested in is men!"

Nicholas laughed once more. "Not Justine!"

Again I felt the chill.

"Nicholas!" I called out before I had time to think. Stepping out from behind the rosebushes, I saw them sitting together on the chapel steps. The place was hot and very still, except for the humming of insects. Fruit glowed in the afternoon light as it hung heavy on the scattered trees. I could smell the sweet juice of the apricots, freshly picked, set on a plate between them.

"Justine!" Nicholas started in surprise. "I didn't know, I mean, I didn't think ..." His cheeks were red. Rhodri jumped to his feet, brows furrowed, turning on Nicholas. His voice was sharp.

"I thought you said this was a secret place!" he said accusingly. Then he sucked in his breath, so deliberately that I could hear it from where I stood.

Nicholas looked crushed. "Well, I meant," he glanced at me, "I meant it was a secret place for Justine, too. We come here together." Then he looked away miserably.

"I see," Rhodri put a gentle hand on Nicholas' shoulder, "Well, now I suppose no harm's done. It is only your sister." Suddenly he was grinning again. He stepped forward with his graceful cat's stride, and reached a hand out to me.

"Ah, the Lady Justine. Come and join us."

I took Rhodri's hand and went with him to the steps. Nicholas quickly moved to the side, offering me his place. "We were about to gorge ourselves on sweet fruit," Rhodri said easily enough. "Here." He handed me a ripe peach, then bit into his, letting the juice run down his chin.

"Thank you," I said, but made no move to eat it. Nicholas reached for his own.

"We were just talking about you," Rhodri began. Upon hearing this, Nicholas nervously bit into the peach, an enormous bite, which sent him choking half to death. I tried not to laugh, and took the opportunity to pound him hard on the back. Sputtering and coughing, he wiped his face with the back of his hand, then scooted down the steps to get away from my helpful blows.

Rhodri continued, "I was just telling Nicholas what a pretty girl you are and how I rather fancy you." He was still sitting next to me, casually leaning back on the step above, his legs outstretched to several of the stairs below. I gathered my skirts in, carefully avoiding his eyes, for I could feel his gaze hot on my face. Nicholas seemed startled by the idea.

"But I'm only a girl—"

"Well, isn't that what most girls are thinking about?" he snorted. "You'll be ready for a husband in just a few years. Would it be so bad if I were that man?" I felt Nicholas stiffen.

13

"But we - we are cousins," I stuttered stupidly.

"Cousins marry all the time!" He reached over and patted my knee.

"Well, I wouldn't marry my cousin!" I blurted hotly, looking him in the eye.

"What?" His voice was edgy and he sat straight up beside me. "Why, what a childish thing to say!"

"Don't call her childish!" Nicholas was up the steps now, beside me, pulling me to my feet. "Justine isn't interested in such things, I already told you." His voice was strong, unwavering. "Let's not talk of this anymore."

At this I smiled, for it was what I had expected of Nicholas, and he had not let me down.

Rhodri, however, seemed surprised at my brother's tone. His brows creased again. "Of course, if it makes you uncomfortable, there's no need to pursue it." Shaking his head, he grinned reassuringly and bit into the fruit he held.

There was a long and uncomfortable silence. "Come now, don't be cross with me, you two. I am glad that Justine came to join us, and glad that we have had this chat. Now we are all *perfectly* clear on the subject. That's a good thing. One can make better choices when one has the right information. Sit!" He reached into a leather sack at his feet and pulled out two flasks. "Come, we must all be friends. Here, I brought one for you, cousin." He handed Nicholas a rather large wooden flask with an intricate design carved into the side. The leather strap was new. "My father gave me mine," Rhodri said, lifting his worn flask for us to inspect, "and if your own father were here, I'm sure he would have given you one as well. Since he's not, I would like to give it to you in his place."

Nicholas took the container and broke into a broad grin. I could see, suddenly, how he had longed for this kind of attention, how, as a boy of his rank, he had no one to look up to. My mother could not provide what Rhodri represented. Something in me softened. My brother glanced at me and I smiled reassuringly. I sat back down by my cousin.

"It's wonderful!" Nicholas exclaimed. Rhodri already had removed the top of his and swigged. I could smell the wine, sweet on his breath, when he was done.

"Go ahead! Drink, Nicholas, to friendship and the future!" He fished a small wooden cup from the bag, handing it to me. "Pour your sister some, too. Justine, you must forgive me for speaking so frankly and being so bold. Come, have a toast with us."

Nicholas did not hesitate now. He poured me a large draught and sat at my feet.

"Well?" said Rhodri. He sounded impatient. "What are you waiting for? Drink it!"

Nicholas grinned and lifted the flask to his lips. Suddenly, a shadow passed over him. Before I knew why, I jumped, knocking the flask from his hands, spilling my wine in the process. The flask fell hard on the steps and cracked, red wine pouring like blood on the white stone.

"What's the matter with you?" My cousin was on his feet. I looked up. His blue eyes looked brutal and keen. "Something was wrong with it. There was something black inside."

He took in his breath sharply, making the sign of the cross.

"So it's true!" he hissed, venom in his voice, "They said you were a witch, that you could see, but I didn't believe them!"

"I'm not a witch!"

Rhodri stooped down, grabbing the spilt cup from me, and stuffed it into his bag. "Stay away from me, you devil's brat!"

Nicholas stood, bewildered. I moved toward Rhodri, a dreadful panic swelling in my throat. "I'm not a witch!" I cried frantically.

"Stay back!" he screamed, turning on me sharply, his hand raised to strike me.

That is when it happened. For one terrible moment I was certain I would be hit, his hand coming toward me in a clenched fist. I heard Nicholas cry out, "No!" It seemed far away, as if I were dreaming it.

Then, as if by magic, the fist stopped in mid-flight, as though an invisible hand had caught his wrist and pulled him backwards. Rhodri screamed as his feet flew into the air and he fell backwards, hard, on the stone.

Nicholas and I stood stunned, not quite sure what had happened. But Rhodri was on his feet in a moment, and for the first time I saw the warrior in him. He turned in circles as if looking for his attacker, reaching for the dagger at his side as he moved.

"Who did that? Where are you?" We were all looking around, but the place was empty. Then the vague thought came to me that I had better run. I turned to the stairs, but Nicholas already had my hand and was pulling me toward the rose garden. Rhodri was fast, and in a moment he was before us, blocking our way.

"Don't move, either of you!" he commanded, a frenzied look on his face, his dagger pointed at me. For a moment, an image of him lunging at us swept though my mind, but then came my mother's voice, strong and unmistakable.

"Stop this!" she ordered, as she came round the hedge of roses, two of her men by her side. She brushed past Rhodri as if he were not armed and in a dangerous state. When she reached us she stopped short. For a moment I thought she would take us in her arms, but she only stood there, collecting herself. Then, with a firm look, she directed, "Go back to the manor."

The two men were at Rhodri's side, swords drawn, and our cousin looked in a rage. We did not wait to see what would come next. Nicholas took my hand again and pulled me toward home. We began to run and did not stop until we had reached our rooms. Pulling me into his, Nicholas slammed the door, bolting it behind us. I had never seen him like this before, shaken and clearly afraid. He went to the chest at the foot of his bed and pulled out his sword. I watched as he clung to the steel, as if it were giving him strength.

"I should have had this with me."

"It wouldn't have done any good."

"But I didn't protect you!" He was in agony. "I didn't even know what was happening, Justine. Are you all right?"

I nodded. "I think so."

"But aren't you afraid? What happened back there? When he was going to strike you, I mean." I shrugged my shoulders.

"I don't know, Nicholas."

"And mother, how did she—"

"I don't know."

We sat together in silence for a long time, my brother holding tight to his steel. Within the hour we heard a commotion in the courtyard, and the sound of men and hooves pounding through the gate. Then, for the first time that I could remember, the great wooden gates of our estate were closed.

AFTER THIS NOTHING WAS THE SAME. It was as if, during that day with Rhodri, our childhood had ended. Nicholas was given his first stallion and hunting dogs, while I was assigned a strict regimen with the loom and a harp. At fourteen, Nicholas had finished his studies and was sent to serve the earl, who dispatched him to London with his men, where he would be trained as a squire and then as a knight. This was a crushing blow to me as, without my brother, I had no voice. For months I was lost in my loneliness, burrowing deeper into myself and my silence, living only for the times when he would return to visit, vicariously alive in the story of his life. When I could no longer bear the discrepancies in the life assigned to my sex as compared to my brother's, I appealed to my mother, but on this point she would not bend. I was, after all, a Lady, and must be educated as such. There were knights and their kin whom we addressed, balls we attended, grand affairs that we sponsored, which maintained our status. Even in the country, one could not avoid one's social responsibilities, Mother assured me. She would remind me that I might not always live in the country, that my life might take me where such skills would be essential.

"What do you mean?" I would ask accusingly, knowing full well she was speaking of marriage.

"Justine, someday ... " but she would not finish. It was as if she knew that the terror from that day with Rhodri remained with me always, ready to burn afresh in my mind. So the subjects of men and marriage were rarely discussed. As the years passed, many suitors came to our door to ask for my hand, but I would turn them down. My mother never forced me. I know she hoped I would come to it on my own, but she did not understand that I would not let myself succumb to such a fate.

So, without the immediate prospect of marriage, or my brother's company, I turned to my mother's determination that I should acquire grand social skills and grace. She patiently ignored my obvious lack of proficiency, unable to understand that I had no knack for such things, because for her they had come easily. She had been born with a natural grace and beauty that drew people to her. It did not matter that she had not been born with a title, for she naturally possessed the social refinement and poise required of her station. Though her father had seen to it that she was educated to elevate her course in life, that was not what made her the success she was. I believe it was because beneath her commanding presence and ambitious nature, she was kind. She would set her eyes upon people, luminous golden mirrors that would take them in and sum them up at a glance. It was then that they would feel it, compassion flooding from her gaze, as if she were saying, "I see you, all the secret parts, and I love you still."

This was what called the people to her; why they bent gladly to her will and welcomed her intuitive nature. They respected my mother's gift as she foretold the Black Death that would ravage England, and prepared our farmers and our fields for the famine that would follow. She fixed herbs for the sick before they arrived at our door. Our people came to her court to resolve their quarrels, for she could see into the heart of a man and tell if he was lying. The villagers did not question these things, but lived quietly at the benefit of her knowing. Even the old prior and the monks did not comment on my mother's gift, as she was a good Christian woman in every other way, and they benefited greatly from the insights she shared.

All this she wanted for me, as well. I knew it, yet in my heart I felt that my destiny was not what hers would be. I was taught embroidery and needlepoint, and detested lessons in social etiquette; it took hours to dress properly, do my hair correctly, learn the right thing to say, the correct way to eat. I failed at each in turn.

I lost myself, then, to my books, to my histories and Church doctrine, searching for evidence of women who had been bold and free. The older I got, the less my life had meaning, just a dull existence of habit and conformity. I became wrapped up inside myself, tight and melancholic. Having no outward voice of my own, I was privately impassioned, my need for freedom pressing from within. As the years passed and the injustices to my sex piled one upon the other, a quiet rage seized me and I determined secretly to live a daring life, to turn away from what was expected of me.

Three

By my eighteenth year, I had become pensive, keeping to myself. My mother tried to draw me out, holding great parties, inviting the finest people in South Whales, but I was not interested. She took other tacks as well. Each year she attempted to give me more responsibility, overseeing household affairs and festival preparations. But I was dreadful doing such things, for they seemed so absurd. Why should I tell the cook what to serve, when she knew better than I what was in the pantry? What possible help could I be in planning a festival? I had no interest in parties and people. I was too committed to my gloom.

Then, one day, my mother sent for me. She was at her loom in the room where the women did the weaving alone. She sat very straight, head lifted, dignified even as she fed the thread through the loom, which clacked, fierce and steady. I had not visited this place in months. I sat down next to the fire, smoothing my skirts to please her. She did not seem to notice the gesture.

"Justine," she began, never lifting her eyes from her work, "I'm not certain that you've noticed, but it's spring." I did not answer, watching her move the shuttle deftly across the threads. "I am going to tour the countryside, as I wish to take count of all our vassals and holdings before summer is through. I will expect you to accompany me."

I sat straight up to protest. "But, mother—"

"I am not asking you, Justine." The steady clacking continued. "We will begin with the Hamilton estate to the east. We have been invited to spend several days there, so pack appropriately."

"Mother . . . " I leaned forward as if to make some point. Seeing me do so, she stopped her work abruptly, giving me her full attention. I found this unnerving, and hesitated.

"Yes?"

The words caught in my throat. I tried to push them out. "It's just that I don't, I mean, I like it here."

"Yes," she said again, annoyed.

"And I am inept at social situations!"

"Precisely why you need more practice. You spend far too much time alone, Justine. I will not have you indulging such a habit!"

I swallowed hard, clenching my fists. "Yes, mother," was all that I said.

THE HAMILTONS LIVED ONLY A FEW MILES from our estate, up the old Roman road. We set out on horseback, with a small accompaniment of servants and the two men-at-arms who always escorted my mother abroad. It was only a few hours until we arrived and, to my dismay, my mother promptly left me, after introductions were made, in the company of young William.

He looked charming, extravagantly clad in a red velvet houppelande — a long gown that was fitted at the shoulders and fell loose below. A richly embroidered belt hung from his waist, and a high, upright collar reached nearly to his ears. I struggled to be polite, making small talk while he showed me about his estate and all through the manor house, which was richly decorated, albeit made of wood. He stopped at each piece of art, each antique, noting for me its worth. All this, as if I had never seen such things, as if I had not been raised in a stone castle on an estate thrice the size of his own. The sound of his voice began to grate on my nerves such that the years of restrained fury in my breast began to rise dangerously close to the surface.

After all of this he led me to a small verandah that overlooked the road by which we had arrived, and there we sat at a table while tea was served. That is when the reason for this *visit* became clear.

"So, Justine," he began casually, "you must tell me what you have in mind for your future." I sipped my tea. "You are the daughter of a count," he continued, "yet your brother will claim title to your family's lands soon, and I wonder what you and your mother will do when this happens." He raised his eyebrows as if asking a question.

"What do you mean?" I asked, coldly. He adjusted the lace at his collar, shifting uncomfortably in his chair.

"I mean," he was not looking at me as he spoke, but fidgeting with a jeweled ring on his finger, "you will soon be left with nothing but the generosity and mercy of your brother Nicholas. I am only wondering what you intend to do. I suppose you could go to an abbey, as my mother will when my father is gone —"

"I will never go to the Church," I snapped, "nor would my mother. Nicholas would never cast us out, if that's what you're implying!"

But he was laughing! "Come now, Justine, you can't seriously think Nicholas would let you stay when he takes a wife and has heirs? He must intend for you to marry then, is that it?"

Hate. Spite. The feelings made me shake. "It's not up to Nicholas to intend *anything* for me!" I was vehement. "I will choose ... "

He was laughing again, and then he tried to cajole me. "Don't look that way, Justine. I'm only trying to help you. No woman is going to choose her husband, especially not one with title and wealth as well. Now, really, I am only asking to see if you prefer the life of a nun because I've heard that you are remarkably well versed in Church canon for a woman, and —"

"I do not aspire to the Church. I told you that already." I could feel my eyes narrowing, my fists clenched on the arm of my chair.

"Now, Justine, don't be angry with me," he said in an ingratiating tone. "It is only that you are so old to be unmarried that one would think your family had plans to give you to a nunnery."

My cheeks flushed. I felt the velvet heat and knew that I was unraveling. "The Church!" I struggled to keep my voice quiet and dignified.

"How could anyone bring herself to ally with the Church? It would be impossible for me to spend my life serving an institution that says we are all born into sin, as St. Augustine would have us all believe. No, William, I could never be party to such hypocrisies as are perpetrated by the *Church!*"

He leaned back in his chair, offended. "Whatever do you mean?" he cried, "You blaspheme, Justine, you——"

"I am perfectly right, William, and if you had an original thought in your head, you would see it, too!" My voice was rising, "What do you make of a religion whose master told his people to 'turn the other cheek,' and to 'love thy neighbor as thyself,' and then ran about the world killing in the name of the Lord? What do you make of a pope that would turn on his own people, fellow Christians, calling them heretics and commanding loyal knights to kill them?"

"What are you talking about, Justine?"

I had read so many times about the horrors perpetrated in the name of Christ that I did not hesitate. "I am talking about popes like Innocent, who called the Albigensian Crusade against the Cathars, good Christians, most of whom were women. Do you know how that crusade ended, William?"

His eyes were wide as he shook his head. "The pope," he stammered. "Justine, the pope knows who the heretics are. His Holiness did the only honorable thing, I'm sure!"

"Honorable!" Now it was my turn to laugh. "Do you know how the 'honorable' pope brought peace to Christendom?" I was bitter. "The Albigensian crusaders in France lay siege to Montsegur Castle, the last stronghold of the Catharist Christians. The castle's noblewomen arranged with the bishop to give them the last rites in the event that they were wounded and could not speak, for they chose to fight alongside their men. Heretics requiring the services of a bishop, now does that not seem strange to you?"

He just sat there, stunned. I should have stopped then but I could not. Something inside me had come undone. I continued pointedly,

"As the situation became hopeless, the castle's military defenders were permitted to withdraw unharmed, but more than two hundred Catharists, men, women, and children, were put to death. They were burned on a pyre, William, in the name of God." I shook my head. "And you would have me choose a nunnery!"

It took him a moment to recover, to raise himself from the chair he was clinging to and collect himself. "Yes, I see your point, Justine, but the pope," he stammered, "knows what is best. If those people were not *true* Christians, loyal to the one true Church, then they were heretics and it was right that they should be burned. And, of course," his voice wavered, "I see now that you will not be choosing a life with the Church." He straightened, regaining his composure, trying desperately to come to the point. "So you will be choosing marriage, then, and I am glad to hear it. You are too beautiful a woman to be locked away, Justine. You should have a husband to take care of you, to keep you —"

"To keep me? I am not a woman to be kept." I stopped with these words, stunned by the truth.

William's face was strained and I could see that he was frustrated. This meeting was not going as he had planned. I could feel the battle within him: he was indignant and confused at my response, but kept himself steady, for he wanted me. It was my dowry, of course.

"Justine," he tried to control his voice, "I realize that you're not like most women and that you've not had the benefit of a father to guide you, but you seem intelligent to me and so —"

"Of course I'm intelligent. What do you take me for, a beast to be bought and sold? I am a woman, William, educated in the great classics of Greece and Rome, where women were writers and poets and rulers!"

"What?" He looked straight at me now, haughty and aggressive. "Greek writers, and women who rule? Who told you such nonsense?"

"I am educated in both Greek and Latin." I paused here emphasizing the fact, for I knew that he probably had not studied either. "I have

24

read for myself Plato's *Timeas* and Homer's *Odyssey*. I've read the poets, and a Latin Bible as well!"

"Impossible!" he exploded so that I stopped abruptly. "Women don't read!" he exclaimed. "You lie! How could you have learned?"

"Don't be so ignorant, William. Of course I read. I learned just as anyone does, from a scholar. If you had any education at all, you'd know that women have been great leaders and have added to our histories as much as any man."

Suddenly I could not bear the inequity of it all. It welled up and I pushed it out with a potent force. "We have been queens, we have ruled. Do you not believe me? Shall I name them for you?" I began to pace in my fury. "Where shall I begin, then? Shall we go back before Rome, even? In Egypt, there was Hatshepsut, and her daughter Senemut, who built temples that still stand by the Nile near Thebes. And there is Jezebel, queen of Israel, who ruled as regent after Ahab's death. What of England's own Eleanor of Aquitaine, who turned over her thousands of vassals to the Abbey Bernard of Clairvaux for a second crusade, which she led herself!" Yes, this was right; I was purging, my body alive at last. "Surely you've heard the tale, William, of how she rode up on a white horse on the day of departure, clad in gilded buckskin boots and armor. How she was surrounded by Sybelle, the countess of Flanders, and Mamille of Roucy, and Florine of Bourgogne, all armored as well. Then she led them across the sea to Jerusalem, where she was welcomed by Melissande, queen of the Christians."

Oh, the look on his face; I will never forget it. Eyes wide, he stood rigid and confused. I could not stop myself now. "What of the Beguine movement, William? It lives even today, though ignorant men continue to persecute it. The Beguines are laywomen, all pledged to chastity, poverty, manual labor, and communal worship, who live in all-female, self-governing communities. No woman is turned away, not for age or class or financial means. There are thousands of women, William, left homeless from the wars, with no men to husband them and without the dowries necessary to join the convent. What shall they do, I wonder?

Where shall they go? They are allowed no property of their own, and no business, and are given no education, yet they have the intelligence to grow their own food, a burden to no one, Christians in name and deed.

"And always, William, we have been mothers, faithful caretakers and protectors of our families and homes." I felt a rush of power move through me as I said these words, and an invisible mouth seemed to take hold of my voice, making me its own. I knew then that my gift was upon me. "Women are creators as much as men! We are the heart of humanity and it is not right that we are not honored! All that is needed is for women to remember themselves and stand up again for what is right, and for men to bind themselves to the covenant of love that they fight so hard to protect."

William struggled to collect himself. "You are mad!" he accused. "This is nonsense, all of it!" He was shouting, "What would a woman make of her life without a man?"

It was an absurd thing to say. I moved toward him then, an unearthly presence upon me. "And what will you make of *your* life, William?" My voice was deep and slow, emphasizing every word. "With your love of external appearances, wealth, and grandeur, you will live an opulent life. You'll marry for money and land. You'll stumble through life, thinking yourself free of sin, taking only what has been handed to you on a silver platter." He tried to interrupt but I did not let him. "You will take from the people you are meant to serve. You will break trust with those who serve you by demanding more than they can give. *And you will sin, again and again, by using your power and position to destroy rather than to create!*" I leaned close to him then, "You will die in fear, William, alone and unloved and easily forgotten!"

His face gone white, he backed away from me as if he beheld a ghost.

"Go away from me!" he cried. "You are a wicked woman, Justine!" He made the sign of the cross as he passed by the servants who had come at the sound of his voice. "See the lady to her mother!"

26

Four

I DID NOT WAIT FOR THE SERVANT, but ran from the verandah to the stable. Pulling my horse from its tether, I was on her back in a moment, galloping down the road toward home. Home. What was that to me? A place that was not my own and would never be. I pushed my horse harder, and she sped through the trees to the familiar hills of our estate. The words I had spoken filled my head. I was confused and angry. I had dishonored my family, and riding away like this was unconscionable, but I would not stop. I pressed forward until my mare had broken a full sweat and was lathered wet through my skirts, which lay like blankets upon her back. Then we were home and I slid from her back, a servant taking the reins, another coming to my aid. I must have looked a sight, my long brown curls wild down my back and my skirts heaved high in my hands as I stormed into the castle, waving everyone away. "Leave me alone!" I ordered in a voice filled with uncommon command.

The servants seemed startled. "But, lady, where is your mother? How did you come here alone?"

"How do you think?" A rude reply, but I did not care. Something had loosened inside of me and I could not tether it now. I rushed to the door of my brother's room and went inside. Pulling off my gown, unlacing the bodice as I went so that I could breathe, I opened Nicholas' chest and took out a long tunic of blue wool, a pair of leggings, and an old pair of buckskin hunting boots. I hardly knew what I was doing as I dressed myself in his clothes. I belted the tunic so that it would not drag beneath my feet, then took his old sword from its sheath, and emerged from his room. The servants were gathered outside the door, and when I appeared they drew back in horror.

"Lady!" a serving woman started, but I pretended not to hear. I ran down the stairs to the old armory, the servants following in a panic behind me. When I entered the room, I turned to them. "Leave me!" I ordered, and pushed the big wooden doors closed behind me.

The room was long and narrow, lined with statues and armor dating back hundreds of years. There were windows on the western side that were shut tight by wood latches. I went to one now and pulled it open, letting in the last light of day. Gripping my brother's sword, I sank down on the floor below, watching as the light fell like a brush across the empty armor and the weapons that hung above. There were flails here, the big iron balls attached to chains that would be swung round and round to destroy an attacker. I stared numbly at the ancient maces, those spiked clubs that would crack a skull in two. These weapons had been wielded by my grandfathers and great-grandfathers and all the men of my bloodline. I felt them in the room with me, their ghosts filling the metal shells of armor, reaching out to me with tales of glory and horrific conquest. I shuddered at the scenes that rose before my eyes, but I did not leave: there was something here that I hoped to find, some part of myself long buried and put down. The sun set, and a pale gray moon stole in through the window. The servants stopped shuffling out in the hall and I was alone. I sat still on the floor beneath the window for a long while, scenes of battle dancing before my eyes, until I heard a sound and realized that the doors had opened and my mother was standing there, an oil lamp in her hand. She paused a moment, fixing her eyes in the moonlight, and then she saw me. Behind her came her man, and the maid that had been distraught at my arrival.

"There she is, ma'am, there as I told you." said the woman nervously.

"Yes, I see," my mother answered. "Leave us now." She turned to shut the doors behind her.

I suppose I knew that she would come, but I do not think I considered whether she would be angry with me. Honestly, I did not care. I had slipped between the worlds of duty and longing. I no longer cared to be what I was. What would she think of me, pitiful sight, dressed in my brother's clothes, clinging to his steel as if it were part of me? I almost cried at the thought of it as she crossed the long room and came to kneel before me. She was everything to me in my mortal years, a force of will that set about me a fortress of protection in an age when women were horribly used. She was both terrible and wonderful and I strained to be like her. But I had failed. Grace and beauty were her weapons, and I had neither. I clung tighter to the steel. She put the lamp down between us and looked out above my head at the night sky as if she were drawing it to her.

"You are unhappy, Justine," she said finally. Silence. "I'm sorry I took you today. I shouldn't have, you're not ready." I struggled to meet her eyes, which bore down on me now so that I could feel their heat. I saw her face then, angular and strong. I ached for her to understand. I wanted to cry out, "I am lost! I am lost and I cannot find my way back!" But I was silent. What could she say that would make any difference to me?

"These last years have been hard for you since your brother has taken his place in the world." It was a statement, for my mother did not make excuses. "I see that you're different, Justine, and that you have a gift. Perhaps that is the legacy you will have from me? We shall see." She stopped there as if that were all she would say. I half expected her to leave, but then she reached out across the candlelight, touching my chin, lifting my head so that I was facing her. It was unlike her, that intimate gesture, and I looked into her eyes. "I know how it feels," she said. "You hate William because he does not know what you as a woman must bear. He is like most men who lack the heart to see injustice and betrayal. And he is trained, Justine, as his father was before him, to look away from love, and to protect the injustice, even to further it, for it is upon that injustice that his very life is built, his sense of himself and his destiny. There is that, too, isn't there? He is free to follow his destiny. You abhor him because he can go where you long to go and do what you long to do."

I felt a cold sensation of pleasure as she said it; a glimmer of understanding broke through. I nodded silently.

"This is something that women share, Justine. Mingled with our love and our passion for creation is this thorn of resentment. 'Why am I not as valued as he?' we ask ourselves. We look everywhere for evidence of our equality, with secret hope in our hearts that a mistake has been made, an awful mistake that we will correct. But where do we look for the answer?" She pushed the lamp over to one side, leaning close to me now, so that I straightened, heart beating fast. I was almost afraid.

She continued, her eyes piercing me. "Everywhere we look, Justine, we see the power of feminine creation. The earth bears, as we do, the fruit that sustains us. The seasons and the tides, the cycles of life, the poetry and rhythms of creation, all reflect woman in her brilliant creative power. Yet this is not enough for us to claim ourselves, for inevitably we look again to the structures around us, and our eyes fall on that singular authority, God. And we are told that God is a man, a man that has cast us out and thrown us down, as men are wont to do. For most women there is then a quiet settling and a life of surrender. They kill what they know, and quietly die. But then there are others, like you, Justine, and like me, who will not lie down in the face of such great error. Those who would face displeasure, even death, rather than live by a lie. Some fight all their lives to prove themselves worthy, equal in power and courage. This is not a difficult thing to do, really. The very experience of being a woman requires a power and courage that few men can understand. To face life with feeling, to live as women do, following a heart whose very nature is to break open, yet to always go on ... such is the courage it takes to love, Justine. It is a different courage than it takes to fight." Her hand rested gently on the hilt of my brother's sword.

"There are things for you to learn about your gift and about being a woman." She removed her hand and stood. The moon must have been directly above her, for she was shrouded in silver light. "There is a woman

I want you to meet," she said, standing to go. "I will take you to her tomorrow." Then she turned and left me as silently as she had come.

Her presence lingered a long time. I remained silent and still, watching the ghosts dance through the hall. When finally the oil lamp sputtered and the flame was no more, I laid down my brother's sword and took myself to bed.

Five

WE DID NOT LEAVE AS MY MOTHER HAD INTENDED, for the next morning
Nicholas came home. He rode in with a half dozen companions who sent
our house into chaos, servants scrambling to attend them. I was only
just out of bed when word came that my brother was through the castle
gates. I pulled on a simple blue gown; I couldn't find my belt, which left
the gown's pleats trailing on the ground. I didn't care. I bounded down
the stone stairs, only to run headlong into my mother.

"Justine!" She collected herself in the most dignified manner and
frowned at the sight of me. Without another word to me she summoned
her maid. "Go with my daughter and see that she is properly attired."
Then to me, "Justine, your brother has brought guests." I could tell
by the look on her face that there was no getting around it, so back I
went, my hair brushed and set, a proper gown and girdle, lace at my
throat, and a diamond on my finger. I looked in the mirror: brown
curls pulled back, freckled skin powdered down. My lips were full but
pale. The dark green mantle I wore brought out my eyes, pools of hazel
and gold. Then, down the stairs at a pace all too fast, so that the maid
cried out, "Lady!" But I did not look back, only heaved up my skirts
and ran faster. I had missed my brother terribly.

I stopped at the door of the great hall, caught my breath, and stepped
in. There he was, taller than when he left, his hair cut short in the style
of the time. He was lavishly outfitted in velvet slippers with gold heels
and a fine embroidered cloak cut short to his waist. He stood in the
center of four young men, his companions. They had gathered in the
hall, a fire blazing, and my mother already in attendance. Knights, most
of them, some familiar, but there was something else, or someone, for

32

as I entered the room a chill ran down my spine and I hesitated. But then there was Nicholas, laughing, reaching for my hand.

"Justine!" He was wonderful, affectionate. My wild country count, whose manners were overlooked for that contagious smile and his charming words. He pulled me into the circle, introduced me to his fellows, and then turned to my mother, who stood by the fire with a stranger whose back was to me.

"Adrian!" Nicholas almost shouted. Again the strange chill. The tall man turned, startlingly slow, his splendid velvet cloak of wine and gold shimmering in the flames. I blinked. Did I know him? He was quite tall, with thick, brown hair that fell neatly at his shoulders. My eyes narrowed and my head swam. Yes, I had seen him before, that thin beard trimmed close, those blue eyes, no, gray, like mist in a dream. He was strangely familiar and it was unsettling. My brother was speaking, introducing me, but I hardly noticed.

"... His Grace, the duke," he was saying. The man was bowing. He had my hand and was pressing his full lips to it—a gorgeous thing. Heat ran through me. My cheeks flushed. I think I said something, something wholly inappropriate, because they were all laughing and my mother was at my side, pulling me to a seat near the fire. And the duke followed. He sat in the chair opposite; I could feel his gaze, splendidly warm on my face.

I was about to meet his eyes when suddenly the mood changed. From the corner of the room came the voice of a man I had not yet noticed. He moved easily into the circle of men, yet I felt them recoil as he passed by. He was a priest, introduced as prior of a large chapel near Kingsbridge.

"This is Father Henry," my brother said graciously. Henry was a pale, slight man with sharp eyes and a thin, pursed mouth. I tensed as he came toward us. Noticing my mother shift subtly in her chair, I knew there was a threatening presence here.

Yet, he was with Nicholas, and there must be a reason, so it was to my brother that we turned our attention as he filled us in on life at court and the news of war in France. Edward was raising a fresh army, and planned to cross the English Channel in summer. I grew uneasy as Nicholas spoke. Of course he would go and join them, of course, he would. "No, no, don't worry, mother, I will be in good hands, fighting with the duke." He was ready to stand with our banner, the eagle and the snake emblazoned in purple on the brooch at his collar. I watched him as he spoke, flamboyant gestures, that dramatic tone; I saw the truth of it, that he was more than ready. He was our brilliant young star, ready to shine in the glory of the purpose at hand. The king required him and our knights to stand ready; they were called to protect our lands and our lives, after all.

Mother was quiet as Nicholas spoke, and when he was done her eyes rested on the duke.

"Your Grace," she began, but he held up his hand.

"You must call me Adrian," he insisted. My mother raised her brow in a gesture that I recognized as a warning.

"Adrian," she began again, "my son will be serving with you?"

"I assure you, Lady, he will be at my side every moment." His voice was warm and gracious. "I will train him as befits his station and his nature." Nicholas was beaming. How could she keep him here? I knew it was impossible, and that this must be the cold dread that lay on my shoulders. Nicholas would leave for a long time now, and I would be alone again.

The priest was speaking. "Your son will be safe, Countess. He could not be in better hands than with His Grace, the duke, I assure you. The duke is high in the king's favor and has fought many times before in the war." He was looking at Nicholas then. "And your son is strong, Lady, and eager to live up to his title." Nicholas beamed, the young stallion let loose in the field. My mother ignored the priest. Her face was grave. There was a long pause, her eyes on my brother, all eyes on her.

"I do not think you are ready for this, Nicholas," she said to my brother, "but I know you will go. I know that you must." She stood and signaled to her maid. "See that our guests are quartered, and tell the cooks to prepare supper." Turning to the duke, who had risen when she stood, she asked, "How long will you stay?"

"Only tonight, Countess. We must rally this country's fighting force and return to London before the month is out." He was candid.

My mother straightened. She looked at Nicholas, who was awkward now, at a loss for words.

"This shall be our last supper, then." She reached out suddenly and touched my brother's cheek, forcing a smile. "We will make it a feast!" I felt her push the words out, emotion held tight in her chest.

"Gentlemen ... " she murmured as she turned and left the room. The fire crackled.

Nicholas turned to me with a helpless look. "Jus," he started, but I reached out my hand reassuringly. "She is only honest, Nicholas. And she will miss you." He took my hand and bowed low. "Of course, you're right." His voice was warming, his companions stepping closer to the fire.

"So tell me of your adventures," I pleaded, sitting back down in my mother's high chair by the fire, gesturing for them to get comfortable. "Entertain me!" I demanded, leaning back regally, giving them leave to relax with me. Nicholas began, and then another chimed in, and then the next, until they were talking one over the other of real life out in the world. I was their audience, properly delighted with descriptions and stories, laughing and clapping, spurring them on in the telling. Somewhere in it all, the duke rose and excused himself, a brief bow in my direction. I felt his presence in the room long after he was gone.

All the while the priest did not move from his chair. He listened to their tales as I imagine he had a hundred times, but that was not why he stayed. I could feel him studying me as I listened. I ignored him and took in my brother's light, his hands moving wildly in gestures of battle, his laugh deep beneath the roar of his fellows. How comfortable he made them, and how easy they were with me. I watched Nicholas as he talked, memorizing the light in his eyes and the ardor in his face, for I suspected, as did my mother, that I would never see him again.

35

Six

I DID NOT SEE THEM RIDE OFF. We had said our good-byes late in the night, and I could not bear to watch him go.

The only surprise that met me when I came finally from my room was that the priest, Henry, had not ridden out with them. He told us that he had come to rebuild the monastery across the river, that he had dreams of building a cathedral there. He had visited the place before supper the night before and was commissioned by the bishop at Cardiff to be its new prior. Our lands were rich and fertile, after all, and our communities remarkably full and prosperous, considering the plague years.

It was precisely this, we later learned, that had brought us to Henry's attention. Nicholas had spoken so highly of our estate and the lands of South Wales, that the priest, who had lost most of his congregation to the Black Death, listened in earnest.

The Black Death had come to Europe in 1347 and had taken the greatest toll of life of any other known epidemic or war. My mother, of course, had seen it coming long before it took hold of England, and had prepared our estate and the town by storing extra food and granting more of our ancestral lands to the peasantry, who farmed them in return. She gave over part of her rose garden to those who were masters in the art of herbs. Most important, she began to guide the shepherds and weavers into farming, stating flatly that, at the first word of the plague reaching England, she would close down the prosperous Saturday market that she had begun. It was essential, she said, to limit trade and travel during this time. Perhaps it was my mother's logical approach and her skillful preparation that kept our village going through those long, bitter years, when the frightening toll of dead across Europe rose by the thousands each day. Or perhaps it was just that my mother had told them that the plague would pass us by. Whatever the reason, people did as she said and our country village escaped the Black Death. By cloistering ourselves we became extremely productive and self-sufficient, even producing delicacies of cheese and wine that later were taken to the neighboring villages and lords.

During that same time, Henry had been a bad prior, losing much of his congregation and all of his wealth. Yet, he had connections in the Church, through whom he maintained his ecclesiastic career, which he would do anything to further. Of course, this I can only say from hindsight. On that day when my brother left us, I had no way of knowing what was to come. The only certain thing was that with Henry came a cold anxiety that pressed itself upon me. Our time of freedom from the watchful eye of the holy Church of Rome had come to an end.

Seven

EARLY THE NEXT DAY MOTHER TOOK ME to meet the old woman, Miriam. It was brisk, late in the spring, and we rode with only a small escort, whom we left at the foot of the blue hills, which ran almost to the river's edge. We called them such because, when the sun had set behind them, in the moments just before night takes evening's place, the hills would appear a mystic blue.

As we neared the hills, my mother reminded me of the legends of this place, of the pagan rituals and gods of a people that once lived here. She told me there had been women, too, priestesses, as there had been in Egypt and Rome and Greece. Deep in these hills they had gathered, worshipping the feminine face of God.

"Before the Romans came to England," she told me, "we worshipped the Goddess, as the legends go for the Irish and the Scots. It was the same here in England, and these hills were a sacred place." Her solemn tone was reverent. "It is high time you know these things, Justine. As your brother is called to his destiny, I know that you are being called to yours. Time to come away from your books. Life wants more from you."

I did not reply, but I remember how extraordinary my mother's attention and the mystery of our journey seemed to me.

It did not take long to reach the base of the hills where our party halted at the foot of the stream. I noticed a lean-to and tether that had already been prepared for the horses, and a fire pit was ready, piled high with wood for our men. The place was clearly familiar to my mother and her escort. I was intrigued. But the real surprise came when she took a basket from her servant and beckoned me to follow

38

her away from the group, toward a path in the trees. We left our escort, climbing a path through solid willows with fern and moss clinging to their branches. I could hear the sound of water flowing over rocks as the stream ran alongside the path. We walked in silence for half a mile until we came to an open field where sheep grazed peacefully in the sun.

Then I heard a sound, an eerie moaning that lodged itself between my breasts so that I caught my breath. "Mother," I started, but she only smiled, lifting her hand to my shoulder. Then the sound again, and another, only this one was low and somehow more human. My mother pointed to a crumbling stone wall across the field and we began to walk toward it. As we came nearer, I realized that the sound was singing, and the voice was that of a man, deep, robust, and penetrating.

Beside the remains of the wall stood an ancient tree, gnarled and covered with nettle. Its boughs were heavy with golden fruit. In front of it was a small pool of water, an old stone plinth above it, where once there had certainly been an altar. A few yards above stood an ancient shrine with the chapel doors thrown wide open. It was a small, oblong building set next to the stream, which even in late spring was running clear. Pines surrounded the building, shrouding it in a wall of shadow. I still remember the scent in the air of sweet apple and pine.

Stone steps covered with shimmering moss led to the chapel door, and there sat a young man and an old woman. The young man was singing some foreign tune, which drew us like snakes from a jar. They were so engrossed with their melody that our approach caught them by surprise. Quickly, my mother began, "We don't mean to interrupt, your singing is enchanting." But the young man scrambled to his feet, bowing slightly.

"Lady," he stammered, and quickly knelt, rolling up a blanket on the ground that held an old scroll and some antique-looking objects. The old woman did not move. She sat, calmly watching us. "No, no, stay where you are, really," my mother insisted. The young man looked nervously from her to the old woman behind him.

39

"Sit, Enoch," said the woman, her accent heavy and thick yet strangely melodic. "It is only the Lady Christine from the town, she will not hurt us." Then, beckoning us, "Come, Christine, we have plenty of room here and bread to spare. Will you join us?" My mother smiled. She knew this woman somehow.

"We would love to join you, Miriam," she said. I was astonished.

I looked at the old woman's face, immediately mesmerized by the large, green eyes, deep set over her defined nose; she gave me the sense of an owl, that deceptive predator. Her hair was a thick weave of silver and red, lying in a long braid that hung over one shoulder. Wisps of silver had pulled loose and curled wildly about her face. She was old but not weathered. Thin lines pulled delicately at her chiseled features, and her lips were full and supple, like a young woman's. She wore a simple white mantle belted low and loose, more like a man's tunic, yet there was a distinct air of feminine dignity about her. Her only decoration was a small, smooth jar, shimmering white, which lay at her throat like a fine jewel.

"Mother," I whispered, now at her right arm, "how do you know her?" My mother nodded absently, a contented look on her face that I was not used to seeing. She looked, for the first time, very young. Without hesitation she sat down at the old woman's feet. It was an odd thing to do, but I followed suit.

"I met Miriam and her nephew, Enoch, a year ago. She and her family were being harassed because they are Jews, so I have granted them a plot of land by the far bank of the river to plow. In exchange she has rekindled the magic of this place, which was originally known to the hill people as the Goddess pool. Over the years it has had many owners, but now I have turned it over to Miriam. She teaches her family every summer, and I, too, come sometimes and listen."

This was a wonder!

The Jews were a people that I, as a Christian, knew little about and cared little for, as we had been told stories, passed down from generation to generation, that they were Christ-killers and could not be trusted. Moneylending was a despised occupation, yet the only work available to the Jews. In centuries past, all great social antagonism had vented itself on these people. They were blamed for everything from the Black Death to a poor crop, and their people suffered seizure of property, forcible conversion, and murder. In Spain, we had heard that to protect Jews in any way was denounced as treason to Christendom, which sent these people flooding throughout Europe, seeking new homes and creating new communities. I knew all of this from books and my brother's tales of travel, but I had never met a Jew. They seemed a fictional people to me.

"You come here to learn from *her*?" I whispered still, even though the woman could plainly hear.

"I do."

I looked to the old woman and back to the young man. He was dressed so strangely, long robes like a priest, and his hair fell in thick curls around his face. And the music ... strange, yet memorable, like something I had heard in a dream.

"I am Miriam," the old woman said to me then. "Or you can call me Mary, if you prefer."

This was outrageous. What blasphemy for a Jew to assume a Christian name, the name of the Holy Mother, no less! I could not help but raise my brows.

"Mary?" I stammered, "That's a Christian name ... " Of course, I immediately regretted saying it. Who was I to judge such a thing? I felt my face go red. "What I mean is," I tried to fix the thing, "it's only that Christians and Jews ... " Was it polite to call them Jews? Was that the right word to use? Perhaps I should have said 'Hebrew'? I was only making matters worse. Gently, the old woman reached out her hand and touched my cheek, a strangely calming and intimate gesture. My mother only smiled.

"It's all right. You are not comfortable calling me Mary. I understand, but that is my name nonetheless, and if you prefer, you may use it." She pulled back her hand.

"That can't be your name." I replied honestly, surprising myself at my frankness. Something about this woman invited me to say it.

"And why can't it be my name?" she asked. "Because it is the name of the Holy Mother of the Christians? Nonsense!" she spit the word out. "You would think Mary and Jesus were Greeks with such names. But they weren't Greek. They were Jews, like us. What do you think they were called in their time, child?" She paused as if to give me leave to answer. I sat silent, enthralled. "Jesus was called Yeshua, and Mary was Miriam. They were orthodox Jews of the holy order of healers called Essenes. Remember that."

Ah, how she put me at ease, immediately in the role of the student, which I would soon take up with zeal.

"Good to meet you, Miriam. I'm Justine." I raised my eyes to meet her gaze, but a shadow fell over me as I did.

"Justine," the old woman murmured my name, a tone in her voice that pushed the shadow into my chest, a wave of dizziness coming over me. The world began to fade as if the moment were somehow undermined and slipping away. I felt another time reach for me, a dark hand summoning. A flash of light and then it was before me: *the man on the cross, wrists broken and bound, his forehead bleeding from the crown of thorns. And the woman at his feet, long red hair masking her face as she wept...*

"Justine?" It was my mother's voice. "Are you all right?"

"Yes, yes," I said, annoyed. My hand went to my head as it began to throb.

The old woman was eyeing me. Then she pulled a small vial from her bag and opened it. A strange scent floated from it, bathing me in a rich, intoxicating flood.

"The sight is very strong in her." Miriam was matter-of-fact.

"As I told you, she's always had it."

Then Miriam poured the oil in her hand and rubbed it on my forehead. Quiet, warmth, and affection moved through me, and my head stopped pounding. Putting the lid back on the bottle, she handed it to me.

"Keep this with you, child, and when it comes sudden like that, anoint yourself with it. It will ease the pain of the vision."

"Thank you," I murmured.

Miriam turned to my mother. "Now let us eat together, and I will share with you the wisdom of our traditions." Reaching into our basket as if it were her own, she pulled out a loaf of bread and some cheese. Her eyes seemed to sparkle. "Ah, Christine, this looks good!" Miriam spoke with authority and tenderness. Even her nephew seemed to relax. Reaching for the bundle in the young man's hands, she revealed the scrolls. Enoch looked confused. "It is all right," she said to him. "They will respect what we share." The scrolls were magnificent, old treasures adorned with silver amulets. I felt the tenderness with which she held the scrolls. Placing them reverently before her, she readjusted the white shawl around her shoulders and began.

"This is my tallith," she said, "my prayer shawl, that reminds me that I am clothed in light, held in the wings of the Infinite One. I wear it when I pray, to be close with my God, to bring my thoughts to holiness. I wear it now to remind you of the light that you are." This she said to me. I knew it was important. I felt as though my life were changing as she spoke.

"This is our holy book," she began, gently touching the scroll. "It is called Torah, which means 'direction.' The Torah is God's revelation to our people. It is our moral code and our law, which you know as the Ten Commandments, that will lead us to a life of holiness. The Torah is rich with wisdom, and many will spend a lifetime studying it. But our core belief is simple. It is said that the great teacher, Hillel, summarized the essence of our tradition by saying only, 'That which is hateful to you, do not do to your fellow humans.' You see? Is this not the root of your own Christian teachings?" She paused only to lift the Torah in her arms. "It is rare to find a woman who knows the Torah, as it is rare with your people to find a woman who can read, no?"

At this my mother nodded, answering, "Yes, it is very rare, indeed. We are privileged in that way."

43

"Yes, you are. And to read and teach the Holy Scriptures! This is something that Hebrews do not allow their women to do any more than any other religion. But it has not always been this way. Somewhere, our tribe as a whole lost sight of the truth, and conformed to the code of their culture rather than to the commandment of God." Shaking her head at this she placed her hand on the holy book. "So I am an oddity, you see, and teach in hiding to the few in my family that will be keepers of the truth." She nodded at Enoch. The young man smiled warmly. There was love here.

"I am the matriarch of my family," she said softly, her tone lilting with the storyteller's hum. "I travel between my family members to assure that my lineage upholds the truth and wisdom that we keep. Summers I spend here with Enoch. In winter and spring I must go up to Ireland, where others of our lineage thrive. Enoch must remain here a few more years, until he has enough money to travel home to the east. Enoch," she commanded, turning to him, "before our meal I will have you tell Justine how you came here. Tell her what happened to your family in Spain. This will be her first lesson."

"My first lesson?" I blurted out excitedly.

"Well, you don't seem to know much," Miriam threw my mother an admonishing look, "and where else will you learn it? Your books will only take you so far, Justine. Your mother should have brought you here a long time ago!" I turned to Mother, expecting to see her ready at the defense, but her face was pleasant and relaxed.

"Yes, Miriam, you're right. My daughter is more than ready." Then to me, "Miriam will be your new tutor. You may come here any day you choose, providing that your responsibilities at the manor are fulfilled. So rest now, and listen to Enoch's tale, and see what he has to teach us today." So this was what she had in mind for me! Days of freedom with a teacher that was a woman; it hardly mattered to me what she might teach!

"Yes, mother." I sat back against the tree, hopeful.

All eyes turned to Enoch, who sat thoughtfully for a moment. His hands reached out absently and touched the holy book. When he opened his eyes a deep and gentle voice began.

"My family was from Spain." He looked at me as he spoke, so that I seemed to fall into his brown eyes, seeing each scene as he described it. "I grew up at the time when the Inquisition became so active in its persecution of our people that it demanded either our conversion to Christianity or our expulsion. This only after they had seized our property, our livelihoods, and tortured and starved us. At the time, most of my relatives had escaped on a boat going to the Far East, hoping to find compassion among the Muslims. My mother's family was very wealthy, a long line of traders and merchants who had connections to get us out of the city of Toledo and take us to the East, where we might find sanctuary.

"My father was a holy man, a rabbi, who was responsible for this Torah and other mystic teachings. We were still waiting for a ship on which to leave when the Christian Holy Week of the Passion came. This was always the worst time for Jews, as the Christians, in their religious fervor, would refuse to sell us food in hopes of starving us to death. But this year, the Christians had such a fear that we would contaminate their Christian society that they began to riot and marched on our small part of the city. No one was safe. With a mandate from their holy leader, the pope, the inquisitors, hiding under those black robes with cowls over their heads, came at us like fiends. They led the Christians to burn us out of our homes and then to torture us to our deaths." He closed his eyes as the pain of remembering fell like a ghost over his face. "I was so young, only seven, I think. My family . . . I had an older sister who was twelve, and I remember my father had taken this Torah and strapped it to her waist, then dressed her in a short tunic like a Christian boy. Then he cut her hair. Tears ran down his cheeks as he did it, poor Papa, the sound of rioters beating down doors, and screams of pain all around us.

"'You must be a boy now, my Rebecca, a Christian boy. You must wait until the rioters pass by and then take your brother to the sea and find a ship.' He kissed her forehead and tied a sack with coins in it to her waist. 'Save your brother and the Torah, do you hear me?' She was crying. 'Papa,' she tried to say.

"'No! There is no time for tears now, my child. You must do as I tell you.'

"I remember Mama holding me, covering me with kisses, and then she placed a pack stuffed with food on my shoulders and put my hand in Rebecca's. I was too terrified and stunned to speak, too overwhelmed to disobey. In my heart I cried out for them, but only stood in silence at my sister's side. Papa bent down and put something around my neck. It was a gold cross.

"'Enoch, do not let go of your sister's hand no matter what you see or hear. Do you understand?' I nodded. 'And do not take off this cross until you are safe across the sea!' It was an impossible thing, my father, a holy man, putting this symbol over my shoulders. 'You must escape!' He explained. 'This Torah must reach our relatives in the East. It must!' Then there was no time left. I could hear flames crackling in the street outside. Papa took us to the door.

"'Mama and I must go first, and we will lead them away. Rebecca, you come only when we are gone. Remember, you are a Christian boy!' Mama was sobbing, holding Papa's hand. She kissed us both.

"'God bless and keep you my children.' They were the last words I would ever hear her say. I gripped Rebecca, horrified. Then the door opened and they were gone, drawn out into a murderous crowd that pushed its way down the end of the block, setting everything ablaze as they went.

"I held my sister's hand and followed her down streets and through crowds, around flaming buildings and dead bodies of people I had known and loved. We went to the river. Sliding down the embankment in the dark, we found a small boat waiting by a bridge. It was a decrepit thing, but it served to take us downriver to the sea, where Rebecca met up with men who took us to their ship. That is how we were smuggled out of Spain. It was a long trip but we reached the

East and found our family there. My sister was amazing: she traveled always as a boy, which allowed us passage and work where there would have been none." He paused here, the weight of grief still ripe in his throat. His voice came more softly, "And now we are here in Wales. We came several years ago, but two of our ships sank, and we find ourselves waiting here until we have enough to pay our debts and return to the East. There are only my two cousins and myself, and, of course, Miriam comes to us every year." He smiled at this. "We have this book, you see, the original Torah that my father had us save, and now I seek to understand it. For all these years I have wondered what is so precious about it that Papa would hold it as important as his own children."

I was spellbound by his story. He was so soft and sincere, I felt the tears pressing at the corners of my eyes. The book in his hands seemed to glow, its ornate tapestries alive now from his words.

Miriam placed her hand on his. "Good, this is a good way to start. Now, Justine, you know what we do here and how our family came to this place. Perhaps you will even be able to understand why your mother has seen fit to help us and even learn from us." A warm nod from my mother at this.

"I had Enoch begin today with his story, for it is from our stories that our people gain wisdom and insight. In sharing we learn. We come to see who we are, and sometimes who we may become. We strive to honor our differences, seeing each other as unique aspects of the Divine. Do you understand?"

There was deep compassion in her eyes, this woman my culture would have me despise. I nodded my head.

"We are sovereign beings that have great power, the power to use our will to direct our thoughts, and the things that we do, toward God, the holy spark. As Jews, we are taught that the holy spark is within everything and is both male and female."

"What?" I interrupted, "God is a woman?" This seemed an impossible thing to say.

47

"Not a woman, Justine. God is *both* male and female; for God is all, God is *everything*. We do not believe, as the Christians do, that we are born into original sin, separate from the one who made us. We do not believe that men are good and women are bad. No," she said, shaking her head, "we listen to the wisdom of our mystical Kabbalah, which conceives of God's attributes as ten sefirot, or spheres, each representing a different aspect of God. It is the tenth sefirah that portrays the feminine dimension of God, called Shekhinah. We refer to her as the bride, to whom we must wed ourselves in every moment. She is the moon and the queen, and we aspire to invoke this presence in all that we do. She is our intimate friend, who accompanies us in our exile, in our suffering, in our loneliness. You understand? We work toward a union *between the male and female* aspects of God. With Shekhinah, we hope to let our whole being become a holy vessel, a throne for the light of the Divine Presence." She leaned very close to me then. "Remember that, child; we honor both the male *and* female. This is how it was meant to be."

Turning then to her nephew, she commanded, "Enoch, sing for us. Pour out your heart to the Spirit of all Life. Robe our feast in radiant garments and sweeten our hearts."

The young man did not hesitate. He cleared his throat and began a long, swollen note that rippled through the air, so alive that I felt its resonance in my chest. My heart beat faster and harder. I felt the blood run to my cheeks as he continued, higher and then deeper, weaving it into one long sound. When he was done, Miriam broke the bread, saying, "Father, bless this food we are about to receive. Mother, fill us with its light."

I CAME TO MIRIAM EACH SUMMER in the years that followed, leaving my escort at the foot of the hill and walking alone up the stream to find her at the old shrine, which she kept. Sometimes I sat silently, watching as she gave the lessons to her nephew. Sometimes I met her alone there, and she would teach me other things, things that she insisted were mine alone. She taught me of the mystery and the magic that filled the old shrine, the power of a holy place where others have knelt in reverence. The shrine had been built hundreds of years before, new foundations laid for each new god it housed. In the stone at the altar appeared the head of a bull, the god Mithras, who came before Christ, and below that on a base of stone, older than the altar itself, was carved the image of the moon in all its phases. This place had served both the God and the Goddess, and now was kept by a Jew, who honored them both.

There were no furnishings, no benches, braziers, or stone carvings, in the little chapel, yet there was something familiar here, empty and haunting in the strong vaulted roof overhead. It was in this ancient place that I learned to use my gifts, with Miriam's commanding presence to instruct me. For some, such skills would take years to acquire and hone, but to me they came easily, and I did not question it. First to come was the magic of the fire, leaping to flame at my summons. Then the wind came at my call, racing through the trees, a ghostly breath of air. Finally, there was my sight: the images that had come so easily in childhood swelled like waves within me, but I remained lost in this sea, tossed about like a storm-driven boat. This, Miriam said, would be my greatest talent, but she was concerned that such a power might go uncontrolled.

I gave myself readily into her instruction. She was warm and kind, giving me a purpose I had craved. It was the attention, too, for I had long been invisible in my brother's shadow. I needed Miriam's smile, the recognition that would meet my success, and the warm hand that would soothe my disappointments. She knew me somehow, this old woman, so different and strange to me. And I was drawn to her, too. Miriam was powerful; one could see it in her eyes. She knew things about me that I did not. Unnerving and wonderful, she knew them just by looking. I came to love her, living each day in anticipation of my time with her in the chapel.

So many glorious afternoons, those, listening to her tell of the places she had been and the things she had seen. She was the keeper of her family's story, and had traced branches of her lineage back a thousand years. Such amazing tales she would share of this great-grandfather or that great-aunt, six generations back! There were stories of royalty and poverty both. Her family was made of Jews and gentiles. Always, she explained, there was a record keeper in each generation. That was her role now, to uphold the records, to watch the families' progress. Most important, there was a holy code that she was bound to pass on, a set of principles that she lived by, and which were her duty to share. Ah, how this intrigued me, that a family should have a code by which they lived, a unifying covenant with themselves and their God. I remember that day, early in our first summer together, when she sat me beside the Goddess pool and placed the tallith over my shoulders, explaining, "It is your covenant with yourself that you are making, Justine. *Make it your quest to serve the highest purpose and the greatest good, and you will find that by serving you will achieve fulfillment of your eternal spirit.*"

How simple it had sounded then. Make choices that will serve the betterment of humanity. Add to, rather than subtract from, the lives of the people around me. Oh, how naïve I was, how life had yet to shape me, how pain and fear and a need for acceptance would motivate my actions.

At the end of each visit Miriam would take me to the Goddess pool, the place of true vision, she called it. I would kneel before the plinth, gazing into the water. Miriam would chant her Hebrew prayer, *Kadosh, Kadosh, Kadosh, Adonai, Sabaoth,* until the water would stir. Sometimes I would see things, images gathering on the surface and then gone before I could grasp them. But I would always try—I would try for her.

Eight

MANY YEARS PASSED, AND I HAD TURNED TWENTY-ONE when the news came: Nicholas had been lost in battle. This should not have surprised us, for, although we did not speak of it, my mother and I had known the truth when he left, but I think we could not bear to give up the hope that in this one premonition we would be wrong. So, when the messenger came, we were silent with shock and something else, a rage, a sharp frustration that we had had to know such a thing. The tension of those years, the unspoken hope and doubt, suddenly broke in on us and pain set in. Nicholas was really gone.

The castle was draped in mourning. Messengers were sent through the gates to tell all the vassals that their count was dead. Something haunted me that day, a salty tide that welled in my throat so that I wanted to scream. As night came, I lay awake letting the dark wash over me, trying to become it. I lay there for a long time until the castle grew quiet, the fires died, and the dead cold that hung between the stone walls engulfed me. I was in a coffin then, some haunting warning that rolled over me, suffocating.... Shuddering, I pulled myself from the bed covers and plunged into the cold night. I was going numb from the news and the isolation. My mother had retreated to her rooms when the messenger arrived. How unlike her it was, and so I was the one who called to the servants, made arrangements, sent messengers, keeping myself busy in my grief. But when it was all done, sorrow filled my heart.

I pulled a warm robe around me and slipped out into the hall. A light shone under Nicholas' door. Gently, I pushed it open, to see my mother leaning against the archway of his window, the dim light from her oil lamp dancing on her face. She was small, soft, and beautifully elegant in her layers of velvet and lace. I had grown a full head taller than her, and for the first time, she seemed fragile to me.

"Mother," I said gently. She did not turn. Louder, "Mother," and I moved into the room. She turned, then stared up at me, her eyes red, her face narrow, and her features strained. Her lips seemed to move as if she would speak, but she did not say anything. Reaching out to her then, my hands trembling, I gathered her delicate frame in my arms and held her tight against me so that she could not resist. But she did not resist; she only cried, silently, her body trembling. And then she pulled back. Looking up into my eyes, she stroked my hair. "I love you, daughter," she whispered, her voice almost a gasp.

Emotion swelled in my throat, but I stood helpless, not know-ing how to feel. Abruptly, she turned and left the room. After a long moment I turned toward the door. A shudder passed through me. Turning back to the window, I saw, perched on the sill, a large black bird, its wings stretched wide as it made a shrill sound and flew off into the darkness.

My heart beat fast. Suddenly I knew I was not alone. A presence was here, ominous, watching. I backed out of the door and into the hall, heading toward my mother's room, but then there was a light at the stairs, and the sound of feet on the flagstone floor.

"Lady Justine, is that you, ma'am?" It was the voice of old Dustin, my mother's loyal servant.

A sigh of relief. "Oh, Dustin!" I replied, "yes, yes it's me." I moved toward him, thankful for his company, but he had the strangest look on his face. "Miss, downstairs, there is a, ah, woman. She insisted you would be up waiting for her. She demanded I come and fetch you. Of course, I said no, not at this time of grief, of, well, but you see she's so demanding..."

"That's all right, Dustin," I said, moving quickly past him. "Where is she?" I asked over my shoulder.

"Still in the great hall, ma'am. She didn't seem the type of lady like you would know—"

I didn't wait to hear the rest. I ran down the stairs and through the dimly lit corridor to find her.

It was Miriam, of course, wrapped in her thick black cloak, waiting alone in the hall. We stood for a moment in silence, grief frozen in my bones. The flame flickered between us. Then she moved all at once, her cloak rising like the wings of an angel falling over me, until I was gathered up in those old, thin arms, crying. She held me fast and rocked me and murmured words in that thick, ancient language that I did not understand but longed to hear. Rhythmic and familiar, her voice soothed the loss, encouraged my tears. My body shook and rocked until I felt the longing for him, my twin and my hero. I missed him, and in the missing, I thought my soul would break. When it was done, a river had run out of me. Miriam pulled out a cloth and wiped my cheeks. "Good." was all she said.

Nine

AT THE END OF THE WEEK WE HELD A FUNERAL SERVICE for Nicholas. A gravestone was laid in our graveyard beside the small chapel. All those who served our banner came, as was custom, to pay their respects. Even the peasantry gathered at our gates, laying flowers before them.

Now, here you must know that in the years that Nicholas was at war, the ambitious Prior Henry had built his church and enrolled our local nobility in its congregation. As was then the custom, Henry graciously allowed his patrons pardon for their sins by selling absolution for anything from gluttony to homicide; or, for the proper fee, he would cancel any vow of chastity or fasting. This common practice in the Church had paid for many a crusade, and it was one reason that my mother insisted on staying far from its doors. The Church peddled salvation, and the new prior was excellent at his trade. More nobles within his congregation meant more money and more land, for no one was free of sin, and who wouldn't absolve himself if he could afford it?

My mother considered herself a good Christian. At our chapel in the garden, we attended regular service led by old Father Peter, who had served my mother since I was born. As well you can imagine, this infuriated Prior Henry, who came to Mother at every turn, to entice her into his fold.

"Lady," he would say, "you must set an example for your people; they look to you as countess to show them what is proper. I have provided you with a church as I said I would, and it is far more splendid then that country altar to which you are so devoted. Really, it is your duty after all ... you must absolve your sins ... be a good Christian."

My mother would listen, patient and cool, until each plea became a cunning demand, which she would ignore. She would not come to his church. She would not turn to him for absolution. She did not like the Prior Henry.

On the day of our service for my brother, we opened our gardens to our guests and gathered before the small chapel for the eulogy. My mother and I dressed in mourning, ready to take our places before the assembly, when Prior Henry arrived unexpectedly. He pushed through the crowd and into the chapel, where my mother and I waited alone. After a cursory bow, he announced that he was prepared to do us the honor of leading the ceremony. This was, after all, his congregation, and who knew better than he how to move them? Old Peter was not used to such a large gathering. Henry was gracious, his voice quiet and convincing.

"Thank you, Father, for your concern," my mother said flatly, staring the little man in the eye. "But we are quite content to have Peter. After all, he has known my son from the time of his birth. I am sure he will know what to say." Abruptly, she turned to leave. I lifted my gown and began to follow, but Henry moved to the door and blocked her way.

"Lady, let us stop and think this through before a mistake is made ... " There was malice in his voice, and I felt the heat come to my cheeks.

"How dare you!" I began, but my mother raised her hand.

"No, Justine, I have been waiting for this; let it come. There will be no good time for it, and I relish honesty, a trait so difficult to find these days." She nodded for Henry to continue.

"I am sorry it must come to this, Lady, but I too appreciate frankness. You see, I have come a long way to South Wales, this isolated little country, because I saw its potential, its ability to grow. I saw that the roads into your village were strong and well built and that you kept them well maintained, offering easy access to the town. Also, I came here because you have a prosperous town and wealthy nobility scattered about the countryside, craving society and a social life. Then there are those who come here by ship, now that we are building a proper harbor. What better way to bring all these people and all this wealth together than through the Church?" A smile flashed across his gaunt face, the jewels on his fingers glistening in the afternoon light.

"When I came here, hearing from your son of your widowed status, I thought you would be in need, Lady, of a friend, a guide, who could help you plan for the future and find a suitable husband for your daughter." He frowned. "Now I see that in this I was wrong. You are *quite* capable."

My mother stood very still. "What do you want, priest?" she said in contempt. I sucked in my breath. No one spoke to the clergy that way. Father Henry did not react, but an insincere smile formed on his lips.

"First," he began, "I would like to lead your son's funeral, so the congregation will know that you and I are on peaceful terms, and that you will now be joining my flock. This will sway those who have remained on their country estates, emulating you and your, dare I call them, *Christian* practices. Second, I would like to offer you absolution for your son, in the event that he did not receive a true Christian burial or last rites and may, as we speak, be burning in purgatory." He was speaking faster, his voice rising, a well-rehearsed speech.

But my mother was only laughing. "Save this for your flock," she told him, "and tell me what it is you *really* want!"

The priest drew back, offended. He fingered the cross at his neck, weighted in gold, then replied coldly, "For your son's redemption I will accept the land by the river and the service of the men-at-arms that followed him."

Again my mother laughed. "You can't be serious, priest. What would ever make you think that I would give you land?" At this Henry looked surprised.

"Why, what else will you do with it?" he demanded. "You certainly do not seem inclined to remarry, and what a small price to assure your son eternal peace at the side of God in Heaven!"

"No, you are wrong again!" There was spite in her voice now. "I will

56

never give the Church land. I will turn this estate into a refuge, a place like the Beguine societies, where women can live in safety and peace; women, Father, that the Church has cast out of her folds. But wait, I'm wrong, aren't I? Women have never been embraced in the arms of the Church. We have been denounced for being slaves of vanity and fashion and for monstrous carnal provocation. We are the Church's rival, the temptresses, distractions from holiness; is that not how it is put? Your theology from Paul and Augustine is the work of males, and this concept of original sin is traced back to the female, Eve. It is all blamed on Eve in the end, isn't it? For what? For giving bad counsel to Adam, who then lost Paradise!" My mother stepped closer, so that Henry stiffened. "It is to women that I will give my land," she stated, stepping around him, then heading toward the door. "And I assure you, Father," she turned in the last step to face him, "that my son sits already in Heaven."

The prior flushed. "You will need me someday, Lady Christine," he said. "You and your girl will need to turn to me for help, and then what will you do when you have treated me this way? How will you manage now without a husband or a son?"

"I will manage," was all my mother said.

That night I dreamed of turmoil in the heat and the dust. A great crowd of people, the sun in my eyes, and then a great black bird, wings outstretched, and I clung to its back, flying away....

Ten

I WAS UP EARLY THE NEXT MORNING, restless, a cold foreboding heavy on my shoulders. I pulled on a warm cloak, took fresh bread from the kitchen, and then slipped through the gates to walk by the river. I needed only to be alone, I thought, to walk in peace and quiet. On and on I went, until the sun was high in the sky and I realized I was already several miles from the castle walls, and the blue hills appeared before me. Miriam, I thought then; I shall go to the chapel and there I will clear my heart.

Another hour and I was at the steps. The chapel doors were closed. Miriam was not there. A bleak wind rustled through the pines as I stepped into their shade and knelt beneath the plinth at the Goddess pool.

I ate the bread in my sack.

Quiet. Just the wind and the sound of my chewing. Where were the birds? I wondered. No sheep in the field. Why was Miriam not tending her chapel so late on a summer day?

Again the foreboding. And fear.

I stood then, my body stiff, ready for something, or someone, but it was only the wind I felt, cool on my cheek, the wind, pushing through me so that I was lightheaded, spinning. I closed my eyes. The ground seemed to move beneath me and I stumbled, then righted myself. There were whispers around me, and I saw it, the circle of women around the pool, yes, chanting, chanting something I knew, or should know. And then a voice — a woman's — deep, commanding.

"Daughter, come to me . . ." the voice resounded in my chest. "Come closer, closer, closer still." The chanting was louder now, and there was a fire, and dancing and wonderful laughter, the laughter of women.

I struggled to breathe, caught between here and there, but the voices grew louder still, calling me:

> *Open*
> *like the water spring,*
> *throat of power,*
> *furious cry of the spirit.*
> *Open*
> *Open*
> *Open*
> *to traditions*
> *of earth*
> *and water,*
> *air*
> *and fire.*
> *Open*
> *like the drum.*
> *Great mother's heart*
> *leads you inside.*
> *Open*
> *Open*
> *Open*
> *to traditions*
> *of smoke*
> *and dance,*
> *blood*
> *and sound.*
> *Open*
> *to the chant,*
> *spirit of life,*
> *Mother's voice.*
> *Open*
> *Open*

Open
To rituals
of birth
and death,
cycles
and beauty.
Open
to the great mother
everything
always
calling you home.

Then I saw it clearly, the women building it, stone by stone, and the altar there by the pool, the stone Goddess set at the foot, looking in, flowers in the water, jasmine in the air. And then they were looking into the pool, seeing, and I was there, too, leaning over . . . .

I shuddered and then my body relaxed.

They were gone. Opening my eyes, I found myself at the edge of the pool, leaning over just as I had seen. The sun, casting shadows through the pines, sent images rippling across its surface, until . . .

It was my mother I saw, rushing through the town square, pushing her way through a crowd of angry men. Then she was through and I heard her cry out, "Miriam, no!" and she was lifting the old woman from the ground. Her nephew, Enoch, lay on the ground beside her, two big men holding him down. I watched as Miriam tried to push my mother away.

"No, Christine," she was saying. "This is not for you. It can only end badly!" But my mother gripped her tighter, lifting her to her feet. Then, turning to the crowd, she threw up her hands and called for silence. Several men stepped back, and old Dustin broke through the mob behind her. There was horror in his eyes, and I saw the cause: Father Henry, standing on the steps of the court, surrounded by his black-robed fiends.

Then Miriam was speaking. "What is it you want, Father? What is it you think we've done?"

I watched as my mother turned around to face him, her skirts dipping into the dirt, sending a ray of dust between the prior and the Jews.

"I have come here today with all these good people," Father Henry began, holding out his hands in a great and benevolent gesture, "to cleanse this town of the wickedness that is amongst us!" Enoch, on the ground, raised his head as if to speak, but several men stepped out from the horde and pushed him down, hard, in the dirt.

"But what have we done, Father? Why do you think—"

"Silence!" he roared, holding his hands out once again. His drawn face had a hungry look. "Heathen!" he cried out, and the crowd stirred again, pressing in on them.

"No!" It was my mother's voice again. She was up on the steps beside Henry then, the countess speaking to her people,

"Stop this at once!" she demanded. "This is a mistake! Leave these people alone!"

Father Henry, a malicious glimmer in his eye, asked, "And how would you know that, Lady? Are you acquainted with these . . . Jews?"

The crowd quieted. Miriam shook her head, was about to speak, but before she could, my mother said it, the words that would seal my fate.

"I do," was all she said. Silence fell. Furtive glances between those who had served her for many years. My mother continued. "As many know," she said calmly, regaining her composure and authority, "I have let them have acreage at the end of the estate, where they keep to themselves. But I imagine many of you must know these people, as I have often heard that money was lent by them to the good people of this town." She looked at them then, the men with stones and rakes and rope, ready to stone this old woman and her nephew to death. I could see it in their eyes, the fever, and the fear. But then there was Henry speaking to *it*, reaching out from the steps above, touching that dark place inside them, enticing it even, justifying its very existence.

61

"You are ignorant, Lady, of these people's origins, their pagan identity and worship of demons. Surely you must know how they steal Christian children in the night for their heathen rituals, their blood sacrifice!"

"Nonsense!" my mother insisted, but the crowd had stepped closer and one of the men near Miriam pushed the old woman to the ground. My mother gasped. Dustin backed slowly away.

"You would defend these filthy murderers?" he hissed. "These are the people that killed Jesus Christ, our Lord and Savior!" His finger wagged in her face. "They threw him to the Romans and begged his execution!"

Anger pushed down the fear that should have stopped her.

"You should be ashamed of yourselves, all of you! Ignorance and superstition! Do you not know what their tradition is about? Why, it is the very foundation of our own! Was not Christ our Savior a Jew? Were not the first fathers of our church Jews, converted? Why, persecuting these people and their religion is like looking at the mother and saying she has no right to exist now that the child is born!" She spoke to the people, her people for all these years, but they only looked back blankly. Of course, they didn't know such things. They had no education and believed only what the Church insisted was truth. Had any of them ever read the Holy Book? They lived in a climate of fear and hostility, and most of them probably owed Enoch money, debt that would disappear if he died. These simple people wanted the Jews gone, hated them; I could feel it wash over me through the water. What could my mother be thinking? Could she not see it in their eyes? But she went on, as if possessed.

"Think before you do this, think of our Savior, Jesus. Was he not born a Jew? Was he not committed to the Torah and the Bible commandments? Doesn't Saint Matthew in his Gospel tell us that Jesus said, 'Think not that I have come to abolish the Torah and the prophets; I have come to fulfill them. Till Heaven and Earth pass away, not an iota, not a dot, will pass from the Torah until all is accomplished. Whoever then relaxes one of the least of these commandments and teaches people so, shall be called least in the kingdom of heaven; but one who does them and teaches them shall be called great in the kingdom of heaven.'"

She spoke loudly in that lulling rhythm that so often put people in trance. So stunning was her delivery, and so shocking was the sight of a woman reciting, that even Father Henry stood speechless. Gaining confidence, she continued.

"I know you wish to do the right thing, and I speak to you only to assist you in following your Christian conscience. We have so many misconceptions of these people and their religion, so many ideas, as if their God is different from our own. Yet is not the Old Testament, their Jewish book of history and law and prophecy, part of our own spiritual heritage? Were not the first Christians converted Jews themselves? You must imagine how it was when Jesus walked the earth. Whom did he preach to? Who walked at his side? *Who made up the first Christians?* Think! It was the Jews." She stepped down into the dirt, and the crowd parted for her. Reaching out her hand to Miriam, she helped the old woman to her feet.

Yes, I thought, leave now; leave quickly, while they are confused. *Leave, mother!*

But Henry had collected himself. He was down the stairs by her side, pushing the old woman to her knees.

"Heretic!" he cried, thrusting his finger, an arrow of accusation, at my mother. "It was the Jews who turned our Lord over to the Romans, and it is the Jews who now trample on the host in their pagan Shabbats!" The crowd closed around them.

"And how, Lady Christine," he said with controlled spite, "would you know so much about these people? How can you know that they do not sacrifice our children?" A wry smile at this as he turned away from her in arrogant dismissal, back to the crowd.

"How is it that your town has escaped the plague? How is it that this shire has thrived while the rest of the country has lost its people and starved? Tell me, please, how this has come about?"

The man holding Enoch spoke. "She told us it would come to pass," he said, his voice shaking. "She knew it, she knew it before it came."

Then, before anyone could think, Henry cried out, "She knew! She knew what could not be known! Who would tell her such a thing? Who? How?" A dramatic pause, and then, "The devil," he whispered, and let go of Enoch to cross himself.

"Satan!" someone in the crowd cried out, and then another, and the men pressed in.

Then it happened as I told you: they took her, Henry leading them to the church, and I watched it in the pool, as they stoned them till blood ran from my mother's cheek. They took the Jews to the stable, where I heard them cry out while others began to place three great stakes in the ground, piling firewood at the base of each.

My mother was taken inside the monastery cell and set down, bleeding, torn, to be given a trial. There were men only, with Henry as the leader.

"Hear you," he said, "you are a witch. Will you confess voluntarily? If not we will bring forward witnesses against you."

"Of course I'm not a witch, I have a pure conscience on the matter. If there were a hundred witnesses I am not concerned, for God knows I am speaking the truth."

I watched as they brought forth witnesses, who described in detail my mother's evildoings. After each one they asked her again, "Will you confess?" She answered, "I have never renounced God and I will never do it!"

Then came the executioner. He stripped her and bound her hands and put her to the torture.

She screamed.

When it was done, Henry asked her again, and again she replied, "I have never renounced God and will never do it!" He signaled the executioner to take her to the stable, where she would be kept. Tomorrow, he was certain, she would confess.

The executioner, a big, round man, lifted my mother to her feet. She cried out.

"Lady," he said then, his voice shaking, "you were kind once to my mother when death had come to take her. I was just a boy but I remember you still, with your healing draught. Please listen to me now. They will not relent, Lady, I have seen this before. They will make me torture you again tomorrow and I cannot bear to do it, but if I turn away they will say I am in league with you and I will surely burn, too! I beg you, Lady, for God's sake, confess something, anything, whether it be true or not. You cannot endure the torture they will have me put to you. Even if you bear it all you will still not escape, not even if you were the queen herself, but one torture will follow another until you say you are a witch. Even then, Lady, you are beyond hope, for once you confess they will burn you."

Lifting her head with effort, my mother looked at the young man and repeated, "I have never renounced God and I never will."

And then she fainted.

Eleven

A RIPPLE SWAM ACROSS THE POOL, and I blinked, coming back to myself. Looking up, I was startled to see a man standing at the water's edge across from me. Scrambling to my feet and stepping away, I began to mumble something, some excuse, and then recognized him, walking slowly toward me, his hand outstretched, his face soft.

It was Adrian, the young duke.

"This is a hard thing for you to see, Justine," he was saying. "But it is done, exactly as you have witnessed, and now I am here for you." He was standing in front of me. I could not speak. "Don't be afraid of me, I'm here to help you." He reached then for my hand but I pulled away, confused and sick. How did he know I was here? How could he know what I had seen? Yet, I knew somehow that what he said was true. He answered the questions as if I had spoken aloud.

"I promised your brother I would look after you, and your servant Dustin told me what happened. I knew you were here because we are not so different, you and I."

Again he reached for my hand, and again I stepped away. It was dusk now, and the sky was aflame behind him.

"How did you come here?" I asked.

"My horse is at the apple tree. Come, let me take you where you will be safe."

I hesitated, my mother's cry burning in my chest. Misunderstanding my pause, he continued, "You can't return to the castle, Justine, they are all looking for you now. Henry will not rest until it is all under his control, and it should be easy enough for him to prove that you conspired with your mother. I have a friend who has a great interest in your family; he has prepared a place for you. Come."

This time I took his hand and let him lead me down the steps to the stallion that waited. He was a strong animal, sleek, black power. He did not shy away when I reached for him, but nuzzled into my outstretched hand.

"You have a way with animals, too, I see." Adrian was behind me, reaching for the reins. "You ride him, Justine, and I will lead. My men are only a mile or so down the river." He reached for my waist, lifting me easily into the saddle.

It was then, when he released me, that I acted, swung my leg over the horse's head, reached for the reins and dug my legs hard into his side. The stallion reared. Adrian fell back. With all the life in me, I gripped with my legs, grasping deep into his mane, the reins tight in my grip.

He charged as if into battle, through the field and down the hill toward the river. Then, like a phantom, I heard a voice, calming, soothing, lulling the stallion to a canter and then to a walk. The horse's ears were perked as if listening to his master's command, but that was impossible, we were almost half a mile away. But it was his voice, indeed; I heard it call the horse's name. And then I understood, *"We are not so different, you and I ...."*

I dug my heels hard into the horse's flank, and called to me the power I had learned with Miriam. It came with the wind, howling up behind me, driving the horse on, drowning the man's voice so that the stallion stirred and then galloped, like the wind, toward my home.

Twelve

I URGED THE HORSE THROUGH THE TREES AS WE APPROACHED, and let him loose when the castle was in sight. The last rays of sunlight hung meager in the sky, enough to guide me to the servants' entrance at the eastern gate, away from the river and the town. I knew precisely what I must do.

I slipped silently through the servants' gate and into the yard by the cookhouse, avoiding the lights that shimmered in the great hall and the kitchen. I waited in my mother's garden until the sun was gone and only the dim light of the new moon could find me. Then I did my magic. Again I called the power to me, and again it came, filling me as though I were a cauldron, stirring my flesh. "Dustin," I whispered, "Dustin, come to me in the garden. Come to me now, in the garden, the garden, Dustin, come." I whispered it again and again, until it became a chant, holy to my heart. The cookhouse door opened and I watched him come, no torch, no men, he came alone.

"I hear you, Lady," the faithful old man whispered into the dark. But I could hear the fear in his voice, too.

"I'm here, Dustin," I whispered back. "I need your help now, friend, please don't fear me!" I felt my voice choke, my throat tighten. Everything now rested on his courage. He stepped timidly into the garden. The rosebushes, tall and adorned with flowers, hid me.

"Faithful Dustin!" I said when he came behind the bush, and I hugged him then despite myself. But he did not draw back, this man who had been in my life since my birth. I needed him now and he was here.

"I'm sorry, Lady, your mother ... but you must know all that by now, else you wouldn't be hiding. But you shouldn't be here, ma'am, they're

68

looking for you." He dropped his voice as he said it, and I realized the danger I was putting him in. "Dustin, I know everything and I need your help."

"Of course."

"I need you to go to my brother's room, into his old chest. Collect some clothes, a shirt, and leggings, and bring his old hunting cloak, the wool one with the hood. And I will need his short sword and a dagger. Wrap them up inside the clothes in case anyone stops you. Tell them you are removing the master's things to the armory. Tell them Prior Henry told you to do it. Yes, that will work."

"Lady," he interrupted, "you don't mean to —"

"Don't worry, Dustin, I know what I'm doing and I need those things. I will wait here for you."

"But, miss, what about money and a horse? Surely there are people you can go to. Why, the duke came by earlier and assured me he would look after you."

I put my hand on the old man's arm. He was a dear friend of my mother's, and I knew that he was confused and frightened, but I had no time for such things.

"Dustin," I said in an even voice, "you must bring me the things I have asked you for. No! No more questions. You must trust me and do as I ask." I had let my voice take on the hypnotic drone that I had so often heard in my mother's speech when she wanted others to follow. "Now go, Dustin, before I am discovered!"

The old man retreated behind the hedge and walked quickly back to the kitchen door. Good. I would just wait here, quiet, under the moon.

I heard a voice, a whisper, soft beneath the roses. I stiffened, listening, straining to hear where it came from, but it was all around me, behind and in front, so that I turned and turned until I realized it was no one at all, just a voice and it was meant for me. I stopped, stood utterly still.

"Justine . . ." Haunting.

69

"Mother..." I was about to cry.

"Go to the herbarium, daughter... to the jars in the back, the ones that are sealed. Go, go now, Justine." Her voice was clear. I felt her presence through the garden, so I turned behind me now to the shed by the wall that held her herbs, and did as she instructed. I went to the back of the little building and pulled down the blue jar, opened it, and listened as she instructed me to pour its contents into the water jug at the door.

"Bring these to me, hurry!" as if she were whispering in my ear.

"Mother!" But then the presence was gone and I heard Dustin amidst the roses.

He had done just as I had asked. I hugged him again. "Dustin, you must go now and collect your things. Get your wife and the servants out of the castle. Leave it now, and hurry!" The old man did not hesitate.

"God go with you, Lady." And as he turned to go, "And with your mother as well."

Can you imagine what I did then? How I pulled out the short blade and sliced my hair, the long strands of brown curls falling at my feet? And how I changed into the clothes so that I would appear a boy, covered my head with the hood, and strapped the short sword to my waist? Tying the water jug to my waist as well, I crept from my mother's garden back to the servants' gate. Now there was commotion. I could see that the kitchen door was open and servants were coming out, carrying satchels, the cook still with her apron on and a loaf in her hand. Dear Dustin commanding them out, a child in his arms, another by the hand. They must have thought him insane, for they protested as they went.

But in a moment I had cleared his name, for a blaze of flame leapt from the kitchen and ran down the side of the roof. The cookhouse was made of stone, but still I sent the flame dancing wildly over the roof and onto the shutters of the old armory.

Screaming then, cries, and carrying on. Yes, that is good, I thought, it would keep them busy all night. Yet, I lingered, focusing my attention on my bedchamber until a blaze could be seen through the window.

Then Nicholas' and my mother's, until I saw the whole second floor alight, the fire licking the wooden timbers above.

The place was in havoc when I left. *I will leave you nothing, Henry,* I thought, *nothing but ashes and dust.*

I called silently to the horse, which met me in the field. I pulled myself upon his back and headed for the road to town, the castle blazing behind me. On the road, I passed many people hurrying toward the blaze, but they did not stop me. As I came to the bridge by the river, I slid off the stallion and let him go.

"Go home now, friend." I told him. "Go find your master," and off he trotted back the way we had come.

I turned toward the bridge. Clutching the blade beneath my robe, I headed over the great stones toward the new church and Father Henry. Two men-at-arms stood at the other side of the bridge, and I could see the yard still full of people, so that my plan looked hopeless. But I could not give up; she was in there, and Miriam, too.

Hatred, red, molten heat.

I looked across the bridge at the church, a large stone building with high, beamed ceilings of wood. Of course. I focused on the timber, the long loft, until smoke rose from the far side and then orange flame. Yes, this is what he loved the most, the seat of his power. I did not care if it was a place made sacred by people's devotion, nor did I care what was lost to the people of this town, for they had lost it already in their denial of truth. I set their church ablaze, the wicked orange flames a ghastly sight against the black sky.

Cries came from the yard, and the monks scattered in a panic; then, buckets and men and women lined up all the way down to the river. I walked right through the crowd, lost in the chaos, and slipped to the back of the stable where the witches were kept. The guard had abandoned his post! I pulled the large crossbar from its home and pushed open the door. Light from the fire outside flickered through the boards that made up the walls.

"Mother," I whispered, "Miriam." A muffled sound and my mother's voice, "Here, Justine, we are alone. They have taken the Jews." I followed her voice to the wall, which held saddles and leather bags on big pegs. In the corner was a post holding up a stall, and there she sat, resting her head on the wall. As my eyes adjusted to the dark, I could see the cut across her forehead, the thin horse blanket covering her, the hand, broken and swollen from the thumbscrews, and finally, the shackles that held her. So, they left her unguarded because of these! I reached for the chain and followed it to the wall. "We have to get these off!" I said evenly, as if it could be done. "We have to leave now while they are busy with the church!"

"Justine..."

I pulled out the sword. "I can cut this out, tear this down," and I prepared to swing the blade blindly at the chain. Tears of frustration.

"Stop, Justine, and listen now, there isn't much time. Come here..." she coughed, her body seized. I dropped the sword, bent on my knees, and tried to hold her, but she writhed in pain.

"They have broken me, Justine, I bleed now... inside." Her eyes were shut. "It cannot be fixed. I will not live through this. But the pain is great and death will come slowly... help me, daughter. Give me the herb at your side. Open the cask and pour it down my throat, belladonna, sweet, simple death. Death on my own terms, Justine...." She shuddered and winced again, so that I could only hold her, sobbing now.

"I can't, mother, I can't, please—"

"Justine," she continued, "you know you cannot undo this chain, and soon the guard will be back and you must be gone. Tomorrow they will come for me and demand something I will not give, and they will take me to torture again, and I will die in agony." There were tears on her face; they glistened in the wisps of light that flickered across the walls.

"Help me die, Justine. Give me the water now. Put it to my lips and then you must go. You must be safe." Her voice a whisper, strained, spent.

I ignored my tears. I ignored the horror in my chest, which gripped me with such force that I could hardly breathe. I pulled the bottle from my side and opened the top. Gently, tenderly, I lifted her head and held the bottle to her lips.

"Yes," she murmured, struggling to swallow. "Yes."

When it was done I rested against the wall and slid my arm around her shoulder, letting her head lie softly against my neck.

"You must go now, Justine." I could hardly distinguish the words.

"I will go in a moment, Mother." I assured her. "There is still plenty of time." My throat threatened to close but I forced myself on. "I have given them their witch, Mother! I have sent the church blazing! It will take awhile for them to put it out, I can stay a little longer—" A sharp breath and tears. I felt her body shaking.

"I want you to survive this, Justine. You must promise me you will go."

"Of course," I answered. But I was so broken now, cut so deep inside that I did not know if I could.

"You must be brave. You will be alone."

"I am stronger than you think, Mother, and I will survive this. I promise you!"

She trembled again. "I love you, my daughter." A ghost of a whisper, "Keep your promise to me."

Suddenly, I knew this was our last moment together. I put my lips to her ear. "Mother!" I whispered.

But she was already gone.

I did not cry. I laid her gently on the straw, covering her with my cloak, then picked up the discarded sword and turned for the door. I knew I could not keep my promise.

Walking as if possessed, from the stable into the yard, the fire still blazing, a procession of hands passing buckets, I moved like a demon through them. At least, that is how I heard it told after. That an image had emerged from the stable, my brother's ghost, sword held high above his head, walking dreamily through the scene, so that some dropped back from the group, crying "Ghost!" and "Demon!" and the monks crossed themselves as I passed by. They say the crowd parted as I crossed the yard, that I went through them savagely, a wicked cry rising from my throat as I saw Prior Henry, how he backed away, and I ran, the sword above me, death in my eyes. Ah, yes, I remember that, rushing at him, his face terror-stricken, and swinging the blade down hard, hearing it whistle against the crackling flames around me, driving it severely, so that it would slash all the way down to his heart . . . . What I remember next was pain, a sharp crack on the back of my head, and then blessed darkness.

Images, then, of being carried back to the stable, and voices, screams, indignant, fearful. And a whip, slicing my skin, and stones, and always the back of my head throbbing, blood wet on my cheek. I think I screamed, despite myself, and then there were torches and the pyre.

"Burn her!" they shrieked, "Burn the witch!" Swooning with pain, I felt my eyes blur, and then I saw them, spirits, hundreds, no, thousands, all women, holding out their hands, stroking me.

"It will hurt," one said.

"It will be unbearable," another added.

"But we are here, you will not go to it alone."

Then they were dragging me, for I could no longer stand, my face in the dirt, and Henry's voice shrieking above it all, "Burn her! Burn the demon witch!"

Everything blurred in the pain as they hauled me up, the stench of death on them now.

"It will be over soon," I thought gratefully, "I'm sorry, Mother, I'm sorry."

And just as the world began to fade, the ropes binding my wrists to the post, kindling already set ablaze, I heard the pounding of hoofs, a stallion's cry and the duke's command, "Cut her down!"

Thirteen

WHEN I CAME TO, I had only a vague sense of my body. A heavy, drugged web hung over me, pressing down on my senses so that I seemed to float just outside of my flesh. I tried to open my eyes, to speak, but I could not. I heard voices, hushed and worried.

"We don't have much time, Cassandra." It was Adrian. His voice seemed to move through me like music, a familiar sound. I shuddered. I felt both of them move toward me, and then one, Adrian, I think, touched my hand. "Give me the oil now," he said, his voice tense. "We must anoint her or we will lose her soul again. I can't let that happen!" He brushed his hand across my forehead and I could feel his fear. *Death*. Yes, that was it, I was going to die, and he wanted to save me. I could feel him pulling on me somehow, through the touch of his hand, as if his will were holding me to the earth, to this room, and to my body, which now seemed farther away. I was suspended between life and death. I tried to think what to say or do. Did I really want to die? The answer slid easily from my bruised and broken limbs, from the memory of torture and pain and my mother's death. Yes. I tried to move my lips, to say, "Let me die, Adrian, let me go." But they would not move, nor would any sound come from my throat. I seemed to be slipping farther away. The two of them were arguing.

"No!" Adrian was angry. "The prince would want this; he has waited too long for her, and he will not bear to lose her again!" His voice was frantic. "Give me the oil now, Cassandra, or I will take it from you!"

"How dare you say such a thing, Adrian!" The woman was indignant. She seemed to be moving away from me, pacing the room. "You are arrogant and stubborn, Adrian. Perhaps you have been too long at the master's side!" I could feel heat surge through his hand, and a sense of uncertainty. He wanted to lunge at Cassandra, to take something precious from her and give it to me. I could feel it. But he was afraid to let go of my head, as if in letting go I would slip away. Cassandra went on, "Perhaps you are not thinking clearly, Adrian. Maybe your feelings for this girl are impairing your judgment? Perhaps you are thinking more of yourself, or what the Master will do when he finds that you let this happen to her. I think the Master certainly knows by now what has happened. He seems to know everything before it happens. Surely he could be here if this were important to him, if he wanted her to be saved."

"Give me the oil, Cassandra. You can lecture me for eternity, but I need the oil now or she'll die, do you understand?"

"Of course. I understand what's happening. Listen to me, Adrian. You aren't thinking clearly. You're overwhelmed by all these years you've been watching over her, and now it's come to this. You feel as though her suffering is on your shoulders, but she chose this, Adrian, and you must let her have her choice. When she dies—"

This was too much for Adrian. I felt something inside him swell and break, and then he lunged, releasing my head, setting me free. I began to float as if in a dream, up and up and up, slowly, gently. Suddenly, I could open my eyes. I was high above the scene, looking down at my body, limp on the bed. We were in a great stone room filled with candles and firelight. Adrian was reaching for the woman's throat! But no, it wasn't that he was going to hurt her, it was the jar she wore at the hollow of her neck, the shiny white vessel. I had seen it before somewhere. The light from the enormous fire threw their shadows, like demons dancing, across the tapestry on the opposite wall. The woman screamed. She grabbed Adrian's hands in hers.

"Enough!" she cried, thrusting him back with the force of a man. "Enough, Adrian! You would force the holy oil from me?" Adrian looked drawn and frail, as if he would crumble. He put his face in his hands.

"I'm sorry, Cassandra. I'm sorry." He staggered back helplessly. The woman softened then.

"I know, Adrian." She was warm. "I see what it is now." She moved toward him. I could see her love for him, flowing like a wave from her chest, encompassing him. "You care for her." She said it simply. Adrian shook his head, coming back to himself.

"Please, give me the oil, Cassandra." He held out his hand. Tears filled the woman's eyes. Reaching beneath her blonde hair, which fell long and loose down her back, she undid the clasp holding the vial to her neck. Then she handed it to him.

"In the name and the power and the glory of the most high," she said.

Turning back to my body, he leaned close to my ear and whispered something I could not quite hear. I was moving farther away, floating upward as if in a dream. The last thing I saw was Adrian tearing the shirt away from my chest and breaking the vial open over my breast. The oil spilled onto me. Even from the dream I was in I could smell the scent, thick with frankincense and myrrh. I felt pulled to it, drawn in and down, wanting to breathe more deeply, a profound urge to taste it.

And then I fell.

In a moment I could feel my limbs aching, my lungs burning. As I breathed in, the aroma seemed to fill my head like liquid, seeping deep inside my body, inside my skin. I began to tremble as it traveled down my throat and arms, rippled down my belly and legs. At first it was exquisite, such a burst of sensation as I had never known, a brilliant light filling me from the inside out. But in the next moment the light seemed to change and the sensation with it. It became a flame, licking my skin, sending a searing pain through my body. Each breath passed like fire down my throat, scorching my chest. I cried out in shock. As if I were an instrument being played, I could feel everything in my body: the light from the fire, the velvet sheet on the bed beneath me, Adrian's voice. I could feel the broken bones in my hand pulsing as if alive, reaching out for each other like lost lovers. My torn flesh screamed in my ears, my heartbeat pounded in my chest as if it would rip through, wanting to be free of me. It banged and banged on my bones, pushing tears up from some hidden place, a box filled with my horror and despair. The pain tore at the box and threw open the lid, unleashing the anguish I had tried to bury. I began to cry.

But there was Adrian's voice, "Justine." I could not open my eyes to see him. "You are in control of your body now, in a different way than you have ever been. You must listen to me." His tone was even. "You are mistress of your body, Justine; you must command it to release the pain and heal itself. You must have the strength of will to insist." I felt him then, searching for a way to help me. "I will try to guide you," he said, placing his hand on my forehead, but a wicked spasm shot through my limbs as he did. I screamed.

He seemed to shrink back. "All right, be still," he said, pulling his hand away. I heard the fear in his voice. "Stay calm, Justine, I won't touch you. You can do this yourself; you are going to have to. Now listen to me. Every piece of your flesh is alive, vibrating like the string of a mandolin. The oil I have anointed you with has plucked the string too hard, made your body vibrate too much. You must slow down the vibration by using your will, the part of you that says, 'I Am.' You must command..." I tried to concentrate, to understand, but the pain was consuming me, running away with my mind. I began to cry out hysterically.

"No," I heard my voice sobbing. "No, I can't, Adrian, I just can't —"

"Don't say that!" Adrian ordered, panic in his tone. "You have to take control, Justine! Everything you say, everything you think, matters, Justine. Concentrate!" But I was trapped inside myself, burning in the pain.

I heard Cassandra. "By the light of Heaven, Adrian, what have you done?" She was horrified. "She cannot leave her body now, Adrian. She will suffer until she goes insane! Look, she is already half out of her mind, my God, and now she is immortal!" I heard the fear in her voice and felt it wash over me like a flame that pierced my skin. I screamed again.

"Be silent!" demanded Adrian. "She feels everything we feel! We must stay calm for her, stay at peace, be confident she will do it!" But I felt his anxiety too, welling up in his throat so that he could say no more.

A throbbing white heat bore down on me, taking away my will, bruising me. I knew I would be lost in it all. Pain. My brother, my mother, and Miriam, all gone. Pain. My body broken, my heritage lost. Pain. My life finished, incomplete.

It was then, when it was all too much to bear, when I was humbled completely, that I knelt finally at the throne of my pain. Tears poured from me to pay homage to each hurt in its turn.

Finally, my body convulsed, then softened as if holding itself, and suddenly the pain was gone.

I gasped for breath, cool, sweet air, and then I relaxed, vaguely aware of a new presence by my side and a hand on my head.

"My Lord." I heard Cassandra's voice in awe. "Master, you are here!"

Part Two

The Prince

One

I CANNOT RECALL CLEARLY WHAT HAPPENED NEXT. It all seemed like a dream.

I know I saw him, the Master, radiant and angelic. I remember gazing into his eyes and surrendering to their familiar warmth. It did not seem strange at all that I knew him somehow, that I felt I had been with him all my life and that I was safe. He traced the features of my face, his soft hand like velvet on my skin. His voice was reassuring, explaining something, that he was my friend, my guardian was it? I listened dimly as he spoke, my eyelids growing heavy, body tingling with fatigue. My eyes shut and opened, now engrossed with the sharp features of his face, all Roman, angular, direct. And those eyes! Of course I had seen them before. I knew him, I was sure of it.

He was smiling down at me, "Yes, Justine, you've known me before." His voice was rich, like the sound of a cello. I wanted to reach out and touch him then, to push my hand through his hair, obsidian black, and to trace his eyes and his lips as he had done to me. I was so drawn to him, yet I could not keep my eyes from closing.

"Listen to me, Justine. Focus on my voice now, darling. Give in to the sleep that is coming for you. Let your body rest now, and know that you will be safe with me for a time. I'm going to take you away from here tonight, away form all the horrors you've been through, and you will sleep, a long and peaceful rest while your body transforms itself. You see, none of this was supposed to happen yet. You were to go with Adrian, and he would have brought you to me. We were to take care of you, teach you for a while longer, and only then would we have given you the oil." My eyelids were impossibly heavy. "But I did not account for your wild temper. I should have remembered … and now things have changed, and to save you, Adrian has anointed you too soon." I was drifting, lulled to sleep by the sound of his voice. "Rest now, precious. Let time pass, let it take you far away from this life you have known. When you wake, your transformation will be complete. You will be as Adrian is, as all of us are," his voice seemed far away …

"Immortal."

This last word I heard in the distance as I slipped into a dream. I was vaguely aware that my body was lifted, held in strong, caring arms, and then there was movement upward and a freeing sense of lightness.

I dreamed then that I was carried across the sky by an angel who loved me.

Two

I AWOKE IN THE EARLY EVENING, alone, in a large, luxurious bed. I opened my eyes easily, instantly alert. Sensation ran through me in a way I had never experienced before. As I surveyed the room, my eyes were keen. Every color seemed to bathe me in its richness. Waves of texture became a part of me, so that I could almost feel the room, as if it were alive, touching me. It was all so different, as if I had awakened to a new body, a new life. I was far from home and *he* was here, I knew it, could feel it. And the remarkable thing was this: I did not feel in the least bit afraid. Rather, I was aware of a growing anticipation, an excitement and giddiness. The pain of my mother's death, the horror, seemed small in me, a hollowness left somewhere far away. It was as if time had passed, distancing me from my life and my grief. No, this evening was not for mourning, I was too alive for that.

I was in an enormous room, torches lit, elaborate tapestries on the walls, expensive rugs, and vases of fresh flowers on pedestals in every corner. I slid out of bed, a silk gown sending ripples of sensation across my skin. I stopped to wonder how I had gotten here, and who had dressed me. I had a sense that I remembered it somehow, or dreamed it — a long sleep, not here in this bed, but somewhere close by, was it in a church? I was attended, and *he* was often there, talking to me, wasn't he? Yes, that was it. I remembered the sound of his voice for a long time, talking, telling stories, reassuring me. There was a woman, too. I struggled to remember her, someone familiar who had come to see me, pressing fresh oils on my skin; and then deeper sleep for a long time. Yes, that was what had happened. I knew it suddenly, that time had passed, much more than a night or a day. I had been sleeping and my body had changed. Now I was someone new, someone different.

I turned to the verandah, streaks of purple and orange melting in the sky outside. Walking to the stone railing, I caught my breath as I looked out over miles of sea. I was high up in a castle of stone, built on the side of a cliff. Waves crashed wildly against the long beach below, their rhythmic crescendo filling me with an unfamiliar excitement. I could see in the fading light the expanse of stone walls with rectangular watchtowers at either end. The gatehouse, to the left of me, was of ancient, crumbling stonework, and the wooden drawbridge was pulled up, leaving a gap in the air between the stone and the land. It was as if the castle was built on an island of its own.

I turned back to my room, my head swimming. Where was I? And where was *he*? I knew that he was here, that I was safe with him, and suddenly I longed to see him.

Back inside my chamber I found clothing, laid out on screens by a dressing table. There was a variety to choose from, some familiar, others in a wholly different style than I was accustomed to. There were richly embroidered dresses in linen, silk, and velvet, robes woven with Eastern designs and colors that leapt wildly into each other.

I chose a simple velvet mantle of green, over a soft gown of white linen that hung loose to the floor. It was cut low at the neck, baring my chest, letting the warm evening air kiss my skin. It was as if the air had a texture to it, caressing me. How luxurious it was in those first moments of my rebirth, to indulge in the sensations of my new flesh.

I stepped out into the hall to find torches already lit. It was warm here; doors and windows were open so that I could hear the sea. I moved slowly down the hall and then down the curving staircase to the next floor, awed by the wealth and splendor around me; magnificent things, with elaborate color, overwhelmed me. Ancient busts stood on pedestals in every corner; bronze statues and masks of gold filled every niche. Indian and Persian rugs covered the marble floors, so that my feet sank into an unearthly cushion wherever I stepped. I wandered through rooms richly decorated, and filled with the most

expensive antiques. Quietly, I moved through them, drawn by an unseen hand, until I entered a long hall, decorated in colored murals with
scenes I soon recognized as historical events. I slowed, entranced by
the colors and the vivid pictures before my eyes. I moved gradually,
every few feet a new story, a different people, a battle, a birth, a death.
The pictures on the walls seemed to be telling the story of humanity.
There were scenes that I recognized, legends and histories I had read.
Sometimes the color would lead my eye up, even to the ceilings, where
figures of epic tales came to life. So real were these figures that I soon
began to lose myself in them, overcome by jungles with wild beasts,
and then lost in Egypt with tombs and pharaohs. There was a people
crossing the deserts, and Christ, there in the manger. The scene was
so elaborate, the light emanating from the child so real that I began to
feel drunk and giddy. The next scenes I recognized were his life, his
ministry, and his death. But the story did not end there; no, there was
the figure of Joseph of Arimathea, taking Christ's body to the tomb,
and then the women were at his feet, crying. My eye lingered on the
woman in black, golden bees buzzing around her in every scene. I had
seen her in earlier scenes, anointing his head, and now she was at the
tomb, but of course, he was not there. She must be Mary Magdalene,
I thought. Then the scenes changed, though the characters seemed
the same. Two stories began to unfold, one following the woman in
black as she crossed the water with Joseph and began a new life, and
the other, following the history of the Church. The one path was filled
with feminine characters, branching out all over the world. Always the
bees were depicted fluttering around them.

It was the other path that was familiar to me. I recognized the early
Christians arguing amongst themselves, and then the birth of the
Church, and its rise to power as the Roman emperor, Constantine,
had his vision of the cross and made Christianity the religion of Rome.
Then the story of the great plague in A.D. 540, devastating Rome and
sending people running to the Church, which explained that the plague
was an act of God, a punishment for the sin of not obeying the Church.

There were scenes of the Church burning books and devastating the sciences, outlawing the Greek and Latin scholars of the past. The murals showed how blind faith had taken over and how the Church prospered from it. Nothing was spared in this visual epitaph. It went on through the ages, until I came upon scenes that I had lived through, marvelous pictures of the story of my own time!

My body seemed to float down the hall as if it knew where to take me. I surrendered to it completely, a sense of my humanity filling me from the images. I smelled life, too, all around me. There were boxes of flowers set at every window, with fragrant vines of jasmine that swept a sweet scent into every scene. I did not know where I was going, only that I was being led, to see this place and these things, and to be touched by them.

Finally, I felt *him* near, an unmistakable pull in my chest. I let myself be drawn by the feeling, away from the hall and the stories I had taken into me there, and down another dimly lit corridor, to a room at the end, its tall wooden doors thrown open, inviting.

Three

I STEPPED INTO A LIBRARY BATHED IN LIGHT, the illumination of a dozen candelabras filling the room. The high stone walls were covered with art with a distinctly Venetian flair. Angels flew across lush landscapes, and Madonnas wept. There were walls of books, hundreds of books, rolled up manuscripts, busts of Greek goddesses, and a large wooden table with a sprawling map. Bouquets of dried flowers filled ancient-looking alabaster jars. A plush couch and upholstered chairs with brocaded wings surrounded the fireplace, now blazing with orange light. A magnificent mirror in a gold frame hung above it, so that I caught a reflection of myself as I entered the room. I stopped, startled at whom I saw. Was that I, my hair long again, falling in wild brown ringlets down my arms and over my breasts, which had now become full and ripe. My body was different, replete with grace and dignity, my eyes a dazzling amber in the light. I caught my breath, anxiety gripping my stomach. Yes, it was I, only older, a woman.

"Yes . . . " his voice was warm and affectionate. I pulled my eyes from the mirror to see him standing only a few steps from me. His enigmatic smile poured over me, washing the uneasiness away. My heart leapt—what a feeling coursed through me at the sight of him!

He was dressed elaborately, a lace shirt with pearl buttons, a crimson cape embroidered with gold thread and shoes with diamond buckles. There were jewels on his fingers and an emerald medallion at his chest.

"Your body is different now," he continued reassuringly. I couldn't answer, just stood staring into his eyes.

"You're not frightened of me, are you?" he asked. My body thrilled with the sound of his voice.

"No," I said. "Should I be?"

"No." He made an offhand gesture. "I'm just surprised at your self-possession, Justine. It's not every day one looks an immortal in the eye." He grinned, and something mischievous crept into his eyes. "No, you are too enamored with the adventure. You have waited so long for it, and now it has come for you, and you can't imagine being frightened of it."

"I feel something," I said, "but it's not fear. My heart is racing. I feel excited, I think. At first I thought I must be dead, but I know I'm not. I feel more alive than ever. I feel more real. Yes, that's it isn't it? I just feel like *more*!"

I could see he was pleased at this. He smiled, and suddenly his face became animated and soft. He reached out his hand to me. Without hesitation I took it. A heat passed through me. He led me to the couch in front of the fire and settled himself in the chair opposite, leaning back comfortably, looking entirely human and at home. Suddenly, the thought struck me — he *looked* human. I felt confused. He had used the word "immortal," hadn't he? Before I could lose myself in the thought, he began, "Let me explain it now so you will understand. There is no need to worry. Yes, you are indeed alive and so am I. But we are not mortal anymore, Justine, in the sense that we cannot die." He paused here and let this sink in. "When Adrian anointed you with the holy oil, he changed your flesh, he made it eternally and forever alive, and in doing so he has heightened your senses, awakened your brain so that it can control your flesh. You will find your physical and mystic skills enhanced. You will hear people's thoughts and glean from them their true feelings, and with time these sensitivities," he paused as if looking for a better word, " ... these *powers,* will grow. You can experience what I am saying in the pulsing of your flesh. It's vibrating, Justine, moving of its own volition. It has its own unique rate and rhythm. Feel it now." He reached out and touched me again, and again I felt a wave of warmth move through me. "Yes, the warmth of my rhythm touching your rhythm. You are feeling my vibration mingling with your vibration." He sat back and I sighed. Yes, I could feel it. I was pulsating with life.

"In time, you will learn to control this pulsing of your flesh, so that you can speed it up, changing your very vibration, which will then allow you to change your form. Do you understand what I'm telling you?"

I nodded.

"You will have the ability to change the way you look to people. You may appear old or young as you wish, simply by projecting the image you desire like a blanket around yourself. I will teach you these things, Justine, and take you out into the world, where you shall have the adventures you have always dreamed of. Nothing can stop you from having what you want. You are a member now, of my court, and you will live the life of a queen."

I was dazzled by his words, and by the concepts he presented, yet I could feel my attention wandering as he spoke, distracted by his beautiful magenta lips.

"Justine!" he was laughing. "Pay attention, my darling, there are things I must tell you first."

"Yes, of course." I blushed, intent on paying attention, yet feeling already the desire to touch him. He said nothing for a long time, merely looked at me, as if he were taking me in. Only gradually did I realize that he was doing something to me. It seemed to come from his eyes, a warm sensation down my legs and then in my chest, until I became completely aware of my own body. Soon, I felt my heart stop racing, and, as I blinked, colors began to look more normal. I was coming back to myself, a sense of calm within me.

"Better?" he asked.

"Yes."

"Good. I have only done what you will soon enough learn to do for yourself." I smiled as the soft beauty of the light from the fire swelled over him. "Now, I must introduce myself. I am known as Prince Illuminare, but my name is Mal'ak."

"Mal'ak..." I whispered. He smiled again.

"I have brought you to my castle in Italy. You will be safe here. Both my name and my court date back thousands of years. We are a branch of an ancient order of priests known as the Melchizedek. There are those from this priesthood who have learned, at different times in history, the mystic practices that bring eternal life to their bodies. They have been sufficiently disciplined and devout to achieve such a state, and have lived for thousands of years, much longer than the history that you know. But their techniques are filled with such rigorous disciplines that few could manage them, and fewer still could achieve the end result, immortality, until I found another way. I discovered the existence of an oil so holy, so pure, that its application brings eternal life into the skin, the blood, and the bones. Its aroma is so rich that hidden places in the brain wake from their deep sleep to keep the body alive. This is how I have made my companions, the Guardians, as we are called. Adrian is one, and you will soon meet others. And now you are one of us as well." His voice dropped as if he were consoling me. "Time has passed since you were anointed, Justine, more time than a day or a week. Your body has changed while you slept. You have aged..." he hesitated. "Twelve years have passed."

I started at these words.

"Twelve years?" I repeated, stunned. Yet, I had seen the difference in my features, the length of my hair, the fullness of my face. "But how?"

"It was necessary to let your body ripen, to prepare it for the oil. I know it is difficult to understand and accept, yet it's true. But you must remember, dearest, that these are not years lost! Your body has matured; you are a woman now, that is all. Eternity lies before you. I have given you *forever!*" He was thrilled by these words, and his excitement calmed me. I did not stop to wonder what "forever" really meant, or to ask myself if it was something I would have chosen for myself. I was completely enthralled by him, his voice, his words, and the desire for his touch. I was giddy in his presence, and let myself settle into the comfort and confidence of his story.

"There are hundreds of us, scattered all over the Earth, working to bring about the enlightenment of humanity. That is our purpose, you see? We are servants of change. We are the guardians of the mystic wisdoms. There is nothing to fear here, my darling. Do you understand?"

I nodded.

"Good." He was almost laughing again. "What you are feeling and sensing helps you to accept what I say. I promise you that in a very short time you will experience enough of your new power to believe in your transformation, for what I have given you is far more than something to understand, but rather, an endless experience. I know you cannot fully comprehend it now, but when you've lived through your first century, and then another, and another ... then you will comprehend the immensity of what I am saying, Justine. You are immortal now. You will never die!"

The fire leapt with his words. He seemed to lean toward me as if he were waiting for me to react, to recoil, or to demand more from him.

"I understand you," I said calmly, "and I'm not afraid, if that's what you're thinking. Perhaps it's the way you said it at first, that I am taken with the adventure before me — this place, these things, and you ... " I moved then, sliding from the couch onto my knees, resting at his feet. My hand slid over his. I watched him sigh.

I have loved you before. I heard his words, though his lips were not moving.

Yes, I thought back, *I remember* ... and then the vision was before me: I saw him kneeling on the earth, in another time and place, the medallion that now lay at his chest was in my hands, the emerald older than that time, carried out of another place. I saw myself reaching down and placing it around his neck, whispering, *"The key to the temple ... "*

"Yes," this time it was his voice, bringing me back from the vision, "Yes, that's right, there was another time, Justine, long ago in Atlantis, the place that is now known only as Plato's great legend. But it existed, dearest, until a great tragedy befell our civilization and you were lost to

93

me. I have waited all these years for your soul to return, to find you again. And now," his voice became soft and low, "I will *never* let you go."

A chill swept over me as if a shadow had broken through the light, and my stomach tightened.

He was looking down at me with so much emotion in his eyes that I tried to push the feeling away. "I will give you everything," he said. "Everything that I once promised."

Suddenly distressed and afraid, I could not look at him. How could this be happening? How could he say these things? How could he love *me*? Surely, I was not now the person I had been then.

"But, why? Why do you choose me now?"

He took my chin gently in his hand and raised my head. "Look into my eyes. There, now, my love, calm yourself. You might think that I choose you for these wild locks," he said, brushing my hair with his fingertips, "or for lips as soft as the petal of a rose." He kissed me softly, barely brushing my lips with his. Then he breathed warm on my check, "Or for skin that flushes from my breath." I shut my eyes and let his words calm me. "You might think that I choose you for these things, for the pleasure that you will give me. But no, it's much more than that. It is the more that you are becoming and remembering. I choose you because I know who you are, your fantastic sorrow, your grief and rebellion." His words lulled me and I felt tears on my cheeks. "I have chosen you for your heart, Justine. It is because I have been loved by you before and I have suffered without you." Lips on my neck, and then his hand gently pulling the gown from my shoulder. I reached to touch his face, shaved smooth, running my hand over his chiseled cheekbone and then gliding over his magic lips. He was such a beautiful man, crisp and charismatic, yet with that soft smile and those radiant eyes.

I wrapped my arms around him, pushing my cheek against his shoulder. "I want to feel you." I said, shocked by my words, so bold and insistent. But in another moment I was laughing at them, too. There was no need to be anything other than that, was there? My life and its restraints were far away and I was free. Then he too was laughing, his arms encircling me, pulling me to my feet.

"Of course you do." He said, slipping his hand beneath my curls, coming to rest, warm, on the back of my neck. A shiver ran through me as he touched my skin.

"Yes," I sighed, "that is what I want now." He wove his fingers into my thick curls and pulled my head back so that I was looking again into those stunning blue eyes. Then, he kissed me, really kissed me, so that I felt it everywhere, felt my mouth opening, my body pulling at him. Yes, that was what I wanted from him. My whole body wanted it, this touch, and sensation merging with sensation. Yet, as I felt the longing for him, my mind seemed to rebel. Questions began to rise, old rules and etiquette moving like black clouds across the landscape of my mind.

"Don't chase these thoughts," he said, as if I had spoken them to him. "Don't go back there, Justine, to what you were supposed to do and who you were supposed to be. Who are you now, my darling?" His lips brushed my forehead, his hands loosening my gown, "And most important, who are you going to become? Free yourself of this hurtful past."

"Yes," I murmured, pushing back the questions, finding his neck now with my teeth, brushing his skin with my tongue. *Delightful! Erotic! Sinful!*

"No," he answered. "You must lose this idea that the Church has imposed on you. *The only true sin is to follow someone else's rules rather than your own... Surrender...*"

"Yes..." I murmured again. And I did.

95

Four

I WAS DELIGHTED BY MY DESIRE FOR THE PRINCE. My old life melted away, and I was reborn into a life of erotic enchantment where pleasure replaced all longing and loneliness. It did not take me long to lose myself in the prince and the new world to which he introduced me. I was drawn to him, as anyone would be, for his alluring flair and handsome show. He wore the decorum of his station with a natural grace, and he inspired in me a confidence I had never before known. But there was something more that drew me to him, something I can only explain as *familiar*. These feelings helped me to understand and finally to accept his explanation of my rebirth. The soul's journey, as he called it, from lifetime to lifetime, could be recalled if one was adept in such things. Often, he said, mortals could not remember with their minds, or see pictures of those other lives, as I could. Instead, they would have a feeling or a sense that a person or a place was familiar. This, he explained, was because the soul remembered and guided each person to meet again the characters he had lived with before, to complete any unfinished business or fulfill a destiny.

I was familiar with this idea called reincarnation. I had read the manuscripts of the early Church father, Origen, who had written widely on the subject until he was declared a heretic for his teachings and burned to death by the Church. There were volumes on the subject in the Hindu texts from India, and the Greek writer, Hermes, and the Buddhist writings that came to us from the expeditions to the Orient. The prince's library was a treasure of such works, and any question on the subject could be explored in the pages of scrolls, crumbling papyruses, and leather-bound books.

Yet it was not this scholarly evidence that made me believe in the great migration of souls; it was the familiar sense that I had indeed known the prince before. This, finally, was what I came to trust and believe in. And so I did not question my feelings for the prince, for as time passed, I became bound to him, as I was certain I had been in that *other* time. Now and then, I would glimpse that past in a dream: *the flash of a sword in his hand, a bull charging, a ring he had put on my finger . . .* moments that meant nothing, other than that they had once been and I had existed in them. I told him of these dreams and would probe for more information, but this he would only answer, "If you are meant to know, you will remember it yourself, my darling. But let it go if you can, and leave the past behind."

In the first days of my immortality, the prince taught me many things about my transformation and the powers that came with it. First, I had to understand that the power of my mind would affect the vibration of my body. He taught me to raise the vibration of my flesh so that it would harmonize with the environment around me, which allowed me to pass through solid substance as if it were water. It was all quite simple, really, once I had learned to control my mind and focus my will. I could touch a stone wall and feel it pulsating, then command my body to pulsate at the same rate. Soon I would quite literally become one with the wall and could pass through it to the other side. This was a most wonderful trick, which I spent long hours perfecting. The prince was a patient teacher, soft and easy, as I took each lesson in its turn. I learned how to seal myself in invisibility and to shield my mind so that others, even immortals, could not penetrate my thoughts. I learned to glean information from my mortal company—their random thoughts and most secret feelings. This delighted me. I could soon see souls, glistening around people's bodies, and intuit their intentions even before we met. My psychic talents abounded and I reveled in it. I could call out the sun when it rained, and send a stormy fever into a clear summer sky.

The prince cautioned me about these powers: "The Christ was wise when he said, 'Do unto others as you would have others do unto you,'

Justine. For there is a law set forth in this universe that even an immortal such as you are cannot escape: *That which you sow, so shall you reap.* It is the one law you must abide by, for it will prove itself master in the end." For the prince to counsel me so was such a rarity that I took his words to heart and used caution with my new strength and abilities.

In the first days of the transformation, the prince did not leave my side. He took me throughout the castle and its grounds, a dazzling historical monument, the architecture of one time built upon the foundation of another. Our rooms were set in the oldest wing, built on the edge of a cliff overlooking the sea. This was the prince's private estate, surrounded by lush gardens and filled with the most lavish possessions of history. His personal library, endless shelves of rare and priceless manuscripts, sprawled through nearly half the bottom floor. Our apartments were lavish, decorated with exotic furnishings and sensual colors. More than an acre of gardens planted around fountains and sculptures stood between the main palatial structure, Roman in its appearance, and our quarters. This modern palace held two ballrooms and several kitchens. Rooms built in rectangles one upon the other could, and frequently did, house as many as a hundred guests. Towers spiraled a hundred feet above the ground, and a wall with ramparts encircled the main courtyard, stables, and several more acres of gardens. The castle was built on a large, gently sloping hill that looked out across acres of farmland interspersed with patches of olive trees. To reach the castle, one traveled on a well-maintained road lined with fragrant pines, holly woods, and cork trees. Below the palace sat a village of square mud houses with red tile roofs. The villagers were almost entirely employed by the prince, working in his fields and his castle. On that first day, the prince took me in his carriage through-out his estate, introducing me to his people, his subjects, as though I were their Lady. I did not question this, enamored as I was with his presence. I took easily to the role, and from the very first, all deferred to my direction as if I had always been there, as if he and I had been wed. From that first day I was referred to as the Lady Illuminare, and overnight became the Lady of his house, though we had entered into no formal agreement.

I was his mistress in the most respected sense. He took me to his bed with a loving touch, pressing me gently to explore the passions hidden in my flesh. There was no desire he would not fill for me, no edge he could not push me over. His lips were sweet and his hands made magic, sending erotic sensations through me that left my heart pounding with devotion. He was, of course, my first infatuation. There was nothing he could ask of me that I would not do, and I longed only to be with him.

After the first few weeks together, I was introduced to his court at a grand affair the likes of which I had never dreamed. It lasted a full month. There were kings and queens at our table, philosophers and poets, cardinals and bishops. The food was rich and abundant. The finest actors and musicians entertained us day and night, performing plays and outdoor symphonies. Hunting and dancing and games were scheduled days in advance. We wore costumes and jewelry from the finest courts in the world, and our guests readily reveled in every pleasure that the prince offered.

On the evening of the third day of the festivities, the prince gathered twelve men in his great library and introduced me to each. These were his companions. They were immortal, made so by his hand and forever in his service. What a colorful mix they were, with their different insignias and accents, as if each came from a different time and place. One dressed as a peasant, the next as a scholar, warrior, clergyman, as if each played a part in a staged drama. Each had the glow that I had come to associate with my new state, his skin vibrant, exuding a sweet and seductive scent. Adrian was among them, but he stood apart, as if uncomfortable with the festivities and anxious to be gone. Seeing him sent a strange feeling through me. Perhaps it was because of the part he had played in my transformation? I tried to speak with him, wanting to assure him that I felt no malice toward him for this new life, but he avoided me at every turn. The festivities were so constant, the new people, names, titles, and faces so overwhelming, that by the time I had a chance to pursue him, Adrian had departed. So, I pushed the thought of him away, for he was the one reminder of a past I quickly dedicated myself to forgetting.

As the weeks played themselves out I indulged in the endless stream of pleasures the prince afforded me. It was as if I were an empty canvas that he was filling with color, layer upon layer, and I gave myself to his brush with total commitment. I had so long subdued my passions out of necessity, that now, in my rebirth, I melted into longing for these physical pleasures. I could not tame my desire to be with the prince, at his side, touching him, or even smelling the scent of him, sandalwood and jasmine. I longed for him to touch me, to bring me again and again to his bed, undressing me, and making me warm with his hands. They were long, beautiful hands, and he liked to run them down my waist and over my hips, coming to rest between my thighs, sending delightful sensations through me. His body, lean with a stark, muscular strength, would prowl above me and behind me, as if stalking my skin. I was captivated by him. How could I not be? He showed me only what I most wanted to see.

But there were other pleasures as well. One evening, when I had pulled him from the banquet, running my hands shamelessly over his strong thighs, he whispered in my ear, "I have a surprise for you."

"And I have one for you!" I laughed, sliding my hands beneath his robe, reaching for his bare skin. He took my wrists firmly and stopped me.

"Not tonight." He whispered again, "Tonight, you will surrender to another pleasure." He kissed me then, long and slow, his tongue lingering on my lips. The music and the laughter of our guests seemed far away as lightheadedness washed over me. He led me from the party to the old wing of the castle. It seemed strangely dark and empty. We entered my room, the bed already turned down, the long row of windows thrown open to the sound of the sea. It was a warm summer night. No candle or oil lamp was lit; only the light of the moon shone through the windows, casting rows of light and shadow across the room. I turned to the prince expectantly, but he only smiled down at me.

"You must know every pleasure," he said. "At first, it may horrify you to go against what so many have taught you is wrong or bad, and it may repulse you to explore what has so long been forbidden. But I assure you, my darling," he reached out and stroked my hair, "you cannot truly enter into life until you know yourself. *You cannot come to an unending love without a caring for everything that is different.*" He leaned down and kissed my forehead. "Trust me."

I was confused by his words, my body full of the sounds and smells and lust of the days of indulgence. I looked up at him, about to speak, when I felt another pair of hands lay themselves gently on my shoulders. My body shivered.

"The Lady Alessandra," the prince said warmly, "will be your pleasure tonight. I leave you in her capable hands." Before I could respond he was gone, as if I had been speaking only to a wraith. I stood frozen on the spot as the woman stepped around me from the shadow and into a beam of moonlight before me. She was tall and slender, with long black hair that fell in waves down her back. Her thin face was pointed and strong, her skin was deep brown. When she spoke, her voice was deep for a woman's, and her words were spoken with a Spanish accent.

"You are Justine," she said, her eyes resting on my lips. I could not speak. My heart pounded in my chest and I only nodded in response. She seemed to like this. "Don't be afraid." It sounded like a command. "I won't do anything you don't like ... I promise." She reached out her hand then, brushing my cheek. A warm sensation rippled across my skin. Then came her other hand, and she cupped my face, pulling me to her lips. They were full and soft, opening with a delicate warmth that made me dizzy. A warm breeze from the window sent soft strands of her hair like a cloak around us. My mind made a feeble attempt to repel what was happening, but as the heat of her kiss spread through me, I found my hands reaching clumsily for her waist. Pulling away, she let out a deep, raucous laugh.

"Good!" she said, *"Esta bien, mi amor!"* Taking my hand, she led me to the bed, letting loose my hair and pulling at my costume, an Italian corset dress of burgundy and gold. She loosened the ribbon on the front of the gown as if she had done it a hundred times.

"Alessandra ... " I liked the sound of her name as it rolled across my lips. "I have never ... " She put her finger to my lips and then kissed me again, taking her time, easing me slowly onto the bed. Then she laid her mouth upon my breast. I trembled. The line between male and female dimmed as she moved her lips over my skin, until finally it was *I* who pulled her into me, and *my* hands that found the ripe place between her legs, pressing pleasure into her. All through the night we delighted in each other, until, at dawn, I rested against her breast and fell into a blissful sleep.

I GAVE MYSELF OVER TO A LIFE SPENT entirely in the pursuit of pleasure. Alessandra came and went, indulging my carnal education. I spent long nights in her arms as she told me rich tales of an Amazon empire that thrived once in a long-ago time—*her* time. She would enchant and entice me with stories of women who lived with dignity and power alongside men whom they cherished. She spoke of the circle of things, the great cycle of life, the Goddess, the mother earth, and the feminine honored as divine. Then she would be gone and I would turn again, starry-eyed, to the prince. Between the two of them I came to know the full range of my desires.

These early years were passed in the time of the Renaissance, the great rebirth. Great ships were built, and men developed instruments for steering them. Trade routes grew as the ships sailed on profitable excursions to new ports on the western coast of Africa, taking slaves and gold wherever they landed. Every country financed grand expeditions. A route around the southern tip of Africa was discovered, and the world as we knew it grew in size. The East met the West, at last.

Then came the great discovery of the Americas, and our Earth grew in shape as we learned that the world was indeed round.

It was a time of wonders—a new art form arose in Europe. We spent years in the great cities of Florence, Venice, and Paris, watching such artists as Da Vinci and Botticelli create a new landscape for storytelling. Books were printed on paper for the first time, and great universities arose where men gathered in a flood to learn. The prince was delighted by all of this. He told me he had not seen such human accomplishments since Rome. Spectacles and watches were invented, and giant public clocks began to ring, ordering people's lives. As I lived through this time, I came to see a change in people, one it seemed the prince had longed for. It was a move toward humanism, a time when scholars and scientists emerged on the stage of social development with the idea that people should be free to explore the world, letting their inquisitiveness guide them. They believed that curiosity and discussion about things were a much better way to live than to go on in unquestioning acceptance.

In spite of their faith, people even began to question the Church and its corrupt leaders. Scholars began to study Bibles written in Hebrew and Greek, the languages in which the Bible had originally been written, and they found that some of the meanings had been lost or misinterpreted. Suddenly, there was a backlash within Christendom as more accurate translations of the holy book abounded. With the spread of printing presses, more people began to study the Bible for themselves.

A horror arose in the papacy! As more people stopped believing that it was necessary to have an intermediary between themselves and God, the Church clamped down, trying desperately to take back control. Once more the Inquisition rose to destroy the heretics. People said the popes and cardinals and bishops spent the money of the poor on lavish palaces, antiques, and libraries. They paid for these luxuries by selling important positions in the Church to the highest bidders, rather than giving them to the best candidates. These practices had existed since the inception of the Church of Rome, yet during this time they had finally become unbearable. A growing number of people, in every country we traveled through, claimed the Church did not offer spiritual leadership; rather, it had become God's banker, selling indulgences to the nobles, documents that granted them a shorter time in purgatory! We watched the faithful struggle with their discontent until there was an uprising, led by the monk, Martin Luther.

The prince kept his companions close to the uprising, close to Martin Luther himself. He was fascinated with the movement, the strength and perseverance of those brave souls who stood up against the greatest power of our time. We were there when Luther nailed his list of criticisms to the door of Wittenberg Cathedral, there when he spoke to the people, telling them that they could only reach Heaven through their belief in God, not by obeying and giving money to the Church leaders. This thrilled the prince. Even when the Church reacted by declaring Luther an outlaw and a heretic, the prince seemed overcome with satisfaction.

"Luther threatens the belief in the necessity of the Church's presence. He tells them to take responsibility for their enlightenment, and they listen! This is a great time, Justine!" he would tell me. "This is what we are here for, my darling!"

People rose up everywhere in Europe in support of Luther's ideas. Soon Europe was divided into two camps: Catholic and Protestant. But there can never be two ways to reach the same goal, can there? Wars began again, only this time it was Christian against Christian, destroying lives and lands in pursuit of holiness. Yes, it was the old story in a new setting. We watched the rest unfold from afar, the prince retreating to our Italian home as Christian neighbor turned against neighbor, all in the name of God. Deeply affected by this, the prince kept us tucked away, far from the sights and sounds of such turmoil. As news would come to us of uprisings and wars declared in Christ's honor, he began to spend more and more time away from the life we lived together. Leaving me in Tuscany to plan some affair, or to sit for a new sculpture, he would disappear for weeks at a time. When he returned, there would be gifts and long nights of lovemaking, but no explanation of where he had been. I did not press him, for I had by this time lived so long at his side that I could imagine no other way of life. He was my compass. I did not know yet that I had my own.

I COULD TELL YOU THOUSANDS OF TALES of the century I spent with the prince — the adventures we engaged in, our journeys through the palaces of Europe, guests of only the most privileged and prestigious. I could tell you of our travels to the East of our passage through pyramid walls to explore the innermost chambers of the holy and the wicked, reading their stories off the stones of their tombs. We traveled the world together, and watched as a new age was born, an age when the torture chambers of the Inquisition finally began to fade and humanity turned toward its inventiveness, toward the sciences and the stars.

As we watched these scenes unfold, the prince told me that the true creation story of humanity, of Earth and the cosmos, would again be revealed one day. He assured me that when that time came, humanity would celebrate their commonality rather than detest their differences. I became entranced with the idea that I would be here to see it, that I could watch the ever-unfolding drama. It did not occur to me that I might become a part of it, or that I had a role to play, a service to offer. No, I had everything one could ever want and a full century in which to play out my lifetime. I was his lady, his mistress, for over a hundred years. If ever I became distracted or confused by my immortal state, or disoriented by the passage of time, he would take me home to our castle by the sea to spend the time as any mortal family might. We would enjoy cold winter days, with fires roaring in every brazier, and hot summer nights when we were treated to ripe melons and glistening bowls of fruit. We had noonday feasts of roasted fowl and thick slabs of beef, dozens of soft cheeses, and bread of coarse-ground flour that we dipped in the freshest oils.

It was the best of everything, always; the finest musicians, paint-ers, philosophers, and theologians would come to entertain us, and the prince's companions would come and join us, like long-lost rela-tives returning home. What tales they would tell me: ancient stories of Greece and Rome, and some older even than that. They became my friends, and some of them family, so that I looked forward to our time together. There was the wonderful, brash Mufassa, an African prince, who came to us with his entourage of servants and friends. He would sweep into our palace, drape the most colorful silks across our walls, and fill the long corridors with drumming and chanting that would thrill me. Ah, what untamed things Mufassa taught me, his black skin glistening in the blaze of a midnight fire, his hands on my hips, guid-ing me to move with the rhythm his drummers demanded. He feared nothing, pulling me closer, moving up against me until the fever of his flesh filled me, and my body responded finally to the drums like a wolf to the moon. And all the while the prince looking on, clapping, smiling approval. How much I came to love Mufassa, his irreverence, and flamboyant, demanding presence. Nothing seemed to upset him, not even the absurd white elite who would come, from time to time, to pay respect to the prince. Once, an older man, a cardinal from the Church, dressed in the most splendid gowns of gold and white, and his entourage, dressed no less regally, graced us with their presence. Oh, what a spectacle that became! After a very civilized supper, Mufassa led us out into the great courtyard, which he had elaborately transformed into a place of pagan ritual. I tried to suppress a smile.

"For the cardinal," he explained to the group, as bonfires were lit and the drumming began, "To show you what your Christian missionaries are up against!" With that he let out a fierce cry, and dancers, their bod-ies painted red, leapt from behind the flames. Well, you can imagine the cardinal's response! The poor man seemed near death as his aides carried him to his room. He left us before sunrise.

There were others whom I came to love as well. In particular I re-member wise Joseph, who had lived a thousand years, and his tales of

Egypt and Rome and the Christian revolution. Now and again Adrian would come, quiet and reserved, staying no more than a night. He was ancient, I thought, but did not like to talk of his past. No matter how I tried to include him, he remained only polite and reserved. When I commanded the musicians to play, and called for a partner to dance with, a dozen hands would reach for me, but never his. When I recited poetry, moving dramatically from guest to guest throughout the room, he would stand and leave!

Just such a scene took place one evening. I had finished my recital, something wickedly sensuous, and left the room to admonish Adrian for being so impertinent. I found him on the verandah not far from the hall, the sound of the others' laughter and the raucous violin mixing with the waves that crashed below. He was seated alone on the wall, looking out over the sea. For a moment I froze. The full moon cast so eerie a shadow across him that for a moment I thought he was someone else, someone reaching out to touch me.

"My lady," he was saying. I blinked. He bowed, and the shadow was gone.

"You left my reading." I tried to accuse but my voice wavered, unsure of its emotion.

"Yes. I didn't mean to offend you, Lady."

"Call me Justine." I was annoyed with him, but wasn't sure why. "Why don't you stay with us, Adrian? Why don't you laugh and sing and smile?" He raised his brow at this and stared at me for a long time. "You are so reserved, Adrian, so serious all the time," I blurted out finally.

Looking hurt, he bowed his head, then replied quietly, "I suppose I don't laugh because I don't feel like laughing. I don't feel a lot of anything if I can help it."

"But why not feel? Why not enjoy yourself? You are immortal and have eternity to watch the world unfold! Why not let it entertain you?"

"The part of the world I see is not so entertaining, Justine." A warm sensation brushed my skin as he said my name. I was startled by it.

107

"Then you are not looking in the right places! You should stay more with us, and learn to enjoy again. I will talk to the prince if you like, I'm certain he'll give you leave —"

"I can't stop my work now, but thank you for the kind offer." He stepped back. I looked up at him. For a moment the world seemed to fade and I saw another time, his hand reaching out to me desperately, tears in his eyes. The sight of it shook me.

"Justine," he said, his hand on my shoulder now, "are you all right? What are you seeing?"

I roused myself. "Yes, yes, I'm fine." But seeing the look of concern on his face, "Really, I'm fine. I was only slipping into vision, it was nothing important, really." His hand remained on my shoulder and I felt the heat pass through me at his touch.

"Are you certain?" Such caring in his voice.

"Quite, thank you." His hand lingered another moment. The sensation it gave left me confused. At last, he lifted it away.

"Shall I escort you back to the others?" Adrian asked gently. "I promise I will try to smile." This made me laugh.

"Thank you for that, my lord."

"Adrian," he said.

"Adrian," I repeated, taking his hand.

It was not until much later, thinking back on the experience, that I realized I had not wanted him to remove his hand. At the time, I told myself that the vision had overwhelmed me and that Adrian's response to me must be from dark feelings of blame or shame. Surely, I told myself, he must blame himself for both losing my brother Nicholas in battle and nearly losing my soul altogether. The prince had told me of their intention to bring Nicholas into immortality with me, but they had lost him. "I swore I would have him with us to keep you happy," he told me sadly.

So, when Adrian kept himself removed, I reconciled his distance with a belief in his shame. I did not see Adrian much after that. It seemed his visits became even rarer, but when we did see each other it was different: I was not so loud, and he was not so quiet, and an indefinable friendship grew. I could not tell you how, for our time together was short, but that bond which rises above time and space was forged, so that I came to trust Adrian, his intensity and kindheartedness. He was an immortal whom, I was sure, I had known before.

There were others of course, who made our lives full. We were not lonely together, isolated, watching life from afar, as I have heard some Guardians keep themselves. Our lives were steeped in pleasure and the comfort of company, both mortal and immortal. It was a good time in its way, letting me forget who I had been, while encouraging me to become more; more confident and unruly and exceptionally bold. It was a time that made me into the person who would bring it all, finally, to an end.

Five

FROM THE VERY BEGINNING, a mystery surrounded the prince, and when I sought to find it out he only laughed and sent me away.

Sometimes I would insist, my hand on my hip. "Where do you go on the winter solstice?" I would demand, speaking in an irreverent tone that no one else would use with him. I had asked the question many times, for each year he and a group of his companions would meet on this pagan holiday, which fell neatly between the Hebrews' Chanukah rituals and the Christians' Christmas ceremonies.

"It is part of my work, I told you, Justine, now let it go," he would reply, pulling a flower from a nearby bush, brushing my cheek with the soft petals.

"Oh, no. You will not seduce me away from this! I want to know where you really go and what you do." I would push him away but he would only laugh.

"No!" he would cry, "you only say you want to know where I go and what I do!" Then he would catch me up in his arms, "What you really want to know, *Justine,*" emphasizing my name so that I flushed, "is why you cannot accompany me." And then there would be a kiss, something long and soft, and I would smile. He knew me too well.

"Yes, well, it's true, and I deserve to know why. Am I not a Guardian, too?" My tone would be accusing, but he would not take me seriously.

"Of course, my darling, but the truth is that this meeting is for the ancients only. One day, perhaps centuries from now, you will be allowed. But *not* today." More kisses, and with his hands loosening my gown I would indeed let it go.

For the longest time I did not let it bother me. I told myself it was not a mystery—he had told me plainly why it was not for me, and I would leave it at that. Years went by, and I grew accustomed to his leaving me for this event. I even knew where he went to attend it, for most winters he would take me with him into the East, traveling from Venice by ship. We would sail south along the Dalmatian coast and then west through the Greek archipelago, arriving about a month later in Jaffa, the port city for Jerusalem. It was always an adventure, for we would don the costumes of different cultures, traveling as Muslims, Jews, Christians, or wild Arabian Bedouins.

The Ottoman Turks took Jerusalem in 1517, bringing an extravagant and educated culture with them. The holy city flourished under her Muslim rulers as they rebuilt her great walls and gates and reconstructed the ancient aqueduct, which brought public drinking fountains into the city squares. What a miracle this was, to find water streaming out of a blue fountain in the middle of a sun-scorched plaza! The city was a maze of exciting activity as we wound through the many narrow alleys leading to colorful markets and splendid religious sites.

At times we explored Jerusalem as Muslims, the men dressing in long black robes and colorful turbans. I would cover my face in public, as was the custom for women. We would spend days exploring the Muslim Quarter, visiting mosques and the great gold Dome of the Rock at the Temple Mount. At other times we would wear the simple layered robes of the Christians, exploring the Church of the Holy Sepulcher, which the people held to be the location of Jesus' crucifixion, burial, and resurrection. There were countless years when we posed as Hebrews, visiting the great temple in the center of the city, a building that held the wisdom of millennia. What a rich place was sixteenth-century Jerusalem, surrounded by her thousand-year-old walls that held the holy places of the world's three greatest religions—and home of the great event that I could not attend.

We would arrive late in November and take residence in our sun-baked palatial home on the edge of the old city, high upon a hill. From the second floor balconies I could look out over the great wall into the expanse of sand on the other side. Near dusk, the endless miles of desert would become an apparition—an ocean of red and gold leading up to Jerusalem's great gates. It was a supernatural sight. The house itself was extravagant. The receiving room held marble columns and colorful murals. It opened into a great courtyard filled with palms and rich couches, so that it was part of the atrium and dining room beyond. Ivory shelves held a mass of magnificent books, and the walls were painted with exquisite murals of the Christian saints.

Always there were servants waiting for us, with baskets of fruit, and ornate plates filled with ripe dates and cheese. We had a grand court-yard with a garden that one could look down on from the second-story balconies. Bringing with us an entourage of servants, we set up house, lingering in the city's wealth of antiquity until the solstice night would come. Then, the prince would kiss me goodnight and disappear into the labyrinth of city streets. Ah, what trust he had in me, what faith. And for the longest time he was right in doing so.

Only a few weeks before the winter solstice in the year 1536, his faith in me became a heavy cloak that I could no longer bear. It was that time of social turmoil when the prince had taken to traveling without me, matters of the world pressing heavily on his mind. He had been away too much that year, and a strange melancholy seemed to hang over him, so I insisted he take me with him to Jerusalem.

We arrived several weeks before the solstice event, and I was looking forward to an untamed month of entertainment—music, parties, long, romantic nights—for these were the center of my carefree life. On the second evening of our stay, however, all of that changed.

The prince and I were having a late dinner in the courtyard, the sky a mass of glittering stars. We lounged in long, thin robes of white cotton gauze that let the cool night air pass through. We had just begun a decadent dessert of sweet dates and honey, when a servant, no more than a boy, came, eyes downcast, to our table.

"What is it?" I asked the boy.

He bowed to me, replying apologetically, "Lady, there is someone here to see the master." He glanced timidly at the prince.

"At this hour? Who—" but I did not finish. I felt a flush of heat move over me from the prince, who had pushed his chair back and was on his feet. Turning to the entrance of the garden I saw the silhouette of a woman beneath a palm.

And then she was gone.

The boy backed away, stammering, "Master, I am sorry, she was not to come in. I told her to wait!"

"How dare she!" the prince hissed, as if the boy did not exist. "How dare she come *here*!"

"Master, I told her you would not see her now, I told her."

But the prince did not hear him. "And with you here ..." he turned to me sharply, his face contorting with rage, his hand flung high in a furious gesture. But then he caught my eye and stopped. Dropping his hand to his side he drew a breath. I had never seen him this way. The boy, who had fallen to his knees and now lay prostrate on the tiles at the prince's feet, began to chatter frantically, "It is my fault, master ... my mistake ... I do not know why I let her in ... I think it was something she said!"

"It's all right." I tried to calm the child who was becoming quite hysterical. I moved from my chair and knelt, putting my hands on his small shoulders. He was trembling. "Go now to the cook," I said, urging him gently to his feet, "and tell him we have had quite enough for the evening. Tell him to close the kitchen." The boy did not move. "Forgive me, master," he said again, his voice quavering. I turned to the prince, who stood cold and aloof. He waved his hand at the boy as if he were an animal on the floor.

"Go!" he commanded. "Do as my Lady bids you." Like a cowering dog, the boy crawled backwards out of the room. It was a shocking sight. As he rose to his feet by the door, I realized he was one of our own servants, a boy I had seen at the palace. He must have been part of our retinue, yet I had not even noticed him. I did not even know his name. To see him so frightened of the prince was ... well, this was new for me, too. Had it always been so? We had always had servants, so that I had come to take their presence for granted. They had always been well treated in our service, or so I thought. But watching this scene, I understood that the prince had a different relationship with them, one that I had not been aware of.

When I turned, the prince was at my side, his hand outstretched to guide me to my feet. Taking his hand, I felt a strange power around him, something fierce and unpredictable.

"Never mind the boy," he was saying as he led me back to my chair. "It was simple enough for *her* to bend his mind to her will."

"But who was she?" I asked. He waved the question away, lifting the decanter of wine and filling my glass.

"It's not important, my darling, I will attend to her thoughtless invasion. Don't let it disturb you."

"But she's an immortal, a Guardian whom I don't know. And why would she come this way? Why —"

"Enough, Justine!" he snapped, in a tone I had never heard him use before. I felt a heat coming from him, something I was not used to, something dangerous. "She is no one you need to know! There are others, Justine, Guardians who are very old, powerful, and foolish!" He sat down and raised his cup. "Now, let's talk of other things."

A chill ran over my body. I could not explain the feeling of dread that hung over me. Something told me not to press the issue. He began to talk of meaningless things: the mausoleum we would visit tomorrow, perhaps a trip down into Egypt or old Alexandria. I listened intently, and as he spoke, I became aware of an anxiety rising in my stomach, something I had never felt before with the prince. Later, I would come to know it as fear, but that night, I began to wonder how many things I had not noticed over the years. How much had I avoided seeing? To me he was kind and loving, giving me every extravagance my heart desired. But who was he with others? A man of immense wealth and power. Where did it come from?

As the oil lamps burned low my anxiety grew so that I excused myself and retired to my rooms. He did not follow. I went out on the verandah overlooking the city, the great wall, and the desert beyond. It was too dark now to see even the wall. On this night the Earth was very dark; only the light of a crescent moon lit the streets. I remember that clearly, for I stood a long time on that balcony until I felt myself blending into the blackness. I did not want to feel the growing dread in my heart. I let myself melt, instead, into the night around me. The muffled sounds from a nearby square floated up over the wall of the outer courtyard: people laughing ... drums ... a Muslim chant.

I don't know how much time had passed before I realized that I had meditated myself into a cloaked state, that is, blended the vibration of my body with the frequency of the night. I had cloaked myself in invisibility more effectively than ever before. Cloaking was a trick that took a great amount of effort and firm concentration to maintain. I had done it before, but usually needed the prince's help to sustain it. This night I had lulled myself so completely into a feeling of aloneness that I knew I was deeply rooted in the magic.

I turned back toward my empty room. What good was this state of invisibility if I stayed here, alone in my chamber? I moved silently through the room and passed easily through the closed door into the hall outside. Ah, this was exciting! I floated down the stairs and into the courtyard, intent on going out into the night to spy some adventure, when I heard raised voices in the prince's den. I stopped short, listening. There was some type of argument ... the prince was emphatic ... angry ... outraged! The other voice was Adrian's. So, Adrian was already in Jerusalem! Straining to hear, I moved toward the arched door that muffled their voices.

"I am not to be commanded!" the prince was saying with vehemence. "I have declined their 'invitation' and that is the end of it! To command *me*? What arrogance is this?"

"It is true, Lord, that they have overstepped their bounds, but it would be better that we attend, to calm them, to show them again why we must do what we do ... "

Closer and closer I moved, until I pressed my head against the wood, only to find myself passing easily through! For a moment I thought they would see me. I had to focus intently on invisibility, but when I realized that I had maintained my cloak and that the two men did not perceive my presence, a strange new power flooded me. Could I be invisible even to the prince? What would happen if they were to find me witnessing their private discourse, no better than a spy? Before I could answer these thoughts, the prince moved toward the door, passing only a few feet from where I stood. I held my breath, prepared for discovery, but he passed by. Adrian followed. They were agitated. It is the only reason I could imagine that they did not detect me.

"All right, we'll go!" declared the prince, waving his hand to fling the doors wide before them. "Never has anyone called an assembly without my permission, not in the sacred place, not in millennia! She has gone *too far,* Adrian!"

"Yes, Lord."

They moved through the atrium and out into the street.

Something was beating so hard inside me that it led me to action before I could think. I followed them into the street, letting my psychic vision open up before me to catch their trail. It would be easy, I thought; because there were two of them, their vibration would be strong. Using psychic sight, I would be able to see a trail of light in the places where they had been. I became a tracker, moving stealthily through the streets of Jerusalem, down old dirt roads, and through abandoned tenements, until they came upon the wall. Seeing them pass right through it and move out into the desert, I followed. Then the trail began to blur, for they had begun to pick up speed, moving as only immortals can, faster than the eye can track. The moon was nearly invisible, and the desert an endless sea of black. Stop here, I thought, but something moved me forward. I strained my psychic sight until I got a glimpse of their fading trail, now a dull beam. Then, with an unearthly speed that was new to me, I was tracking them again, far into the sand. I moved with expectation, as the prince had taught me, knowing that I must imagine myself the wind, blowing faster and faster toward my destination. I had no time to wonder about my way or to think of the consequences of my actions—whether I would be caught following or end up lost in the desert. Onward I went, mile after mile, until I was far from the city, no sign of humanity anywhere in sight. Finally, I slowed, as the floating haze of light that was their trail came to the edge of a long valley fringed with steep cliffs. The air was different here, it was moist, and I smelled salt and seaweed. We must have been near the Dead Sea. I walked down a path, straining to use my intuitive sight in the utter darkness. Passing through a tunnel in a large stone wall, I came out into a courtyard, well lit with torches. Steps hewn from a luminous pink stone led up to a temple carved into the face of the steep rock wall. Here I saw the fading trail of many immortals. This must be the sacred gathering site. I went inside.

I could feel the vibration of the place pulsating beneath my skin, as if the temple had a sound that was singing itself into me, and I was becoming a part of it. The temple was simple: a round room with an altar, a large obelisk of black stone against the main wall. Torches burned on the walls. I could see a residue of many different vibrations here. I was close to the gathering, I was sure. But where were they? I moved to the obelisk and, without thinking, reached out to touch it. My hand moved easily through the stone! Through here, I thought. I raised my vibration only slightly and began to move through the wall. I traveled deep into the stone, guided by a sound, a heartbeat within the temple, in the very stone itself. This place was so alive!

Then I came out into a long corridor lighted with oil lamps. I walked slowly, quietly, concealing myself again in a shield of invisibility, cloaking my mind lest anyone sense my approach. At the end of the hall I began to hear voices; someone was yelling, and then another, and then there was Adrian's voice calling for order. My heart pounding, I took a deep breath and stepped from the corridor, across the threshold of an ancient, circular stone room with a huge round table in the center. There were almost thirty of them seated there, the prince sitting across from the door. I froze for a moment when I saw him, then calmed myself. He can't see you, I told myself. He doesn't know you're here, so stay calm and listen. I knew there was no turning back now. I was here, I had done it, and now I wanted to know who they were and what this was about. No, I would not have left then. Instead, I moved silently to the side of the door and doubled my invisible shield.

The prince sat opposite me, so that I could see his face. I could see most of their faces, except for that of the woman who sat opposite him, her back to me. She was tall and elegantly poised, with hair so orange in the shimmering light that it looked like flame itself. As the conversation wore on, it became clear that she held a place of honor here, a place of power.

A woman was standing near the prince, her blonde hair pulled up sharply from her face. I recognized her immediately: it was Cassandra, the woman who, with Adrian, had anointed me. She was speaking.

"But you must interfere," she was saying, waving her arms passionately toward the Master. "We cannot stop it without you. The tribes can't withstand your Church and its fanatical army of conquistadors. We beg you to make them stop! Look at Cortés and the Aztecs. In just two years after his arrival in Mexico, the Aztec civilization has been destroyed. And for what? Gold. But even though they control most of Mexico, the Spanish will not relent. They are the wealthiest nation on Earth today, yet the pope urges them on. He tells them to push into the interior and convert the natives while he steals their riches to build his churches. Please ...". Contempt was clear in her tone.

The prince nodded sympathetically, as if listening to a child.

"I know it is difficult to understand, Cassandra, but we are working for the greater good here, we are waiting for them — "

"There is no more time for waiting!" Cassandra cried with exasperation. "Do you know what has happened to the Inca?"

The prince smiled indulgently. "I'm sure you will tell me."

Oblivious to his tone, she went on. "It was this Francisco Pizarro and that fiend, de Soto, who heard tales of the riches to be found in the Andes Mountains of Peru. They took a few hundred men into the Andes to find the Inca Empire. When they arrived at the Inca capital they found the leader, Atahualpa, and his vast army already waiting for them, with friendly intentions. Seeing that the Inca warriors were too many, the Spaniards devised a trap. They set up camp in a protected area of the town square, and invited the emperor to meet with them. When Atahualpa arrived the next evening, with unarmed soldiers and attendants, he found only a priest holding up a wooden cross. As the emperor approached with a small band of attendants, the priest held up the cross, demanding that Atahualpa convert to Christianity!" Here Cassandra threw up her hands as if to emphasize the absurdity of the demand. "And when the emperor refused, hundreds of Spaniards leapt from the surrounding buildings where they had been hiding and fired on the crowd. They killed most of the Incas and captured Atahualpa. Then your conquistadors held the honorable leader for ransom, asking thousands of pounds of gold and silver, which was delivered to them." She looked from the prince to the assembly around the table.

"And when the ransom was paid, the Spanish broke their word and executed Atahualpa." She stopped there, turning slowly back to the prince.

"These are your people; you can stop them. If they did this to empires as great as the Aztec and the Inca, what will they do to this little tribe?" The man sitting beside her stood then, bowing slightly as he did. He was tall and dark, his hair falling to the middle of his back. I had never seen a man with his features before; he was stunning, really, with dark brown skin and a sharply etched face that reminded me of a regal bird. He spoke slowly, calmly, emphasizing his words with a simple nod of his head. He spoke of his people, of the land across the sea, the *New World*. He told how the tribes lived close to the land, respecting the Earth as mother, how the tribes trusted the newcomers at first, even welcomed them, and how disease from the Europeans was now sweeping over the continent and killing his people. Then he described the deceptions, the lies, the Christian faith forced on the people. Women raped and forced to be whores, children sold into slavery, people tortured until they would convert to Christ. My stomach tightened as he told his story, going on and on, recounting the atrocities inflicted on his people, until even the prince began to shift in his chair and finally held up his hand.

"Thank you, I think we have heard enough." The man paused and glanced at Cassandra, who turned to the red-haired woman. I watched her nod to the two and they both sat down. Now I was intrigued. Clearly there were two different groups at this meeting: there was the prince, with Adrian at his side and several others I had seen come and go over the years; and then there was this woman opposite, with her contingent. But who was she? I wanted to move and watch her, to see her face. I could feel warmth coming from her, a sense of calm that was somehow familiar.

Others were standing up to speak, arguing the new man's points, but the prince held up his hands again.

"No. Sit down, all of you!" His voice was firm. "I assure you it is as the king has told you. Every horror is true." His voice filled the room. Then he turned to Adrian. "Tell them, Adrian. You have watched the armies for yourself, tell them it's so."

All eyes turned to Adrian, sitting stiffly at the prince's right. Slowly he stood. "My Lord," he said, bowing his head to the Master, then with a long, graceful sweep of his arm he bowed to the woman with the red hair, "my Lady." I saw the prince smile as Adrian continued.

"I have traveled with the Spanish conquistadors for five years now, and all of this is true. We have lied and raped and pillaged." There was a long pause as he let this sink in. "And we have done it all in the name of God." He said this flatly and sat down. No one spoke. The silence was frightening

Then the prince began, "So you see, we know exactly what is happening in the New World, we are even an active part of it! As I have said a hundred times, it all serves our master plan. It is temporary

120

suffering that will serve a much greater good."

"I don't believe it!" Cassandra blurted, "How can you say this is temporary? How can you condone suffering for any outcome? We are their Guardians!" She almost spit the words at him. I felt uneasy. Others stirred in their chairs. But the prince remained calm, his gaze bearing down on Cassandra so that, finally, she dropped her eyes.

"I know you don't agree with my ways, Cassandra." The prince looked around the room. "Many of you can't understand what we are doing, but I assure you, we are only agents of their growth, giving them opportunity to become better, finer beings! We are taking our lead from the old Hebrew tradition of the Satan, an angel sent by God to stand in their way to show them the path of error. Adrian is my general, my emissary of Heaven by exemplifying hell! If you would try to understand—"

Shaking her head, the red-haired woman interrupted, "You don't really believe that anymore," she said quietly. The prince shifted uncomfortably in his seat, and grimaced, meeting the gaze of the woman across from him, her voice soft but commanding. Everyone seemed to stiffen from the tension in his movement. The woman continued.

"You had faith in them at first, Lucifer priest, thinking they would see the error of their ways and be led, so much more quickly, to the light. It was a noble enough theory, I grant you that. And as the millennia have passed you have thought your Church a wonderful success, its dogma and treachery suffocating the world, the darkness so overshadowing the light that humans would eventually band together and rise up against it. You were ecstatic when the Renaissance swept through Europe, followed by Martin Luther and his Protestant reformation. You thought it would happen then, that those with a conscience would stand up against injustice, ignorance, and intolerance! But they have failed you, haven't they? *They have given in to horror upon horror and pretend that they have no part in it.* And so you doubt them and even yourself." She paused and I felt a wave of heat move from the prince toward her. A wisp of her hair trembled as if a wind had stroked it.

Then she laughed.

"Does the truth sting, my Lord?" she asked, leaning forward brazenly in her chair. The others looked horrified, and several stood and backed away, but the woman did not seem to notice. She only went on.

"You are afraid, aren't you, Lord of the Light, that you have done your worst and still they don't respond. I can see it in your heart! You are saying to yourself, 'I have created more evil than I had imagined it would take, more hypocrisy and lunacy than I could have calculated in the beginning. And still they don't respond!'

"So you yourself don't believe in your cause, or your people."

Her voice rising in volume, she stood, her long hair falling to her waist, hand raised in a delicate gesture of peace. Then her voice softened. "You had hoped that humanity would see that the wealth of the richest of men could be used to create equality, a shared dignity to be had by all. You thought they would find genuine compassion, which would lead them to right action!" She stopped and sighed deeply. "But you were wrong. You've failed in your task, and now you will not admit it and stop the growth of this evil. Humanity will never remember their royal nature this way, Mal'ak. You can't force them into it. You must *show* them the way."

"Enough!" roared the prince, smashing his fist down on the table so that it shuddered and cracked, a long, jagged seam splitting the stone in two. The Guardians scrambled away before it fell to either side. Only the woman stood still, an aura of dignity around her. He glared at her then, so that I shivered from his look.

"I am Guardian to them all!" he raged. "I give meaning to the suffering of the weak and the sick and the poor! I seek to answer the question that burns in their hearts as they ask, 'Why am I cold on the street with nothing to eat, no food for my family, when over there they are warm and have more than enough? Why do I suffer and they do not? Why do I toil and they reap the reward? Why, why, why?'" He had leapt up from his chair, shouting, so that the objects in the chamber began to shake. "Let their suffering and their struggle and every injustice they endure serve a purpose! Let some suffer so that the others might learn compassion and kindness and come back to themselves. It is opportunity that I give them; an example of how *not* to be. I love them, each and every one, and if you cannot see that, Miriam, if you cannot understand my way..."

But he did not finish. As he spoke her name, a flame of recognition swept through me and I knew who she was. Miriam, my Miriam, and the realization so stunned me that I dropped my shield of invisibility and was suddenly standing for all to see in the doorway of the chamber.

"Justine!" It was Adrian, I think, who threw up the alarm, and then there were others, and the prince's eyes glaring into my soul.

It is difficult to recall what happened next. I remember running, terrified, back down the long corridor, his voice right behind me. "Justine!" But I did not stop. When I came to the stone, when I tried to think myself through the wall, I stumbled in my mind, crying out, "I raise my vibration to- to- to the temple!" It was all that I could think as my body touched the stone.

"No!" I heard the prince's voice from far away. Suddenly I was moving up and out, expanding in all directions, my body contorted, then liquid and free. What a lightness and joy overwhelmed me as I moved up and up, through the rock that the temple was carved into, and then out into the night, toward the sky, and up into the stars. I heard his voice again, closer this time, calling my name, and suddenly I could feel his hand grasping my leg.

And then I fell.

Six

I AWOKE IN MY ROOM IN JERUSALEM.

Adrian was sitting by my bedside, his hand holding mine.

"Adrian?" My voice was soft and strange. He smiled down at me.

"Yes, Justine, it's me. You're safe here."

"But where ... how?"

His voice came to soothe me. "You're in the city, in your suite of rooms. The prince has gone on to Rome and left you safe with me. He will be back soon, and I will take you to him."

"The prince," I began, remembering the meeting, the table cracking in two and then *her*—

"Stay calm, Justine. Let your body get used to your being back in it! Your consciousness was not prepared to go where you sent it, and we are lucky to have you back at all. No,"—I had tried to move—"not yet, just rest for now. You believe me that you're safe?"

"Yes."

"Good. Then you can give yourself the time you need to come back. Shut your eyes again, rest now, sleep." I did as he said while his warm hand stroked my forehead and his voice calmed me.

I dreamed then of something beautiful and far off. Some place I had visited and longed to go to again. For days I slept, with Adrian waking me now and then, pressing a bitter drink to my lips, his calm eyes coaxing me back to my life.

∞

WHEN I AWOKE ON THE THIRD DAY, I lay very still in my bed, feeling my body with my mind. My feet were warm, calves tingling, legs aching to move. This was good. My mind felt clear, refreshed, and restless. I opened my eyes. No one was in the room, so I threw back the sheet and went to the washbasin, where I bathed myself. My body felt fully alive. Ah, the wonders of immortality, of flesh that vibrates an aliveness beyond pain and fatigue! I brushed out my hair and put on the white linen robe waiting for me. Soon there was a knock at the door.

"Come!" I noticed the tone of my voice as I replied to the rapping. It was more a command than an invitation, my voice cold and aloof. I wondered, suddenly, if I always spoke this way, but before I could speculate further, Adrian entered. He looked different, wrapped in the cool white Egyptian linens, his skin dark like a native man's.

"I have been playing the part," he said, as if in answer to my observation. Ah, yes, my mind, it was open for all to see. I took a moment to shield myself, while he looked away respectfully, as if sorry for seeing it. I wondered then how much he might have seen in my days of sleep, when my mind lay vulnerable and exposed. But this was Adrian, I reminded myself. He would be respectful, regardless.

"Lady," he began, "it is good to have you back." What a smile, and those quiet eyes, laughing.

"Yes, but what happened?" I asked.

"The temple you were in is not for the uninitiated," he explained, "The vibration there is much too high for the untrained mind. It is a wonder that you were able to move through the stone at all! Actually, we aren't quite sure how you did it to begin with. But once you were unnerved and frightened ... " he hesitated there.

"Yes, I was frightened, it's true." I urged him on.

"Yes, and your mind could not control itself and you merged with a much greater vibration, a sort of mammoth wave. It's because you aren't yet trained to manage such a wave that it took you the way it did. It was *extremely* dangerous," he shook his head severely, "for once you were a part of it, you could not have known how to bring yourself back."

"How did I get back?"

"The prince."

I put my hands to my head and paced the room. The prince!

"But how, Adrian? And why? I have broken his trust and found out his secret — if he had wanted me to know who he really was, he would have told me a century ago!"

Adrian shook his head. His eyes looked sad. "I don't know."

"How can you not know? You know everything, don't you? You've always known who he was! All of them have, our royal court ... all this time, they've known we're *devils*!" The horror of it shook me. I had lived all these years in splendor and ease, playing the devil's concubine. It was too much.

"We are not devils," Adrian said gently. "Come, I will take you to the prince and he will explain it to you."

"No!" I turned on him heatedly as he reached for my arm. "All this time, you could have told me, warned me, but you did nothing, Adrian. You serve him in his evil plot! I heard you say it! You're the one he trusts the most, aren't you?"

"Justine, you don't understand."

"No, I don't," I declared coldly. "And just what is it I'm to understand Adrian, that I have been the devil's mistress? That I have believed him to be good, that I have followed him, cared about him, lived to serve his cause and his companions? How am I to understand a hundred years lived as a lie?" There were tears behind my eyes, and my voice caught in my throat.

Adrian clenched his fists, but his voice came low and gentle. "I know this is hard for you, Justine, to find out this way. There are still things you don't know, things that will help you to accept it. You think you were the devil's mistress, that you have conspired to some unholy purpose, but I tell you, we are not devils, Justine. Our allegiance is not to darkness, but rather, to the light!

Moving toward me, he shook his head. "Before you judge us and yourself, remember that we have tried for thousands of years to guard them from evil, leading them instead to their hearts. We were faithful to the task until finally, when the Anointed one came, the Christ, and fought for them, and wept with them, and showed them it could be done, and people still turned their backs on love, the prince devised for us a new service. *We began to create a darkness so obscene, so appalling, that mortals would be shocked awake by it.*" He grabbed hold of my shoulders then and spoke with gravity.

"It is not easy or simple or enjoyable, but we do it, because we have tried everything else and nothing has saved them. We must force them to be splendid, choosing love over hate. There is no other way for them."

I was stunned by the fervor in his voice and the passionate expression on his face. He dropped his hands from my shoulders. "Now come Justine, I'm sure the prince will explain it better than I." He turned toward the door, but I did not follow.

"No." There was defiance in my voice and pride. "I don't want to see him."

Adrian took a deep breath and shook his head.

"The prince did not ask," he said quietly.

Ah, there it was, the unspoken dread. In all the years I had been with the prince, I had never felt like his servant, or even his comrade. I was his partner, his lover, and his delicious joy. The truth was, I had never known fear with him, or of him.

But now I did.

I felt it, cold, in the center of my chest. An image of him crashing his fist through the stone table in the temple and cracking it in two flashed before my eyes, but there was something more. It was the way the others had backed away from the table, their eyes averted, the most outraged of hearts losing the courage to face him! When he had recognized me standing there, and I had looked into his eyes, yes, right in, past the shell of the man I knew, I had seen something else. *Someone* else.

"And what will you do, Adrian, if I don't come with you now? Will you take me to him by force?" My tone was cold. He only shook his head sadly and replied, "I would not."

"And what if you return without me? What then?"

"He will be angry."

"Yes, but what will he *do*? If I were to pack my bag right now and leave, take a ship to Alexandria, or lose myself in the streets of Florence or Paris...just disappear!"

A distressed grimace pressed at his lips.

"He can find you anywhere and at anytime. He has been with you long enough now to know your particular vibration, your unique signature." I was silent.

"He could have sent another for you, Justine, and he still might. I can't tell you what they will do, but if you come with me now..." he hesitated, then reached out his hand again, "I will be with you."

"It's a kind offer, Adrian, but tell me, how can I trust you?"

"I can't tell you to trust me," he replied. "You have to learn to trust yourself, Justine. If you would rather face him alone..."

But I had already made up my mind. I moved swiftly across the room and took his hand.

THE PRINCE SAT WAITING FOR US in the small courtyard below my rooms. He got to his feet as I entered and moved to take me in his arms, a familiar gesture. I threw up my hand warily.

"No, don't touch me!" I insisted. The smile fell from his face. He glanced at Adrian, who shook his head slightly. So, the prince had expected Adrian to sway me! Moving to one side, the prince pointed to a plush Roman chair at the table, which was laden with wine and food. It looked as if he were expecting to celebrate!

Moving slowly, gracefully, I took a seat. The turmoil in my stomach seemed to calm as I took note of the prince's charming manner. Still, I was glad that Adrian was close at hand. He had taken a seat by the door.

"Justine," the prince began, "I should be angry with you, very angry, that you disobeyed me."

"I was not aware I was under your command," I retorted hotly. A smile pressed at his lips.

"I think you know what I mean."

"No, my Lord, I do not think that I do! Apparently, there is much I do not know about you!"

"You are as angry with me as I am with you!" He threw up his hands exasperated. "I should have known," he groaned. "The mystery of it was too much for you! I should have known that one day ... " but he stopped there. "Come now, Justine, you must not be angry with me. I had hoped that Adrian might explain things to you, but I will do it myself—"

"Explain what? Adrian has told me why you play the devil. He has explained quite enough!" I had lost all caution, my voice bursting with outrage.

"You're overreacting, Justine!"

"She called you Lucifer!" I hissed. "You are Satan and I am your mistress! You have played with me and I ... " Ah, the truth was so close, "*I have let you!* I have taken your lavish life and traded it for decency. Where is my honor? Where is my dignity?" I glared at him accusingly, "And where are *yours*?"

This last was too much for him; he threw up his hands, commanding, "Enough! You still don't understand, do you? You call me Satan with disgust because you are ignorant of what it means!" I was moved by the passion in his voice, the look in his eyes, yearning for me to understand and accept.

"Lucifer is just a very old name, which was my title as a priest in a long-ago time and place. And the idea of Satan is just a myth made up by the Catholic Church to frighten people. How else could they get people to join them? They needed a dark force for God to save them from. Everything is blamed on this 'devil' and, of course, the ultimate fear that keeps people coming to the Church is the idea of hell, the devil's domain. No, Lucifer is the Greek word meaning "light-bringer,"

Justine, and that is my intention. That is what we are all working toward. We are guardians of the *light*."

I tried to reason with myself as he spoke, telling myself that he believed what he said.

"But how can you be guarding the light if, in fact, you are working against it? You tell me the Church has created this devil, yet now I know that the Church is your own creation! And the worst part is, the Church is the very thing that leads people away from themselves. I have heard you say it yourself!"

"Yes, that is exactly right. Justine, you must try to understand that we have watched civilization after civilization rise and fall, humanity cresting on waves of enlightenment, only to fall back down into its darkest nature. For thousands of years we have tried to help, kept alive the mystery schools and ancient initiations that would deliver the sincere seeker to the truth. So, I decided on a new course of action. Difficult as it has been to serve in this way, I have seen the wisdom in this new direction. I intend to guide humanity back to the light by forcing them up against their greatest darkness. In this way, I am, it's true, the Satan. Do you know the meaning of the word, or its origins?"

I shook my head.

"Satan is the word used by the Hebrews to describe a guardian angel. God would send a Satan to stand in a person's way to dissuade him from going astray. Remember the Old Testament story of Job, who sets out to do the very thing God tells him not to? It is the Satan that saves him in the end. God sends down an angel to stand in his way. You see, the Satan appears as one of God's obedient servants. He was never described as the Christians have come to see him, as the leader of an evil empire opposing God and man." He shook his head, half-smiling. "Satan is a messenger. In Greek you would call him an angel, a word that is a translation from the Hebrew word "Mal'ak," or messenger. That is my name also. So, I am, in the truest sense, a Satan, in that I create an opposition that people must overcome."

His reasoning exasperated me. Shaking my head sadly, I leaned toward him. "And you intend to help humanity by perpetuating pain and suffering?"

"If that's what it takes." His features hardened. I could see he was hurt, disappointed that I did not agree. But I could not.

"I'm sorry. I just can't understand how hurting people can be a good thing, a helpful contribution." I was infuriated. "I don't want to discuss this with you anymore. I'm sure you're right that I shouldn't have followed you, but I did, and now everything has changed. I don't want to be with you anymore. I won't go on with you like this!" My voice shook as I said the words, but the prince did not react. He sat back in his chair, lifting a goblet to his lips. He took a long, slow sip. Resting his elbows on the velvet arms, he made a steeple of his fingers, resting his lips upon them.

"And what *do* you want, Justine?" he asked finally. I felt Adrian shift uneasily.

"I don't know," I answered. "I need some time to think."

"Well, you don't have time now, my darling. You have been to our sacred place without permission, and for that you must leave Jerusalem." His tone was oddly warm. I did not understand. "I will send you with Adrian," he said. "He leaves at the end of the week for Spain, and in the spring he will go back to the New World. I will send you on an adventure with him, and perhaps you will come to understand better why we must do what we do. Adrian!" He raised a beckoning hand.

"No!" I said, "I won't go with Adrian, either."

"Justine," Adrian began, but the prince held up a hand. "My darling, there is no better person in the world to watch over you while —"

"I don't need anyone to watch over me anymore!"

"Of course not, but I will send you with Adrian, nonetheless." His tone was precise.

"And if I refuse?"

Now a serious look crossed his face. "And why would you refuse? What else will you do? I don't think you will go to Miriam." His tone was sarcastic, "Not now that you know she is alive and well, and has been so since your mother's death. You don't want to see her, do you?"

I shook my head. The fear churned in my stomach again.

"A wise decision, my darling, but I didn't think you would. Not after you consider all the time she could have come to you, the comfort she could have been! It's best you stay away from her now." He moved from his chair, all charm and congeniality. Taking my hand in his, he continued tenderly, "I know how difficult it was to lose your mother so soon after you brother. I did my best to be there for you, Justine. I wanted only to make you happy. Was that so wrong?"

"No," I pressed back tears. "You gave me a good life, Mal'ak...." I could say no more. "I'm tired," I whispered, getting to my feet. I was becoming vulnerable, visibly shaken.

"Yes, go rest, Justine," he said, rising to his feet and nodding his head. "You will go with Adrian and have the time you need. When we meet again, you might feel differently toward me, and better understand my cause."

I turned and ran from the room.

I kept to my room the rest of the week, brooding over all I had heard. I wanted no more of the prince and his companions; no matter how I turned it over in my mind, I saw that I had been lied to. I had been part of something unspeakable and I blamed them for it.

The prince left early in the week for Rome, and when he did, I sank into a deep depression. By the week's end I did not even rise from my bed. I lay there in semi-darkness, the sounds of the street pressing at the drapes. I turned my morning servants away and lay for hours alone. Then, there was a knock at my door.

"Go away!" I cried, "Leave me be!"

The door opened.

"I said go away!" I snapped.

"I heard you." Mufassa stood in the doorway, dressed in bright orange robes, a thick green turban wrapped round his head. Without so much as a look to me, he strode to the window — slow, sensual strides — and pulled back the thick blinds. The muffled noises cleared, and the sounds of horse's hooves, laughter, a child crying, accosted me. It must have been well into the afternoon, for light flooded the room.

"What are you doing? I told you I want to be left alone!" I was angry.

"You have been alone too long, Justine. We are worried about you."

"Like hell, you are! You're probably here because *he* sent you. He wants you to make me go with Adrian, right? The ship leaves tomorrow, Mufassa, and I am not going with it!"

He walked to the bureau and pulled open a drawer as if I had not spoken. He reached underneath, pulling out my travel bags.

"What do you think you're doing?" I challenged, sitting up in bed. He did not answer, but began pulling clothes from the drawers. I threw off the sheet and stepped from the bed, my hair falling loose to my waist. "Mufassa!" I stormed over to the bureau and pulled the clothes out of his hands. "You have no right to be here!"

"No," he said deliberately, as if containing his anger, "you are the one who has no right to be here. It is time for you to go."

"What?"

"This is an important time, Justine, and you intruded on a meeting that you were not invited to. You have seen things that you were not prepared to see, and certainly you have heard too much!" His passionate accent pressed the words into me as if they were alive.

"Too much!" I threw down the clothes in disgust. "You mean I have heard the truth and know finally that you, all of you, have lied to me. I know, finally, that I have been living a lie and have been party to unspeakable evils, whether they have been by my own hand or not!"

"Is that what is troubling you?"

"Of course, that's what's troubling me. That, and the fact that it doesn't seem to trouble you!"

His expression solemn, Mufassa nodded. "And how, Justine, can you know what troubles me?" his voice accusing. "How naive of you to assume that pain and suffering is lost on me." Shaking his head, he bent down to the floor and picked up the clothes I had thrown. He walked over to the bag and put them in. Startled by his words, I hesitated.

"In my time, Justine, I lost my family and my tribe. I am the only survivor of a Christian rampage. In the name of God, the men of my village were slaughtered when they resisted Christian conversion and slavery. My mother was raped as my father's dead body lay across the doorway. My little sister was taken away by a Christian priest to be his mistress. Every child who was too young to serve or to take care of itself was murdered. Nothing remains of my village, or my people, or our art and customs. There is no trace of us left on this Earth." He did not look at me as he spoke. He just kept packing my bags.

"I didn't know," I began, but he held up his hand.

"I don't tell you this to make you feel sorry for me, Justine. It is only that we have all had our losses and felt suffering, fear, and pain. No one of us is immune, *not even the prince.* Especially him. He has felt it far longer than we have."

"Are you going to defend him now?" The edge crept back into my voice.

"He needs no defense. He has chosen his way as I have chosen mine as you will now choose yours. He is an old one, Justine, and because you do not agree with his way does not mean it is wrong."

"How can you say that?"

Turning to me then, he spoke with a sternness that I was unaccustomed to.

"Who are you to judge what I say or do? You have spent the last century surrounded by the finest things that life could give. You have had no end of wealth and luxury, and what have you done with it? Whom have you helped? What have you made of yourself, Justine? Hmm?" Turning to me sharply, he stretched out his hands in a flamboyant gesture. "Has the world offered you no opportunity for service? Have you not seen a child crying, or a woman bent over by age, struggling against life to survive? Have you never thought on the lives of those who have been cooking your meals, or sewing your clothes, or dressing you each day? What are their hopes and dreams, Justine, tell me. *What has been within your grasp to give that you have withheld?*" I was silent, stunned. "It's so easy to say that you were trapped, or lied to. Do you tell yourself that we withheld the truth and you were our victim? Did we use you to amuse ourselves? How is it that you have convinced yourself that the conflict and pain you feel now is our doing, hm? How do you reconcile your choice of a lifetime spent with your head in the sand like an ostrich?" He turned away once again. His words hurt, but they were giving voice to the feeling of dread that lay buried inside me.

"I didn't want to know or see," I whispered, shaking. "It was easier to forget, to live apart from the struggles of others. My life with the prince was so . . . easy. It just seemed normal. I knew he had power, of course I did, but I didn't want to know what he did with it!" There were tears in my eyes.

"I know."

"I feel guilty that I have been so spoiled, so self-centered."

"There's no reason to feel that way. You're not bad because of what you have, Justine, but with it comes a responsibility, a choice that you have not been willing to make. We have made our choice. We have chosen our paths, right or wrong. We are serving in our own ways, and we don't expect you to agree with us. Just don't blame us for your choices. That's not fair."

"No, it's not, Mufassa." I began to cry. Finally, the tears that would ease this pain began to flow. My body shook. In a moment, Mufassa's arms were around me, my head on his chest, the anger slipping away. He held me for a long time. When I had quieted he began to stroke my head.

"I suppose," he said gently, "that we should have told you what we, as immortals, did as groups. But you were so new to your power and your gifts, our shining star, that I fear we were selfish, too. We wanted you to come into your immortality with joy. Not all of us were so lucky. And the prince, he wanted to protect you from the harshness of life. He wanted to give you everything. He has searched so long for you. That was not right on our part, Justine, for you are a woman, and you must live with what you do and do not accomplish." My tears slowed, but still he held me.

"There is so much life ahead of you now. I want you to go out and discover it! We will pack your travel bag and send you out of Jerusalem. The truth is, it's not safe for you here anymore." I pulled away from him, wiping my eyes.

"What do you mean?"

"Some of the others are upset with what you've done. You didn't have permission to be at that council or in the holy place. They don't like that you know where it is, and where the sacred things are kept, and that no one is certain how you could have achieved such a feat!" He laughed at this. "Even the ancient one did not detect your presence! Justine, you must have a gift that is very strong! But now, it is best that you go." His smile was infectious. "Adrian leaves for Spain at dawn. He's preparing a place for you on the ship as we speak. You'll excuse my interfering, but you must go now, until we've sorted things out with the others. And to go against the prince, Justine ... " he hesitated. "Go with Adrian as the prince suggests. Adrian is very old and there are many things you may learn from him." He kissed my forehead. "And Justine, don't come back to the East. Not for a long time. There are old ones here, immortals you have not yet seen or heard of. They are very strong and gifted, and they will know if you trespass again. Mind what I say now!" He lifted his smooth hand to my cheek and caressed me. "We may not always be able to protect you."

Seven

It took six weeks, even with Adrian calling the wind, for our ship to reach Spain. We sailed first to Italy and then on to Barcelona. I spent most of my days out on deck beneath the enormous canvas sails, my hair undone beneath a wide-brimmed hat I tied on with a scarf. This was a particularly undignified way to present myself, but I did not care and Adrian would not chastise me. It was made clear that I was traveling under his protection, so the raucous sailors left me to myself.

It was good to be left alone.

At night I lay very still in the rear cabin of the vessel, listening to the boards creaking as the ship cut through the night. With the little round window open, I would let the scent of the sea bathe me. The days wore on. I knew I did not want to go to Spain and spend the spring languishing as the Lady Illuminare. Who was she? No. There was something else calling me.

I would not speak of this to Adrian. Although I knew he would not try to stop me from leaving him, I could not disappoint him. During the voyage the intangible friendship that bound us was rekindled. When I felt social and joined him at the evening meal, he would ask me to recite my favorite poems and stories for him, anything to pull me from loneliness. And I felt somehow that in my doing so, Adrian was pulled, too, from some lonely place inside himself.

At times I watched Adrian on the bridge before the mainmast, the lovely deep blue of the twilight sky behind him. He wore a deep purple cloak, and his thick brown hair was blown back by the wind. I was captivated by the fierce focus in his eyes as he stared toward the horizon, as if willing the ship toward it as he would a stallion. There was a forbidding majesty to his face, a loftiness that humbled his men and, I think, made them afraid. He wore his rank like nobility, for it was not something one would question. But there was something else I saw in him, too, in the shape of his mouth, soft and full, which spoke of gentleness. And when he looked at me, when he turned on the bridge and caught my eye below, his face gave off a faint light, his expression warm and comfortable, so that I would smile despite my gloom.

Then one night near month's end I had a dream. I was walking at dusk in a great rose garden, cut back for the winter. Frost was on the ground. And then there was a building and a cross and then, yes! I recognized the old mausoleum that my great-great-great-grandfather had built in the cemetery behind my family's chapel. I looked around at the graves; familiar old stones, hand-carved, elaborate with metals, some in the ground, some with statues raised above. Yes, I was standing in the cemetery behind the chapel, and there was my father's grave, and next to it was my brother's. But there was another. I traced the name and the epitaph on the stone. "CHRISTINE," it said, "LOVING MOTHER." I was shaken. A grave for my mother? But there was more. I watched as my hand moved from her stone to one next to it. And the name the hand traced was my own.

"Justine . . ." I heard myself say, and horrified I tried to pull away. "Justine . . ." I said again, only this time I was above, somehow, watching. "Justine!" I cried out with a sob, lowering my head to the stone.

And then I woke up.

I did not speak of the dream for several days, but in the last hours of the voyage, the cragged outline of land emerging in the distance, it came to me, finally, what I must do.

I mounted the deck and moved toward the bridge. A tall, blond sailor reached out to help me to the platform, but Adrian waved him away and took my hand.

"So, you've come to see the view from the bridge before we land." He was smiling, pleased. "I'm surprised you've waited this long!"

It was good to see him happy. He guided me to the rail, which I gripped with my left hand; I did not let go of his with my right. He squeezed it reassuringly.

"You'll like Spain, Justine," he said. "I will have the finest rooms set aside, and I will show you Barcelona myself."

His face was radiant, his stance strong and comforting. He looked back to the water as a great white froth splashed against the front of the ship. This exhilarated him. Still, I did not let go of his hand, and he did not pull it away.

"Adrian, I don't want to stay in Barcelona with you." He continued to stare at the sea. "I want to go back to Wales. I want to see what's become of my home." Still he did not turn to me. "You have been so good to me, and I want to thank you ... ."

He simply squeezed my hand. "You're sure?" The ship dipped and lunged, and he tightened his grip, steadying me.

"Yes."

"And you will go alone?"

"Yes."

We stared at the horizon for a long time, watching the land grow bigger with each leap of the ship's great hull over the waves. When the men began to move like soldiers toward their stations, and the orders were called out above and below deck, he turned to me, his face kind.

"My ship will leave for the New World at the end of May. There will be a place for you aboard."

Another gentle squeeze of my hand and he let me go.

I did not know how much I had missed my home until my small ship finally made its way toward the familiar port in South Wales, but I could see, even from a distance, that things were very different. The port had grown in size, and the harbor was large with a long dock that extended like a bridge into the sea. I saw the blue, ragged line of the town against the glowing sky. It was very cold, even though the snow was gone. I could see my breath in the air like a cloud in the night.

The fact that I had been gone for more than one hundred fifty years was obvious as I made my way through the burgeoning town, the low-hung roofs of its cottages gleaming in the moonlight. Silver designs adorened the iron gates of the fine new houses made of stone and wood. Lace curtains hung in windows made of glass. Rows and rows of new houses spread out beyond the old fortifications. I hardly recognized the streets or the old square where my mother had brought the first real markets. Behind the windows I spied gilded furniture and other bits of wealth that made my past in this place seem barbaric and sad.

On the first night, I traveled the muddy streets and stone sidewalks until I found a decent inn. I kept to myself, going largely unnoticed and unchallenged. I was discreet, traveling in a simple shift and a large, hooded cloak carrying only a small, worn bag at my side.

On the second day, I went out of the town toward the old church. In its place stood a large cathedral. The bridge was wider than I re-membered and I could see that the town had spread out around the building as if it were its center. They had rebuilt it in stone.

I would not go in. Old, bitter feelings welled dangerously inside me. I continued down the road, the river on my left, our old wall still standing on my right. When I came finally to the castle, I saw that it was occupied. The gates were not the same, the tower had been completely rebuilt, and, of course, there was a new roof. Peering through the gate I saw that the place was full of people, horses, and carriages, and large groups of servants running between what looked like a new cookhouse and the castle. Ah, so they had blamed the fire on the kitchen. I watched as the main doors were flung open and a train of black-cloaked men escorted a man in red robes and glittering gold down the stairs, into a very expensive coach. The gates were opened and the Church official's carriage was pulled through.

I shuddered. So, the Church had taken control of our estate after all — and the town. I brooded over this, wondering what I should do. These were my first days alone, really alone. I was not used to thinking about my life or planning what I would do beyond the next pleasure. For the first time in all the years that had passed, I wondered what had happened to our staff, our loyal servants, after we were gone.

I waited most of the afternoon outside the great iron gate, until a group of servants came with their carts loaded with foods and linens. As the gate swung open for them and they passed through, I fell in step behind them. Once inside, I slipped into my mother's old rose garden and headed to the back of the chapel, where our family cemetery had been. It was still there. The wall was green with moss, just as it had been in my dream, and the mausoleum was cracked and the paint faded. I walked over to the old graves where my ancestors lay. Thirty-or-so graves marked generations, some with elaborate crosses, others simple. I went first to the familiar stone crosses that marked the graves of my father and brother, just as I had in the dream. But as I neared them I froze: there beside the crosses sat two ornately carved square stones. It was impossible! On the first was my mother's name, and the other held mine. This could not be! Two heretics, witches no less, given burial sites in a Christian cemetery? The only explanation was the prince, but why? What would he care whether we were honored in this way or not? A chill ran over me as I realized something much more incredible: how could I have dreamt such a thing? My head was spinning and emotions swelled in my chest. I ran from the cemetery, returning to the inn.

The next day, I bought an old pony and cart, and filled the cart with cheese, bread, and wine. I bought a warm sleeping roll and some tools—an ax, a shovel, some bowls, a knife, and a cast iron pot. Ignoring the curious questions and looks, I departed the town without looking back. Heading past the castle, I took the road that would lead to the blue hills and the little chapel tucked away from the world. I was not afraid to do this alone. I longed for it. I knew it was what I had come here for the first night I had looked up at the mountain, a magical mist hanging low over the shadows of trees.

I remember little of what happened during this time. I spent three months alone at the chapel, which had long since been abandoned, doing ordinary things—cutting away the brambles and bushes, cleaning away the old nests that had been built on the altar, unblocking the stream, and re-consecrating the goddess pool. I learned to enjoy my solitude rather than fear it. The loneliness I had felt began to melt away, and I felt the Earth reach up and out to hold me. I sat with the spirits of the place, the women who had come before me, and I thought back on my life before I became immortal. I remembered the people who had helped me, and the ones whom I had helped. I had cared then. And finally, I came to know that I cared still.

Eight

EARLY IN THE MONTH OF MAY, when spring had taken firm hold of the hill, and the nights had grown warm enough for me to sleep under the stars, Miriam came to me. Dressed in black, her long red hair loose about her shoulders, she walked up the hill to the shrine, the sun setting behind her. I knew it was she, I could feel the heart I had so loved beating in her chest. She appeared younger now, a woman of forty or so, the lines on her face smoothed away. She was elegant; even wrapped in the plain robes of a peasant traveler, she brought grace and power with her.

I knew that she would come. I had felt her drawing close. I had wanted her to, hoping to confront her, to say the thing that would break her heart. But when she stooped at the visioning pool, dipping her fingertips in the water to anoint herself, a familiar warmth washed through me. I moved my hand toward the fire pit, bringing it to flames in the old way. There was something comforting about it. Looking at her then, my old teacher, I was not so sure I was ready for this meeting.

"I am here." Her voice resounded in the open air as if we were in a temple.

"So you are." I tried to say it coldly, for I had meant to keep my distance. It was my anger I wanted to vent, but she did not give me time.

"Justine," she said, moving nearer then, reaching out her hand to brush my cheek. "I have come because, finally, you are alone."

"I don't care ... " I whispered, my throat tight. "Now that you're here I have nothing to say!" Miriam only shook her head, moving closer until she almost held me in her arms.

"You are angry with me! Of course you are, but you love me, too. Is this not the moment I trained you for? This is the moment that will

143

make you your own woman, the moment you will choose love over hate! You already know what you must do. Didn't I teach you all those years ago to go within, to seek answers from a Presence, a God that would answer you? To stand up for truth, even in the face of personal danger?" Her voice softened then, "Isn't that what your mother gave her life for?"

I reeled at this, turning sharply to confront her.

"My mother! How dare you bring her up now! You were there, weren't you? You were with her and you did nothing to save her. It was because of you that she died!"

"No, Justine, that's not true." Her voice was calm, even as I pulled away from her and began to pace, my tone becoming frantic.

"But it is true! I saw you there, you and Enoch, and she spoke up for you, she tried to save you, and then you left her there to die!"

She shook her head sadly. "Your mother died because it was her choice to stand up for truth. I could not help her or dissuade her from her purpose, Justine. I could not save her, for it was to Enoch and a greater purpose that I was pledged. No, Justine, it was your mother's choice to die for what she believed in."

I turned on her violently. "No!" I cried, "No! I hate you!" The old pain rose up in me, bitter and rank.

"But you know what I'm saying is true, Justine. Your mother was exceptional in that she did not fear death. Because she knew the wisdom, as you do, she knew that there is no such thing as death. It is only the shedding of one's skin. Cry because you miss her, Justine, but don't cry *for* her. She died with honor, standing up for what was right and true, and her soul lives still, with the dignity of knowing that."

Yes, it was all true, every word she said. Of course my mother's soul lived on, of course it did. She was free to grow beyond this life, immortal in so many more ways than I. But there was still pain in me, an arrow let loose from the bow in my mind. There was something else I wanted from Miriam, something I could not forgive ... suddenly, I blurted it out.

144

"You have been here all this time, all these years and, and ..." I could not finish. Grief was pressing hard on my chest and I realized I was crying.

"And I did not come for you," she finished, holding her arms open to me. I was shaking, then moving toward her, letting my body fall into the soft folds of her embrace. She held me while the tears spilled from the cup inside me.

"You must forgive me, Justine. I did not know how to approach you while you were with the prince. He and I do not always mingle well, and you seemed so happy with him. I have been watching." She brushed my hair with a soft hand. "You have chosen a life with him that I could not offer and would not wish you to miss! He is a very old soul, Justine, one you have known before, and I felt it important for you to complete something with him." I quieted with her words, softened in her embrace. I pulled back and she wiped away my tears.

"Try to understand," she said, "it isn't that I have not loved you."

I nodded, knowing that it was true. What made it so hard was that I had loved her, too.

"I want to go with you now," I said. "I have left him. Whatever I was to complete is done! I will not return to that life."

"Yes, I think you will leave him now, Justine, but it is not time for you to come with me. You must find your own way now." I was crushed at this. Panic gripped me.

"But, Miriam, I have to go with you now! I don't know where else I belong."

"Be calm," she said, reaching out to touch me again. "Remember what I taught you. Command your courage forward, you will need it now. I have faith in you, Justine." Her eyes were smiling.

"But how shall I find my way?"

"You must trust yourself, living as the mystic does, listening to what is inside of yourself, rather than what is outside. Inside is where God lives. Inside is where you will find the answers you seek. And above all, you must not fear pain or struggle. They are your temporary teachers.

They will break you open and carve you out."

I knew she was right, but I had not wanted to hear the voice inside because what it called me to would have destroyed the life I had. It would have led me to confrontation and rejection, and I could not bear that. Well, I would bear it now.

"I will not stay long with you now, for my work takes me back into the East tonight," she continued.

"But Miriam, I have so many questions, there is so much I don't know!"

"You know all you need to know! Keep your life simple, Justine. Go now with Adrian to the New World. See what you will learn with him. He too is an old soul whom you have known before. Haven't you felt that?" I was surprised by the question.

"Why, yes, I suppose."

"Well, trust that! Don't question what you feel. Your feelings are linked to your heart, and your heart knows the future. Does your heart really want to come with me, or are you simply afraid of going with Adrian?"

"But Adrian works with the prince!" I protested, but Miriam held up her hand, shaking her head.

"Justine, *everyone* falls from grace. There is no soul born to this Earth that does not make a mistake on its way to enlightenment. Adrian doesn't need your judgment; he needs your compassion. Perhaps that is even his gift to you. It's certainly something you're ready to learn!" She was blunt. "Are you not drawn to him?"

"I, ah, yes, I guess we're friends," I stuttered. She eyed me for a long moment, as if looking beyond me, or into me, at something I could not see.

"I remember when you first met him, more than a century ago, at your family's estate. He had come in with Nicholas, yes?" I nodded, remembering the scene, the sense of warmth that had come from him. "And he was the one who came for you when your mother was taken, and again, he was the soul who saved you from the cross."

"Yes ... " I replied absently, remembering his voice crying out through that wicked night, "Cut her down!"

"And have you never thought of him over these years? Have you never missed him?"

I blushed and pulled away from her. "He is a good friend. I have been loyal to the prince, surely you know that!" My tone was defensive, but Miriam was only laughing.

"Yes, I am aware of your loyalty. But I wonder what would happen now if you were loyal to yourself, instead?" Her face was warm and her eyes glittered. "Go with Adrian, Justine! Go and see what you find! I know it is not your time to be with me. You can trust that."

I sighed. Yes, I would go with Adrian.

"Will I see you again?" I turned to her, pressing my head to her shoulder. Her arms came around me again.

"Yes, but I think it will be some time," she answered warmly, stroking my hair.

"When you really need me, I will come."

Part Three

Adrian

One

ADRIAN WAS EXPECTING ME.

I had taken a small craft from England, arriving in Spain just a few days before he would set sail. As I walked down the long plank to shore, Adrian stepped through the crowd gathered on the wharf. It was quite a sight: raucous sailors, merchants with baskets of fish, and whores hanging on their soldiers' arms all moved out of the way respectfully at his approach.

"Lady," he bowed slightly, reaching out his hand.

"Adrian." I could not suppress a smile. It was good to see him. The crowd lingered, watching, so that I felt myself elevated by the reputation of my escort.

"I had hoped you would come!" Lifting his arm for me to take, he began to guide me over the creaking wooden wharf toward the crowd, which again parted deferentially as we passed.

"How did you know when I would arrive?"

He laughed at that. "I was the wind that brought you here!" he answered. Looking up at his face I saw that he was perfectly serious.

"Of course you were," I said.

He took me to his ship, a monster of a thing with three billowing sails, each bigger than the next. I had never been on a vessel so large or with a crew of so many. There were no low galleys with slaves dipping their oars; this was a ship of war, loaded with food and water to sustain us for a voyage that would take months.

The ship was divided into three sections. The long stretch of deck in the front and all the space beneath was for the crew and supplies. A second deck, raised several feet above the first, housed the captain

151

and his staff; behind this, separated from the Spanish soldiers and sea-
men, was an aft cabin that was to be my own. I was relieved for this
separation, as I was conspicuously aware that I was the only woman
aboard. Yet, I could see that I would not be bothered on the voyage,
for I was secure in my position as Adrian's ward. The men would
hardly look at me when I spoke to them, let alone behave inappropri-
ately. No, if anything, it was quite the opposite: they treated me with
a kind of reverence one would not expect from a group of seafaring
men. Later, I came to realize that they felt themselves a distinguished
company, honored to be of Adrian's troop. They looked at him as a
hero, their lives well spent in his service. This realization touched me
deeply, for what was it in Adrian that could make a man look on war
as a privilege, killing as an honor? They loved him, these men, and
that love gave them the will to override their lust, and sometimes even
their common sense.

So, from the beginning I was not threatened by the long months of
this journey. On the contrary, I looked forward to it. I spent much of
my time with Adrian. I told him of my journey to England, of my time
at the chapel, and the things Miriam had said. Well, not everything—I
did not mention her reference to him. In his turn, Adrian spoke of his
journeys into the New World, his conquests, and his hopes for a new
renaissance of the spirit. I listened as he spoke, sensing in him the
genuine desire for change. He believed it could be done, and that his
way, the prince's way, would ultimately succeed. At the mention of the
prince I stiffened, a cold apprehension rising up from my stomach. I
tried to discuss other possibilities. Did not Miriam have another sug-
gestion, another plan, another path? Yet, I could not persuade him that
there was a different way.

"You are angry still with the master," he replied, "so you cannot see
the wisdom of his way. But soon, perhaps, you will."

I did not pursue these conversations, knowing in my heart that
there could be no other way for me. At these times, I wondered why I
was doing this, why I had put myself on this path with him. But when

Adrian softened, offering a tender smile, I would see it in his eyes, the reason I was really here.

It is difficult to describe how the intimacy grew between us in those months. The isolation of the shipboard life, and the long days together, gave us a familiarity that was more profound than I had known before. My heart opened as I watched Adrian with his crew and his maps and his long, silent evenings reading the stars. He looked up at them like old friends who whispered the news of the cosmos into his open ears. Many nights I would sit with him as the ship rolled with the waves, singing the songs that Miriam had taught me long ago: songs that would call the wind or calm the sea, and make the stars twinkle in the sky; lullabies and hymns my mother had taught me. The crew would gather on the deck below, some humming along, one striking up a tune on an old wooden flute. When the voyage became too long and the men grew restless, clashing with one another, Adrian would soothe them with stern direction and the promise of a future they would own. We never faced the hardship that I have heard some travelers endure. Adrian kept us moving swiftly along the sea, our water supply replenished by a freak rain when it ran low, and never did we encounter another ship or a storm to confront us.

As the weeks wore into months, I found myself absorbed into a life that was unique. The prince, and the life I had lived before, seemed farther away with each passing day. And so did my inhibitions.

One evening, Adrian came to me, announcing that we were only a few weeks from our destination.

"Then your adventure will really begin, Justine," he said. He put a book down on the narrow wooden table, pulling over the oil lamp. "Look at this." His voice was excited. Opening the pages of the book, he showed me pictures of wild beasts and overgrown jungles. "This is what it's like around the capital city of Mexico ... all this is jungle to the east, and here," he pointed to a map on the back page, "this is where the mountain rises to the sky. This is where I'll be taking my men. You'll be safe in the capital, I have a small palace there and ..."

he continued talking, but I was not listening.

My eyes lingered on his long, thin fingers as they turned the pages. His words began to flow together so that I heard his voice as an instrument playing, lulling me gently toward him. I was standing by his side, my hair loose about my shoulders. I sat down beside him and watched his face, warm and animated, as he spoke. His broad, angular forehead trimmed neatly by coarse brown bangs, creased with lines as he quite seriously pointed to a page with images of snakes. "And these are the worst, look here at their marking so you'll recognize them ... " My eyes traced the curve of his cheek and fell, finally, on his full, sculpted lips.

"Justine ... " he had paused, "what is it, what's wrong?"

I did not answer. Gazing up into his eyes, I watched him flush, and seizing the moment, I leaned over and kissed him. It was a simple thing, a brush of the lips, but a fire shot through me that left me yearning for more. In a moment, Adrian was on his feet, the book falling to the floor. He knelt awkwardly to pick it up. I stood quickly, reaching out my hand for his arm, but he stiffened, placing the book in my palm.

"No, Justine." His voice was low, seeking command.

"But, Adrian," I began.

"No." he said, "this cannot happen. If I have led you on in any way—"

"You haven't," I said. "I'm the one, I just wanted ... "

"No." he said again, a finality to his tone that hurt me. He had been so warm, so kind, I could not understand that he did not feel the same way. How could I have misread the way he looked at me? Did he not feel the same excitement when I came into his presence? I was embarrassed that I had so misconstrued him.

"I acted foolishly," I stated flatly. "I just felt ... I just, just wanted ... " I hesitated; I was not at all sure what I wanted. I could not imagine that I was really here to see the New World, or to watch the Spanish conquest that would surely ensue. No, I was here because of him, because my heart recognized him, and I was no longer willing to hide such a thing. A terror ran through my breast as I realized this. What could I say to him in the face of this rejection? What would he think of me?

He raised his voice then: "You can't do this to people, Justine. It is a cruel thing to play with a person's heart!" His voice was harsh and he had an odd, faraway look in his eye.

"But, I'm not!" I insisted.

"Justine!" he cried, exasperated. Moving toward me, he took hold of my arm, a startling gesture. "You're unkind! You would take your pleasure regardless of the consequences!"

"But, I don't—"

"You belong to the prince; you're his woman, as you've always been."

"I'm not! I'm not *his*, I'm not *anyone's*!" I shouted, trying to pull away, but he held me fast. "How dare you say this to me, Adrian! I've done nothing to you, nothing but reach out with my heart, and now you're being cruel!" I accused.

"It's impossible!" He raised his voice now, and his cool, collected exterior shook with heat. I had never seen him this way.

"Maybe it's impossible for you because he's your master," I said, jerking my arm hard, releasing myself, "but I am free. He doesn't own *me*," I hissed. "What can he do to me, Adrian? I'm immortal; my body cannot die. So, will he make me suffer? Is that the kind of man you follow? A man who would torture an innocent soul finding her own way? A man who would persecute the woman he loves just because she loves another?" I was in a rage.

"What? What are you saying?" He seemed incredulous.

"I'm free of him, Adrian! I'm not going back to him, not when we reach the New World, not ever! I will face whatever the consequences of my choice may be, but I will not stay with him. I *will* follow my heart." My voice was powerful and direct. "And if you don't care for me, if you don't feel the way I do ..." but I stopped there suddenly, for a look passed over Adrian that quieted me. It was a shadow of some long-ago pain that glimmered in his eyes, and it chilled me.

Slowly, he ran his hands through his hair, closing his eyes. He took a long moment to collect himself. The ship rocked us gently in an even rhythm, while the golden glow of the oil lamp sent shadows across the cabin door. I sucked in my breath, waiting. Adrian opened his eyes, a strong, quiet presence animating his face. In a low voice he asked, "Are you telling me that following your heart has led you here to me, Justine?"

My body shook slightly as he said the words.

"Yes, that is what I am saying."

There was another long moment of silence between us as we stared into each other's eyes. This was the first moment of equality we had ever really shared. He owed me nothing, neither protection nor deference to my station, and I could not command him as I once could. What we shared now would be only the truth.

"I think you're right about the prince, Justine. I don't believe he would ever hurt you, not directly. In the end, he will only do what he thinks he *must*." He took a step toward me and almost whispered, "Justine, you must understand that I struggle with my past and my loyalty, even though I know what my heart longs for, too."

I shivered.

"You care for me, too!" I blurted, as if in victory. What a blunder! Trying to correct myself, I continued. "I mean, you have feelings..." But he was only smiling, moving toward me again, reaching for my face. Cupping my cheeks in his hands, he leaned down and kissed me, a full, smooth brush of the lips. Then came the fire again, an orange flame leaping from my hips. I pressed my mouth hard against his, letting the passion run through my flesh. My hands found his shoulders and his chest, sliding down his long, narrow waist. Gorgeous!

Love me! I said silently with my mind and my body. I heard his answer inside me, filling me with a delicious and memorable heat. It said, *I do love you!* His lips moved to my cheek, his hands pulling away my shift. I pushed my body closer to him, pressing my breasts against his chest as if we would merge. *Yes! Love me* I thought again, sliding my lips like water down to the hollow of his neck. *I do, Justine.* I heard his voice inside me again. *I have always loved you . . . .*

156

Two

WE BECAME LOVERS, each night spent in my cabin languishing in the delicacies of each other's body. Sleepless nights rocking with the waves, long caresses, and sometimes tears. There was no boundary, or limit. I fell deeply in love. Those were precious days and nights, before the realities of the world, and the life Adrian would choose, were before us.

We reached New Spain by the end of the summer. The city of Tenochtitlán, Mexico, the great capital of Spain's New World, was sweltering. We were taken through the streets of the massive city by carriage, surrounded by legions of soldiers protecting us from the Indians whom the Captain-General Hernán Cortés had left alive. There were not that many. Most of the people I saw were women and children, working under the crack of a whip. Adrian tried to divert my attention, and at another time I would have let him. I would have ridden with the curtains closed, arriving at some palatial estate with no care as to how I had gotten there or who had paid the price. But as I rode through the streets that day, I would not look away.

"What are they doing?" I asked Adrian.

"Not many Indians, or Aztecs, as this tribe is called, survived the siege on this city. Now the women and children are left to rebuild it for the Spaniards and the Church. The real power here lies in the hands of the bishop. His title is Protector of the Indians and Apostolic Inquisitor. He is here to instruct the Indians in their worship of the one true god, his god, of course."

Looking out the window, I saw a group of Spanish soldiers goading an old man; one raised a whip above his head and let it fly. I turned away as I caught the sound of it slicing through flesh.

"Adrian!" I shuddered. "How can you let this happen?" I could not conceal the horror in my voice.

"I'm not *letting* it happen, Justine, it's their choice to behave this way. I didn't swing the whip."

"You might as well have! You have the power to make them stand down."

"That is not the point. They have the power to stand down as well; it's up to them to use it! I can't do it for them. I can't be their conscience or their guide. I can only hope that what I do awakens them to it."

"By condoning this?" I was incredulous. The sight of people slaving in the heat and the echo of the whip grated on me.

"I don't condone it." His voice was cool and in command. "You miss the point, Justine, this is the way I serve."

A cold tension rose between us. I bit back the angry words that pressed on my lips. Arguing was not going to make my point. And there was a strange sensation in me, a desire to hold onto the infatuation I felt for Adrian. I did not want to let this come between us ... not yet. I knew from the moment I set foot on the ship that Adrian would not be dissuaded from his purpose. This was his life; he had invested centuries in service of this plan. If he were to agree with me now and admit that his efforts were misplaced, or worse, decide that he were wrong, it would negate all the years that had gone before, and this he would not do. From this he must protect himself, I could see it in his eyes. But it was something else that kept me silent. I sensed that were Adrian to see the pain he had helped to create as purposeless, well, I did not know if he would be able to survive, for it was a sense of *purpose* that kept his defense in place. So, I held back my words, deciding to bide my time and stay close at his side, seeing where this would lead me.

We spent two weeks in a villa that was considered a palace of Cortés, in the city of Coyoacan. There the great church of San Juan Bautista was being built, and across the square was the local city hall. Soldiers paraded in front of it day and night. A Dominican monastery lay just outside the town, built with thick, heavy walls of stone. Like most monasteries I would come to see, it echoed the stern imperial mood of the Spaniards. The monastery itself seemed to speak Cortés' famous proclamation: "We are the emissaries of a great king, a great God, and a great Church, and, as their spokesmen, we are right and have rights which cannot be denied us."

The city itself was lined with cobblestone streets and square mud buildings called *adobe*. Ancient trees branched out in the square, giving their shade for the noon *siesta,* which the heat made us strictly observe. It would be a safe enough place for me to stay while Adrian set out on his quest. Afterward, when he returned, we would face the prince together. This was Adrian's plan, but on the night he came and told me he was to leave, I was ready with a plan of my own.

He came to my rooms very late. The temperature had cooled and my windows were thrown open to the night air. I left only a few candles burning low, so that the room was suffused with a dreamy light. Adrian came cleanly shaven, a fresh white shirt hung loose over his broad shoulders. When he kissed me, the light scent of rose water lingered on his skin. He did not speak, but ran his hands gently through my hair and down my back, sending chills across my skin.

"My love," I whispered as his hands found my waist.

"Yes?" His voice was soft.

"I've heard rumors today and watched your men preparing to leave ... " He pulled his lips from my neck, hesitating.

"Yes, they're making ready. I was going to tell you ... " he dropped his eyes, "we leave at dawn."

"I see."

"It has to be done, Justine! I've given my word that I would see it through!" Turning away from me, he went to the window. He leaned his shoulder against the thick clay wall, his profile lit by streaks of silver moonlight.

"I understand," I said neutrally, moving to his side.

"You do?"

"Of course." I smiled and nodded as if my acceptance were a thing to be taken for granted.

"You understand?" he sounded incredulous, a smile breaking over his face. Then he reached for me, his controlled exterior disappearing in a sea of kisses. I kissed him back, long and slow, my hands reaching up around his neck and pulling gently, teasingly, at his thick hair.

"Yes," I murmured, pulling him to my bed. The candles wavered as a light breeze stole in through the window. I dropped the mosquito net around us and loosened my cotton gown so that my breasts were in his hands. Then there was a rush of sensation as I pressed him down and moved over him, a ghost of pleasure. Adrian kissed me.

"My love," he whispered, "I'll return soon. Then I will take you away from here, and we'll have time ... " My lips brushed his forehead and his cheek and then, softly, deliciously, my tongue found his ear. I whispered back, "My love."

His hands moved down to my waist. "There is no need for you to concern yourself with me," I said. He pulled away my robes. "Because I'm going with you." He began to laugh, reaching up to kiss me again.

"Justine, you are incorrigible," he murmured. "How wild and outlandish you are, how—" He stopped. "You *are* joking aren't you?" he said, grasping my hands, which were pulling away his shirt. "I mean, you can't be serious? You don't intend to—"

"But I *do* intend to," I said simply, smiling down at him. "I like the way you're holding my hands," I teased, leaning down to take his lips again, but in a moment he had shifted his weight and pulled me down beside him. My seduction had taken a wrong turn.

"You can't be serious!" His voice was rough. "We're going into the jungle, Justine, with two hundred vicious men!"

"I'll go as a boy again."

"You can't possibly!"

"I'll go as your servant, I'll attend you." I reached for his cheek. "That way I'll be allowed to sleep in your tent ... " This seemed to give him pause, so I continued, running my fingers down his chin and neck to his chest. "I won't get in your way and I won't try to stop you, Adrian. I know what you're setting out to do. Even though I don't agree with it, I want to be with you." I was telling the truth about this, for although I had first determined not to support Lucifer's dark deeds, I felt inexplicably drawn to this. I had gone this far and opened my heart, and now it seemed to be singing truths to me that I dared not disobey. For whatever the reason, it told me to go with Adrian, and I would follow it, no matter the outcome. Oddly, he did not continue his argument or try to dissuade me further.

"That could work," he said, relaxing as I gently pushed him down again. "Yes, I can see how it could work."

Three

IT TOOK TWO LONG MONTHS to find the mysterious tribe. Because many of the men had seen me as a woman at Adrian's side, I had to take great care with my disguise. My hair was cropped close to my head and I had to use my psychic skills to lay a web of deception about myself. I was seen as a male servant, and I waited hand and foot upon my lord commander. Needless to say, Adrian liked that part. In the evenings I would retire to our tent and let him make it up to me. In this way I kept myself distracted from the horror of the task at hand.

The Spanish bought native guides, but they were no help in finding the tribe. In the end, Adrian had dreamed the course that would lead us to them. We climbed up out of the jungle, most of the men on foot. Then it was into the mountains, through lush fields of green, up and up, until the air seemed to press upon our lungs as we breathed it. Past the clouds we traveled, until finally we came upon a trail. Then it was easy. A few more days led us to the base of a steep slope. At the top, stone buildings marked the perimeter of a community built right up to the edge of the cliff. This is important to understand, for the soldiers saw this to be an easy victory because there was no way out of the village if not down this slope and through our camp. Cliffs surrounded three sides of the settlement, so the air of triumph filled our men even before our tents were in place.

Early the next morning, I saddled my horse, riding at Adrian's side as he led his men up the slope and into the village. The troops spread out like a fan, sweeping from dwelling to dwelling, but all was quiet. Minutes dragged on, and the only sound came from our troops sifting through the emptiness. I became hopeful. Perhaps they were not here,

I thought. Perhaps they have escaped. But how?

There was a commotion at the end of the plateau where a raised structure, a small, flat pyramid, stood. It must have been their temple. My heart sank.

"Sir, we've found them!" the captain cried as he approached us.

"Good." Adrian was brusque. He seemed uneasy. "Go back to camp and wait for me there," he snapped at me over his shoulder. My horse began to move at his command. A shiver went up my spine. He urged his horse forward before I could reply. I pulled hard on my reins and willed my mount to stop. Something was happening here, something unusual. There was a pressure on my head and chest, and I realized it had nothing to do with the altitude. It was energy that I was feeling, just as I had sensed it at the great temple in the desert. Yes, there was a frequency here, pressing in on my body, raising its vibration without my willing it to do so!

I turned my horse around and dug my heels in hard. Racing through the empty corridors that were the village streets, I headed for the temple, and then urged my horse up the small slope to its steps. But he would not go; he reared and turned and started back down the hill.

"No!" I cried, willing him around, but he only circled and reared again, so that I lost my grip and fell to the ground. I rolled away unhurt as he sped back through the streets toward camp. I leapt to my feet, calling forth a force field of protection and invisibility, and then made my way to the top of the steps.

Reaching the summit, I came upon the most startling scene: hundreds of people, their deep-brown skin wrapped in beautifully colored robes, standing hand in hand at the edge of the cliff. It must have been the entire tribe, mothers holding babies, fathers, daughters, grandparents. Our conquistadors stood in their immaculate rows, spears at the ready, swords drawn. Yet, they did not move. They seemed suspended in time. And there was Adrian, his stallion pacing back and forth as he cried out to them in an ancient tongue. We waited, but no one moved. Then, in Spanish, he cried out again.

163

"Come away from the cliff! Come peacefully and your lives will be spared!" The soldiers were uneasy. I could feel their fear clinging to them. This was not what had been expected. This tribe was different somehow, and the men could feel it.

There was movement amongst the people, and the group began to part. An old man stepped out from among them. His hair was long and white, as were his robes, and he was powerfully built. A wave of warmth passed through me as he moved forward. I heard Adrian gasp.

"Adriano!" the man cried out to Adrian, smiling broadly. And then in Latin, a tongue impossible for him to know, he continued, "My son. So we meet again at last!"

Adrian had gone white. He stared at the old man who held out his hand to him.

"Adriano," in Greek this time, "you know these people cannot turn themselves over to these men. You know they cannot become slaves and whores to the Spanish. These people have too much dignity for that. Surely, you have felt their vibrations . . . " Adrian's horse began to move, unbidden, toward the man, who continued, now in Spanish, "These people are holy and will not submit to fear of death or give their lives to serve evil men." He laughed then, a thunderous sound that made Adrian's stallion give out a high-pitched shriek as it reared. Then he was back at the edge of the cliff, though I did not see him move!

The old man turned to Adrian and held out his hand again.

"Come with me this time," he said, then turned to the cliff and took hold of the child at his side. The tribe lifted their hands in a long, fluid motion, and all together, young and old, they stepped off the edge.

Four

IT TOOK HOURS TO REGAIN ORDER OVER THE MEN. The village was empty, and a cold, eerie silence hung over the dwellings. The men were afraid to take anything, afraid even to be in the village. I watched from the shadows, cloaked in invisibility, as Adrian ordered them back to camp and then rode, with the scouts, to search for bodies. It was dusk when he returned, and I heard the rumor before he reached our tent—no bodies had been found!

I had a candle lit and food laid out when Adrian pushed back the flap of the tent. Usually, he would have been accompanied by his captains, but tonight he entered alone. I helped him pull off his breastplate and uniform. Then, in silence, I washed him with warm water I had infused with a sweet perfume. He closed his eyes and let me bathe him. I tried to wash away the dull, quiet pain that clung to him.

When I was done and began to dry his skin, he opened his eyes suddenly and pulled me to him roughly, frantically, kissing me hard. Then, he was pulling loose my boyish costume, and pulled me down to the soft bedding we shared on the ground. He did not speak, only pressed himself onto me in a fever, burying his head in my neck and breasts. I could hear a thousand tears screaming in his heart, and I struggled against my need to ease them.

"Wait," I said, taking his head in my hands. "No, Adrian, wait..." I hushed him gently as he began to protest. "No, my love, you can't use me this way. You can't bury your pain in me." I spoke the words without thinking, and we were both shocked by them. Yet, I knew they were true. I stroked his head, "Please don't be angry, don't pull away from me." I could sense a cold, aloof air coming over him. "Don't do that, love, not now, not when I'm here for you and I know that you're hurting."

"What do you know?" His voice was aged and broken. "What could you possibly know of my pain?" Abruptly, he sat up, putting his head in his hands. I lay still, my heart breaking. I did not know how to reach him. It had to be his choice to open up to me.

We were quiet for a long time. The sound of fires being lighted and frightened men singing Spanish songs for comfort floated through the canvas walls. Adrian turned back to me.

"I'm sorry," he whispered.

I burst into tears — I was so in love with him!

He pulled a blanket up around us and took me in his arms.

"I have to tell you something, Justine," he began, cradling me. "I want to tell you who I am and how I got here. I want you to know — I think this is why you are here with me." He waited until my tears calmed. "I can feel that I'm awakening in the presence of your love. Some long-dead part of me is resurrected! I struggle to turn away from it, to put the voice of my conscience to rest once again. But I cannot!" I laid my head on his chest and listened to his immortal heart. I felt frightened. I knew that this was why I was here, too. This was somehow my destiny, and now that I faced it I was afraid, for I knew that I would be changed by it. Yet, I felt it pulling me forward.

"Tell me, my love," I murmured. He shifted to look at me, the light of the candle on his face.

"I was young when it happened. Only thirty-five, but already I was a colonel in the Atlantean military."

"Atlantean?" I interrupted. A slow smile drew across his face.

"Yes," he answered, "I come from the ancient legends of a great civilization. You've read about it, no doubt, in Plato's *Timeas*. The tales of a continent that existed in the Atlantic, and a people so advanced in the sciences of the mind that they had accomplished remarkable feats in the metaphysical arts. Then came the deluge, the horrific cataclysms that took their land and its people beneath the sea." He paused, staring into the candle flame. Silence. Images began to stir before my eyes. A great city at the foot of a mountain, high walls of green stone built along the sea, towering columns of iridescent pink holding marble archways, a great temple high on a hill .... And then there were shadows, dark, horrible things. I shuddered and my vision cleared. Adrian stared at the candle like a priest making his confession, as if in the flame he were calculating his sins.

"Adrian!" I whispered.

He took a breath and woke from the dream. His face warmed, and he looked at me affectionately.

"I'm here. It's all right," he said, taking my hand reassuringly in his. Turning it over, he opened it and traced my palm with his finger. "You have the same hands..." he murmured absently, and a chill ran through me. He looked up into my eyes. "There's much to tell you, Justine, before this night is over. Now I'm sure that I must tell you the whole tale.

"As I said, I am from Atlantis. I was born into a military family, and the direction of my life was decided for me long before I was born. I was very good at what I did, for I was clever, and driven by an overwhelming desire to please my father. I was a natural leader. Men trusted me. I had a keen sensitivity to know what people were feeling, which most military leaders lacked. Sometimes, I could even feel inside of them, as if I were the blood in their veins. I rarely spoke of this, for it displeased my father greatly, but it was a talent that helped me understand the men I led. They sensed this somehow, and performed feats for me that far exceeded my expectations. It was their devotion that moved me through the ranks, establishing a brilliant military career.

"Now, this talent was not so mysterious or magical a phenomenon in my time as it is now. In Atlantis, there were temples and schools devoted to such things. We all understood that what you now call God was not a figure or a personal being like a man or woman; rather, God was seen as energy. We referred to this energy as the Mighty Presence, which animated all matter. Thus, the Mighty Presence had created the

167

cosmos, the Earth, and all living things. To us, *everything* was alive. A talent such as mine meant only that I had an affinity for merging with the energy that lived in all things.

"In Atlantis, we had specialists in the intuitive arts, those who could heal or find water, or sense the weather. Those who could see the Earth's energy waves would direct us in our architectural design and guide us in the placement of our homes and temples. The principles of geomancy governed the placement of our cities and holy shrines, which were absolutely spectacular. Never before has such architectural beauty been produced. Even the great cathedrals of this time could not compare with the splendor of our temples. The finest artisans, guided by the creative force, the Mighty Presence, built them all over the countryside. Some were small alcoves built as part of the landscape, others, in the cities, were enormous, gathering places for our schools and courts.

"I loved the temples. I was drawn to them even as a child. Built of marble and precious metals, and inlaid with stones and gems that served to magnify the waves of Earth energy, which they attended. Always they smelled of the holy oils, frankincense, myrrh, sandalwood, and rose. Reverence, that is what they were made for. Not a place to bow down beneath a God that judges, never that. They were shrines to the Great Presence that inspired and animated all life. Places to uplift us, reminding us that we, too, were the creative force through which the creator worked. Ah, here I go, speaking as a priest, something I did when I was young, but that my father never tolerated. It was not seemly for a boy of my lineage and position and obvious military future to espouse the esoteric understandings of my time. No, my father, who saw this predisposition toward the metaphysical world, removed me from its influence at a young age.

"I became a warrior like my father. I took life after life until I was numbed. As I rose through the ranks I ordered others to take lives, and distanced myself from the killing. But I was a killer, nevertheless. This went on for years, and I became a cold and hardened man. I had few friends, and my intuitive skills began to leave me, as if, the more

I killed, the farther I went from some central part of myself. I think now that I was afraid, for had I acknowledged my choice of allegiance to my father and my family name over allegiance to myself, the weight of it would have defeated me.

"So, I carried a sense of dread that something in me was dying, something irretrievable that I could not live without. I struggled against myself and buried my fear.

"This was the state of my life when the events that led me to the prince and to immortality began. I was in my late thirties, very young for that time, and, as I said, already in a position of command.

We had planted two Atlantean communities in the Pyrenees, as it was clear then that our Atlantis of the sea was in danger of the ever-rising waters of the Atlantic. Our need to settle these lands and relocate our people was pressing on me and had served to justify my war on the native tribes of this place. The new city leaders had chosen an excellent site for its construction: the junction of two rivers, which had served as a ceremonial meeting place for the surrounding tribes. I had agreed on the site, as it assured us a great supply of water and perfect military defense, and only a mile or so beyond that point lay a valley that would serve as a reservoir.

"So, I sent my legions to prepare the site. We removed the people who would not leave, and desecrated their ceremonial lands. I ordered this without feeling; it was after all, the obvious and necessary thing to do. The tribes were stubborn and would not leave the place, so my troops slaughtered them. On this bloody consecration we laid our city's foundations. For more than a year, thousands labored on the temples and homes and defensive walls, even through the bitterly cold winter months. In the summer we set to work on a magnificent dam a mile below the city gates. All that remained was to remove the small tribe that lived in the valley below.

"Now, at this time I had been having a love affair with a beautiful young recruit named Japheth. Having a male lover was not unusual in Atlantis, for we did not live with the judgments and beliefs of your time. Only men were warriors in the Atlantean army, and we were often separated from women for long periods of time, so it was only natural to take a man as a lover. It was the same for women: during periods of war, there were fewer men than women, so the women would partner and raise their children together. It was not uncommon in that time to find three people, or five, making families, sharing the responsibilities of life as a community. So, for me, a decorated colonel, always in the field, it was expected that I would have a man as a companion. In fact, I had taken many, always new recruits, and always under my command.

"But Japheth was different. He had only just enlisted in the spring and had spent more time building than defending. He was against the building of the great dam, concerned for the welfare of the valley dwellers. He would often suggest alternatives, silly propositions, really, that we could never have employed. I would listen, enamored with his eyes and the deep, rich red of his lips as he presented plan after plan. I did not encourage him, of course, but took my father's military explanations and laid them like a cloak upon his shoulders. But the remarkable Japheth shrugged them off. Perhaps it was this innocent persistence and his refusal to yield to my ideals that made me love him. Whatever it was, I let myself soften to his naiveté, and was gentle when I should have been harsh.

"So it was on the day that the dam was completed. I sent interpreters to sit in council with the tribe, making one last attempt, for Japheth's sake, to get them to move. It seemed ridiculous to me that they could not comprehend their eventual annihilation if they remained where they were, but they were quietly insistent: we would have to kill them to have their land. What a position they had put me in, I thought. I blamed them, called them stupid and barbaric. I demeaned them in my mind, thinking of them as no more than ants in the ground, to be washed away by the rain. That is how I was able to set the date for the opening of the dam. We announced it to the new inhabitants of our growing city, explaining that the valley tribe had been given plenty of time to relocate. The choice was theirs. Those were the words that laid our hearts to rest that night, knowing that at dawn, the tribe would die in the crushing waters we would release. Japheth, dejected, came to me that night. I was quartered in a fine house by the eastern wall next to the river, dinner laid out on a table beside a warm fire. I was at the table, ready to eat, when I felt him, standing alone in the door. He was in shadow still, so I beckoned him in.

"'This is their home,' he said from the dark, not moving. 'I told you they wouldn't move, any more than we would move from our temples and our towns. That land is their sacred place, the canyon walls are filled with their dead. They can't leave, Adrian.' I put down my knife.

"'Enough!' I demanded, getting to my feet. 'Enough of this, Japheth, there is nothing I can do about it. They have had plenty of time to relocate themselves. I have offered them assistance and even opened the city gates to them if they would join us! What more can I do?' I was agitated with his childish response to life. He did not move.

"'You're wrong, Adrian, we are all wrong. It is their land, Adrian, the Great Presence comes to them here.'

"'Don't talk to me about the Presence! The Presence is making the waves rise in the sea, driving us here, too!' I scowled and moved toward him. 'You are young, Japheth; you think we have choices where we do not!'

"'No,' he said it firmly so that I stopped halfway to the door. I could see him now, the firelight casting a haze of gold about his face. There was something there that I did not recognize; something was different. 'You are wrong again,' he continued, 'we always have a choice, Adrian.'

"'Japheth,' I began more gently, reaching out my hand, but he still did not move.

"'No,' he said again, 'You have lost faith in human kindness, and use the words of a priest to justify this evil action.' His voice was filled with despair. 'You are like a dead man walking about with power and knowledge that could unite and inspire, but instead you destroy and degrade. I want no part in it, Adrian.'

"He lifted his hands and threw something at my feet. I bent and picked up his legionary badge. 'I am not in the right profession,' he said. 'The council has accepted my resignation. I'll be leaving tonight to join a group that is observing the tribes just south of here. I've only come to say goodbye.'

"I was stunned. Leave? I hesitated, gripping his badge, then slowly got to my feet.

"'Goodbye, then,' I said it coldly, turning my back to him, returning to my table. I was a commander and he was dismissed. When I looked up, the doorway was empty.

"At dawn the next morning I gave the signal to open the dam. Water poured out in torrents, down the steep embankments, rushing into the valley, and swept away the proud people of the Pyrenees. There were no survivors.

"IT WAS A YEAR BEFORE I HEARD OF JAPHETH AGAIN. The city was weathering its second winter and our people were being imported from the lands by the sea. It was late at night when I received word that a group of our people had been left at the great gates. The tribesmen from the south had carried them there and laid them on the ground before the gate. Moving without orders, my men had brought them inside the city, rushing them to the hospital. 'Fools!' I thought as I hurried to the hospital, 'What if they are diseased? What if they are contagious?' I was fuming by the time I crossed the threshold of the healer's temple and into the hospital door. In my time, we had two kinds of doctors: the healers, who used only their hands, and the surgeons who addressed the physical body with instruments and medicine. The healers were sent for first, as they were by far more effective in most cases, simply laying their hands on the body and sensing what was wrong. Rarely were surgeons necessary.

"This night the hospital corridors were so full that even I had to push my way through to see the mage, the leader of our healers. She was a small woman with deep-set eyes and a calm, professional manner that put one at ease — but not that night. When I saw her in discussion with a group from the city council she was tense, a deep furrow between her brows told me that things did not go well. She nodded when she saw me.

"'What is it?' I demanded.

"'It is not good, Colonel. Come.' And she led me from the group into a smaller room, which looked through a small pane of glass into the healer's den. Everyone who entered this room would be quarantined. This was not a good sign. I turned to the old woman.

"'What do they have?'

"'We don't know. Her voice was low. 'We've never encountered anything like it. None of us can break through. It is viral and contagious. My finest healers can see it being transmitted through the air.' She put her hand up to the glass that separated us from the large room filled with beds and robed physicians at their sides. 'They all have it now.' Her voice grew quieter. 'I did not realize how deadly it was; even the healers are being attacked through their psychic fields of protection.'

"I was stunned.

"'Are you saying that not even the healers are safe from this virus?' She nodded her head.

"'And how many of them are in there?' I demanded, my fear and frustration growing.

"'All of them,' she replied. 'It never occurred to me that they would be susceptible. It has not happened in hundreds of years.'

"This took a moment for me to digest. It was well known that the healers and surgeons of my time could face the deadliest diseases and remain immune due to their strong will and honed intuitive abilities. I had never thought of a disease as 'attacking' someone or the role of a healer being that of a 'defender,' yet the words were easy for me to understand now. Looking at the woman beside me, I suddenly sensed her grief and confusion. I bit back words of accusation. She should have known, she should have thought … but this did not matter now. I was faced with the grim reality that my men, and who knew how many others, had been exposed, and that some thirty of the city's finest healers were going to be lost. My mind worked in numbers then, not in terms of the human heart.

'"Why are you not affected?' I asked the mage. She shook her head.

'"I am the only one who has yet to be exposed directly,' she said. 'They did not send for me until it was too late, and now they will surely die in there if they cannot find an energetic cure. They need a pathway to the virus, they need a way to get in, to see it and name it, exposing it to the light.'

I was trying to think, to take command of the situation, but found myself staring through the window at a form that lay just opposite me on a makeshift cot. I did not recognize his body, so thin and frail that his ribs shown through his skin. But his gaunt, fevered gaze held me as I looked into those familiar eyes.

'"Japheth.' his name pressed against my lips so that he half-smiled, then winced in pain. My body seized suddenly as he tensed. What was this? My hand was at my side, my stomach burning. The mage reached out and touched me, then drew back.

'"Colonel!' I heard her voice, but suddenly was doubled over in pain. I struggled to regain my composure, but only staggered, falling heavily against the glass. I saw him again then, brutal suffering etched on his face. His lips moved and I could hear his barely audible voice, 'Help me.' And then the pain was gone.

'"Colonel!" the mage said again, 'I feel it in you? How?' But I did not answer, only pushed her away and moved toward the door to the den. 'No!' I heard her cry, but then I was through it and standing at his bed, my hands outstretched. I took him in my arms. Something moved inside me, some heat long submerged that longed to be let loose. It was a fire that knew its way around the closed places in my heart.

'"Colonel, what are you doing in here?' Someone's voice, hands on my shoulders, and then they pulled back. I could feel their eyes on me, in the room and through the glass, but I did not move or open my eyes. And from my hands a force moved violently, plunging inside Japheth, until I breathed his breath. Searing pain shot through me; blinding waves of red assaulted my vision, so I could not see. I reached for my sword, but of course it was not there. I was disoriented. Then I heard a voice, like a whisper in my ear.

"'No,' it said, and I felt a presence that was not my own or Japheth's. I was not alone.

"'You will not heal him with a sword, Adrian.' The words were warm and strong, a man's voice, quivering somehow in my hands. 'Feel,' he directed. 'Trust yourself, this is your true gift.' I relaxed at the sound of his voice, familiar and calm. I would follow his directions, I would do as he said … but how? His voice came in answer.

"'Adrian, just turn back to your heart. Turn back to the feeling that led you to lay your hands upon him. *Love him, Adrian.*' An image of Japheth, his kind eyes laughing at me, his hands stroking my hair.

"I do love you, I thought, and a pain ripped through my chest, a terrible horror loosened in my heart, and I felt as if I would break open. Suffering. Dread of every tomorrow hollow and alone. There were the deaths I had caused, thousands of them, falling away like pieces of stone.

"Then I saw Japheth's face, smiling again.

"'Forgive yourself,' he was saying, but I turned away, the pain in my chest breaking me.

"'Yes,' he said. 'I forgive you.'

"'I think I was crying then, for somehow I sensed myself still in that dimly lit room, and a circle of healers were now set around me. Tears were warm on my cheeks.

"'But I am a commander, a great leader!' I tried to cry, *'I cannot feel!'* But it was too late. Something had loosened in my heart, and the tears were washing it away. I cried. Even as I held him, my officers looking on, I did not care. I rocked him and wept for everything I had not given him, every drop of love that I had withheld. And I softened as I

175

wept, pain falling like rusted armor at my feet. When I was quieted, I heard the voice again.

"'Good,' it said, 'Now you must find the virus, Adrian, and love that, too.'

"I did not fight it. I only did as he said. It was spontaneous and easy: I opened my heart and the Great Presence rushed through it, a mighty river that flowed from my hands. I was back inside of him, glowing gold against the red. Brighter and brighter I became, until the red softened into tones of pink and faded into the gold itself.

"Hours must have passed when finally I opened my eyes. My body was hot and soft. The healers had, indeed, surrounded me; they were chanting quietly, rhythmically, and the man in my arms lay staring up at me, smiling."

Five

"Japheth lived and so did the others. That night and all the next day, I went from person to person, and I loved them, one as much as the next. The healers came with me, forming a circle around us, intoning the words of power and protection. I did not tire until it was all done, and then I lay down and slept long and deep.

"When I awoke, I was not alone. A tall man sat next to my bed, white hair falling to his shoulders. He wore a violet sash across his white linen robe, the sign of the healer. On his wrists I saw the violet tattoo of the dragons, symbol of a high priest. He smiled down at me.

"'I am Thoth.' He sent the words telepathically. 'I am master of the Temple of the Seventh Ray, home to the healers of Atlantis.'

"I recognized his voice at once. It was the voice that had been guiding me through the night of healing. What a marvel to be touched by the master, this legend of a healer. He bathed me himself, then clothed me with a white robe similar to his own.

"'Your destiny is with me now, Adrian,' he said. My heart leapt. I felt my desire to leave this place, and my command beating on my breast. I was done here at last. I looked to Thoth and knew that I would go with him. It would be a simple matter; he would make it so. There was no resistance within me. Nothing could have torn me away from the master's radiant look and gentle hand. His was the voice that had guided me in the healers' den, but mine, he assured me, were the hands that had done the healing. This was what I had been waiting for, longing for, all of my life. I no longer cared what others might think of what I did. I knew that I was, for the first time, truly free.

177

"So, I left my command, and dear Japheth, and went with Thoth to the great city of Caledocea, to the temple of the healers. There I devoted myself to learning the art, and did not miss my old life. I excelled as a healer, moving quickly through the priestly ranks. It was a sweet and beautiful time, the best I had ever had. Thoth loved me and I him. He had my loyalty. For many years I was happy serving Thoth and happy with my life at the temple. It was the most peaceful time of my life.

"Then one day, walking through the great courtyard that led to the temple gardens, I came across a young woman arguing with a belligerent soldier standing guard at the gate. I had come around the corner of the wall, so neither saw me. A chill ran over me as I rounded the corner and first caught sight of her. I will never forget that moment. I was stunned by her presence, captivated by her beauty. She was dark skinned with thick black hair pleated down her back. She wore a simple toga, short at the thigh, and the band on her arm was of Mithras, the white bull. Ah, she was an athlete, a bull rider, yet I could see that she had the deep-set eyes and high cheekbones of the old Lemurian families. Usually, the Lemurian women were priestesses, trained in social graces. I realized immediately this was not the case here.

"The young woman was roaring at the guard, 'Let me pass, you idiot! I tell you, I have an invitation! I simply can't find it! Now hurry up, I'll be late!'

"The guard only laughed. 'Sure, you have an invitation, doesn't everyone? Now look, if you don't have it in your hand, you don't get through this gate! Move on!'

"He pressed the end of his spear to her breast. It was an outrageous thing to do, the sort of thing we had worked to train out of our ranks in the army. He leaned in closer, following the point of his spear, and in a lowered voice he made a remark that brought the girl's hand hard across his face. He backed up, stunned, then lifted his hand as if to strike her.

"I was at her side immediately. 'What's going on here, soldier?' I snapped, as both he and the young woman turned to me. I noted her look of relief.

"'This girl,'" he stammered, 'she's out of her mind! I think she's—'

"'I don't care what you think, soldier, stand down!' The man hesitated, unsure.

"'That's an order, soldier.' My voice was full of its old command.

The man lowered his spear, and I took hold of the girl's arm, pulling her through the gate. She moved easily beside me. When we came to the garden, out of the guard's sight, I stopped and turned to her.

"'Are you all right?' I asked.

"'Yes, thank you,' she said. 'He was brainless and dull!' she continued, rolling her eyes. 'I thought I would have to run for it!'

"'Well, I will see to it this never happens again. Our soldier friend will soon find himself digging holes in the snow in the Pyrenees!' I laughed. She began to tell me where she was going, some meeting by the lake, but as I tried to listen, I found myself tracing her sunburned face and losing myself in her eyes. They had an unusual amber hue.

"'You're a healer,' she said, nodding at my white robes and brazenly pulling at the violet badge.

"'I am.'

"'Then you are called a priest in that order?'

"'Yes,' I answered.

"'Sworn as a celibate?' Heat stung my cheeks.

"'No!' I said too strongly. She only smiled.

"'I'm Jael,' reaching out her hand. 'Thank you for your help.'

"'My pleasure.' Such a sweet sensation as her hand touched mine. 'I'm Adrian. I serve under Master Thoth.'

"'I'll remember that, Adrian.' She moved as if to go, then hesitated. Turning back to me, she continued, 'I am one of the finest bull riders in Caledocea.' She said it plainly, as if it were matter-of-fact. 'At the next full moon I will be riding the white bull. Perhaps you will come to watch?'

"'Perhaps.'

"'I think it would do you good, Adrian the priest.'

"This startled me. "Why do you say that?'

"She stepped very close to me so that I could smell the sweet scent of jasmine in her hair. 'It's something about your look. You seem so ... serious.'

"I smiled. 'And that bothers you?'

"She smiled back. 'Yes, I suppose it does. I'm not sure why, either.'

"She seemed annoyed at this, yet, as a priest of a metaphysical order, I understood why she had said it. I felt it in the aura around her, a familiarity that went back before this life. I could sense it pressing into her consciousness, but she seemed to shrug it off.

"'Anyway, it doesn't matter,' she said. 'If you come I promise you an adventure! Maybe I'll even see you there.' With that, she turned and moved toward the garden.

"My heart beat hard as I watched her go. I felt a longing stir in my body, a desire to reach out and stop her. I wanted to touch her skin, to kiss her ... but this was madness! I had only just met the girl, and no bond could be that strong, especially for me, a trained soldier and priest! I was master of my mind, was I not? Chiding myself, I turned back toward the temple, but as I did, a pain ripped through my chest, so strong that I stumbled and fell. Struggling to breathe, I covered my heart with my hand and focused on my inner sight. I could see there was nothing physically wrong; it was an emotion that had taken hold of me. I looked deeper. The image of Jael flashed before me, reaching out her hand. And then, a deep aching and a wretched craving to be in her presence again.

"I opened my eyes and stumbled to my feet. Turning to the path she had taken into the gardens, I began to follow, using my intuitive skills to find my way. I had to see her, to try to control what was happening to me. As I neared the lake, the pain in my chest began to ease. My breath calmed, and I began to reason with myself.

"It's simple,' I told myself. 'You've known her in some other life, and your soul recognizes her. There is nothing more to it than that!'

In Atlantis we believed that the soul was immortal and that it was born again and again upon the Earth until it was enlightened, so it was assumed that a conscious person should recognize the souls he had known before. But even as I reasoned, I knew there was much more to it than that. My life had changed from this meeting. This feeling was not simply recognition of her soul, but rather, recognition of my destiny.

"When I reached the lake, I stopped short. There she was, a rose in her hand, stunning in the sun, and at her side, his hand laid intimately upon her waist, stood the high priest of the great Melchizedek order. I recognized him immediately, his deep-set features and long black hair accentuated by the rich blue robes of his rank. He was the Lucifer, leader of the brotherhood of light. I had seen him from afar at the great councils in which he debated heatedly with my own master, Thoth. The Melchizedek had a plan to save the wise ones of Atlantis from the disaster by administering a metaphysical elixir that would cause their flesh to become immortal. He wanted the masters to live on, to serve those who remained on the Earth in regaining the great wisdom and truth of their divinity. But Thoth disagreed with any kind of metaphysical intervention. He argued that death of the body was necessary, and that it did not matter how that death came about. It was what we did in the moment of our death, the consciousness we would maintain, that mattered.

"And here he was at the lakeside, just a man, with his arm around his woman. Suddenly, he looked up and caught my eye. It was as if he sensed my longing and confusion. Embarrassed, I began to look away, hoping he would forgive my intrusion, but something stopped me. I felt a warmth move from him to me, and then I saw him smile kindly, nod his head, and look away. There was no venom or malice in his look, only an understanding that was kind.

"I went back to the temple, spending the next few days absorbed in my prayers and meditations, studies and incantations. I had to prepare for my initiation with Thoth. There were long hours at the clinic, laying my hands on the sick, and more hours with the master, honing my psychic vision. Through it all I was aware of a nagging desire to see this girl again.

"I watched her ride the white bull at the full moon. The arena, much like Rome's great coliseum, seated thousands, and was filled. As the dangers that threatened Atlantis mounted, our people turned to what was familiar for comfort, and nothing excited us more than the courageous acrobatics of the bull riders. Dozens of them took turns with different animals, somersaulting from the back of one beast onto the shoulders of another. The crowd would shout its approval as with each hour the tricks and the animals became increasingly more dangerous. Finally, at the climax of the evening, when the moon had taken her place above our heads, the champions rode bareback into the ring, leaping from one steed to another in a show that sent the audience cheering wildly. Then came the drums and trumpets, and a chorus singing a melody that filled the stadium and silenced the crowd. It was a magical moment; the ground in the middle of the field seemed to open, and out from a cavern beneath us the white bull charged. On his back stood Jael, her arms outstretched as if she were flying. Her body was taut, painted half in black and half in white; she was meant to represent the moon. Around the arena she rode, rolling deftly on her heels, doing backflips while the enormous beast charged red-clad runners. She leapt to his shoulders, taking hold of his powerful horns, pulling herself into a handstand. The crowd went wild, and still the bull charged on. She was fearless, this goddess of the night, with a strength of will and feminine grace that I could not turn myself away from. She was indeed the greatest bull rider I had ever seen, and the crowd made her their heroine; their applause thundered at the end as she rode the beast back into the center of the Earth.

"I was changed after that night. I could not concentrate on my sacred practice or the rituals that would prepare me for my initiation. There was no peace; even in my dreams, her stone-white body and the palpable force of the crowd cheering her on haunted me. For weeks I struggled to focus my mind on my practice, but inevitably found myself daydreaming about that night—her face, her eyes, the sound of her voice. I suddenly longed for something that I had forgotten in the years of priestly training: it was a sense of the world, of power and presence. I had felt it many times as a soldier, facing death. This longing drove me to a great distraction, so that I began to fail in my studies and my metaphysical progress.

"Then, one day, as I struggled in my meditations in the temple, Master Thoth came to me. He sat cross-legged on the floor beside me, an intimate gesture for it intimated that we were equals. He was a unique teacher in this way, as most of the masters maintained a rigorous discipline and hierarchical nature in their orders.

"'Adrian,' he began softly, 'my son, we must speak.' He passed his hand before the incense bowl and a strong scent of frankincense filled the air. 'You are troubled in your heart.'

"'Yes, master.'

"'You are falling behind in your preparation.'

"'Yes, master.' I took a deep breath and lowered my head. Having always excelled, I was ashamed to admit this.

"'Though I have not spoken of this in a long while, I sense the hour is drawing close when Atlantis will meet its destruction.' I looked up at him. 'You know this?' I nodded. 'And still you are not able to concentrate on your practice? If you do not go through your initiation, you will not be ready to stand in the ascension with me and with the Lemurian priestesses when the time comes.'

"He waited for my response but I was silent. I had known for years that he had aligned himself and the healers' temple with the Lemurian priestesses, who, through rigorous practice, would go to their deaths in consciousness. This was called the ascension. For a very few, like Thoth, it would be through the physical transformation of the body; he would quite literally transform his body into the vibration of light and maintain a conscious sense of self. He would then be a part of all realms, the visible and the invisible. Through the ascension, Thoth would truly be immortal. But this could be done only by those who could already move between the inner and outer worlds, those who had taken such control of their minds that they could surrender their personal will to the will of the Great Presence, or as you would say in this time, to God.

"But as I said, only a few would go to their ascension this way. For most, the ascension would be a physical death of the body, yet a conscious rebirth of the soul.

"Either way, to stand with Thoth at the ascension meant I must have complete control of my mind, so that when I gave the command to transform, I could see it and feel it and believe that it was so. And to do this I must be initiated, and in this I was failing.

"'It is the woman that occupies your mind,' Thoth said impassively.

"'Yes,' my voice was filled with grief. 'I am working at putting my focus back here on the temple and my preparations. I've worked dutifully at it, Master, truly...' I could hear the emotion breaking inside me. Thoth put his hand on my shoulder.

"'Adrian, perhaps you are working too hard at it. Perhaps another destiny is calling you, a life you have yet to live? The ascension is not to be struggled toward, it is to be surrendered to. Do you understand?'

"'Yes.'

"'Then perhaps you should stop struggling and turn instead to *her*.'

"My head snapped up and I exclaimed, 'But I can't! She belongs to another!' I was shocked by these words, suddenly realizing that I had already thought of this. I knew in that moment that if the way were made clear I would have left everything to be with her.

"Thoth began to laugh. 'No one *belongs* to another, Adrian. Surely you have learned that from me by now! She has only *chosen* another, my son. And that should not matter, for who knows how your destiny with each other will unfold? What if you are simply not meant to be beloved of one another in this incarnation? What if there is another path, and yet another, that she is leading you to? *Don't ask why you are led, ask only where.*

184

"'Now, there is something I have decided, and it will be hard for you to hear, but it is the right thing.' I grew cold, afraid of what he would say.

"'I see you are not being led to your ascension with me.'

"I began to protest, but he held up his hand, 'No, wait, let me finish. This may be difficult for you to face, Adrian, but now is not your time. I sense another destiny before you, and I have been told to let you go.'

"I stared in disbelief.

"'But I'm one of your top students! I've come so far in such a short time, Master, how can you ...' but he only held up his hand again and shook his head.

"'There is nothing to discuss, Adrian. The Great Presence has spoken to me, and I am responding. It must be enough for you to trust that. This has nothing to do with love, Adrian, for truly I love you as my son. But your time with me has come to an end. I am sending you to another temple, where you will be of great service to those who will be relocating.'

"I didn't know what to say. I was furious, and yet I believed what the master said. For years I had trusted his wisdom. I could not stop now.

"'Where?' I asked. 'Where are you sending me?'

"'I have been told to send you to the temple of light. You will serve under the Master Lucifer.'

"'What! But, Master, he is the one,' I broke off suddenly as Thoth slapped me hard on the back. A blaze of white heat rushed through me and I heard a voice, my voice, say, *this is right*.

"'Don't question your soul, my son.' Thoth's voice was gentle, 'It will lead you always toward your enlightenment. If you resist it, you will only prolong the journey. Now go. Lucifer is expecting you. Your destiny awaits.'

Six

ADRIAN STOPPED TELLING HIS STORY at that point and looked at me. The candlelight was growing dim, and his face had fallen into shadow. There was more, I could see, something he was close to telling me, something important.

"You went to Lucifer?" I pressed him on softly.

"I did."

"And were you ever with Jael?" My heart was beating hard. I had to know the end. Familiar images unfolded before my eyes as he spoke.

"No," he answered sadly, shaking his head. "Over the year that followed, I worked closely with Master Lucifer and came to be trusted by him. He raised me through the ranks of his order, so that I spent much of my time as part of his inner circle. It was, from the very beginning, a familiar relationship, as if I had always served at his side. We were easy with each other. He spoke to me as an intimate, giving me such power and privilege as I had once enjoyed in the army. But instead of killing, I was now intent on saving lives. I suppose I liked being a part of something again, something outside myself and my metaphysical pursuits. I found a great pleasure in being with *him*: his brash and charismatic personality drew me in, so that I felt important in his presence. He was as kind as he was brutal, a self-assured politician one moment, and a poet the next. He was a radiant man, and people vied for his attention and his favor. Whatever the reasons, I had both.

"I grew loyal to Master Lucifer and to my position at his side, aware that I was on purpose in this work. Master Thoth had been right in sending me here, for I knew instinctively that this was my proper place

186

and that in this work I could thrive and make a difference.

"And yet I suffered.

"In the face of *Jael,* passionate and inspiring, I was shaken. No matter how much time I spent in her presence, my feelings for her did not change or quiet in my heart. Watching the prince with her was my only consolation, for it was clear to me that he loved her. I could see it in the tender and adoring way he looked at her. He seemed to drink her in, sated by her beauty. She would speak to him in the most frank and impertinent ways, but he would only laugh. There was a palpable intimacy between them, something fertile and warm that I could feel in their company. Jael was his Lady, and I had no hope of that changing, yet I felt a pull toward her, a soft, warm glow in my body when she would enter the room.

"So, I persevered in my work, trying to keep my time with Jael as formal and polite as I could. This proved difficult, as she was not the courteous sort. She seemed not at all affected by me, reaching out her hand at every opportunity to touch me affectionately, or to tease me about my humorless demeanor and sense of decorum. She seemed to think me dull and passionless, so that I came to wonder why she bothered with me at all! At the time, I assumed it was because of him, Master Lucifer, for he did value me and my skills. Whatever the reason, I resolved myself to stay loyal to my work and to my master, living with my desire for Jael as best I could.

"The prince ran the affairs of the Temple of Light largely from his own chambers, which I visited daily. I would carefully avoid the early morning hours when Jael might still be about, dreading the tenderness I would feel in her presence. Late one morning, long after she should have been gone, I stepped into the courtyard that led to his rooms, closing the door behind me. As I was about to pass through the curtains that separated it from the main room, they began to move faintly in the breeze, and as they stirred, I saw Jael inside.

"I was captivated, watching as she crossed the room. A thin, pastel robe tied loosely about her waist fell gently from one shoulder. Her skin was bronzed from the summer heat, and her hair fell, disheveled, down her back.

"I should have announced my presence immediately, but I did not, shamefully lulled by the scene. Then, I realized it was too late. From the room behind her, the prince's voice boomed, 'Jael!'

"I hesitated then, stepping back into shadow. I could not open the door behind me unnoticed, and if I made myself known she would be aware that I had been watching her. I stood, stiff and silent, trying to cloak my presence.

"The curtains stirred from side to side so that I caught glimpses of her pacing, back and forth. Her voice was strained,

"'I tell you I can't do it!' she was almost shouting. 'You are the Lucifer, one of the most powerful men in the dynasty! If she will listen to anyone, it's you!' The prince was in the room now, taking hold of her arm, pulling her to him.

"'Ah, but she won't. Your mother is stubborn and set in her ways. She will protect the Lemurian secrets, even if it means they are lost forever in the catastrophe that is to come. Our last meeting did not go well. She is not going to give me access to the oil, Jael. I *must* have your help.'

"'But, Mal'ak!' she sounded exhausted. 'You can't possibly expect my mother to give *me* the oil. I'm a great disappointment to her, and have no interest in the traditions and training it would require to even be allowed into the Emerald Temple. Even if she does agree to initiate me, which she won't, I can't possibly go against hundreds of years of tradition. The women of my family have always been priestesses of the Emerald Temple. I'm the first one to go against such a tradition, and if I were to break faith with them now—'

"'Jael, I'm not asking you to break faith with your family, or even to leave the bullring and turn to a life in the temple. Dearest, you know I would never ask such things of you.' He laughed, 'Why, you wouldn't last a day under such restrictions, and I'm certain that your mother knew that when she gave in to your passion for the bullring in the first place! No, Jael, calm yourself now.' He reached out, touching her cheek, but she looked away, sullenly. 'I will get the oil myself, Jael. I will go to the temple and take a jar with me. Here, look.' His voice had dropped into that conciliatory tone I had so often heard him use in council. It was the voice he used after an argument, when he had asked for something outrageous and been denied it; then his attitude would change, his voice pleasing, and he would ask for something else, something smaller and perhaps more reasonable, which he would inevitably be granted. It maddened me to hear him take this tone with her!

"He had pulled something from his robe. I strained to make out what it was. 'There, you see?' he said sweetly enough. 'An alabaster jar just like the high priestesses wear. I will be respectful in every way possible, honoring the traditions of the oil and its people. I will go to the temple and fill this jar, and then I will bring it to you, a woman of the holy blood, and you shall wear it until we are called upon to use it. No one even needs to know that we have the oil, you see?' He had let go of her arm, and she was holding it, the alabaster jar.

"It was a tradition that women would wear such jars, strung like necklaces about their throats. Different jars contained different holy oils; some would be used to anoint the sick, some to increase fertility, others to baptize a child, or consecrate a marriage. But it was known that the high priestesses of the Emerald Temple, the Lemurian bloodline, wore only jars of alabaster, anointed by the sea, and that the oils they contained were more precious than any other. Of course, both the kings and priests of Atlantis had sought the purpose of these oils, as well as the secrets the priestesses kept, for it was well known that the Lemurian lineage had the gift of longevity. Their women outlived, by as much as a century, even the Atlantean priests. You see, Atlantis was ruled by ten dynasties, each led by a king who wielded the powers of science and war, and a high priest who sat in council, deciding how to use such powers. For all of our technology and luxury, we were still a society dominated by men and the mind.

"The Lemurian priestesses had recognized the limitations and the dangers of such a system long before they came to our continent. It was said that they had made a pact with the ten kings of Atlantis, preparing for them an ointment that would lengthen their lives in return for their power and protection. It was not uncommon in our time for a king to live a hundred and fifty years, or for his queen to bear him a child at the age of ninety. Judicious use of this kind of power insulated the Lemurians from the priests and the affairs of our world, allowing them to keep to the life within their great temples. There were occasions when one of them would come into our world, marrying into a royal family, mixing their blood with ours, but their secrets and their magic had remained, for hundreds of years, behind their walls.

"'But, Mal'ak, they *will* know we have it!' Jael was pleading with him now. 'I tell you, my mother will know. You misjudge them, they are very, very powerful. I know. Growing up inside the temple I have seen things, Mal'ak, things I have never seen here. And there are thirteen of them, powerful high priestesses, each with an oil of her own. How could you possibly know that *my* family's oil is the one?'

"'I know,' he replied calmly. 'And I do not misjudge them or their power, Jael. I have ways ... '

"'What ways?' Her voice was sharp.

"'I cannot tell you that. You will have to trust me. I know your mother has the oil I seek. And she will not give it to me or to anyone else! The oil will perish with her, Jael, and the good that we could do with it will never come about! It's that simple.' He was behind her now, his hands around her waist as she fingered the jar nervously. 'We could do so much good with that oil. We could leave Atlantis before the deluge and take our teachings and the ancient wisdom to other places on the Earth, helping other civilizations to rise. You still want to be a part of that, don't you?'

"'Yes.'

"'Then you must do this thing for me, Jael. It will be a simple thing, for I would never let anything happen to you. You know this, too?'

190

"'Yes.'

"'All I need is for you to give me your emerald medallion.'

"'What?' She seemed surprised by this. 'You mean the amulet my mother keeps for me?'

"'I do.'

"'But what good is that?'

"'It is more than an amulet, Jael; the emerald is a key! All the women in your family inherit such a key, but only those who are initiated know what it is and how to use it. All I ask of you is to claim what's already yours, to take it from your mother's house and bring it to me.'

"She shook her head slowly, 'I don't know, Mal'ak...'

"He turned her around. 'Dearest, won't you trust me with this? You are my lady, my love, and I will not go into this work without you by my side! I love you.' For the first time, his voice broke, as if with injury.

"She looked into his eyes for a long moment. Then, as if satisfied by what she found there, she replied quietly, 'Yes, I know that you love me, Mal'ak.'

"He pulled at the tie around her waist, letting it fall to the floor. Reaching his hands inside her robe, he leaned in toward her neck, kissing her softly.

"'All I need is the medallion, Jael. Is that not a simple thing for you to give?' He had pulled away her robe, his hand finding her breast.

"She caught her breath, 'Yes, yes it's a simple thing.'

"Her breast grew round, the nipple hard as he kissed her, full on the mouth.

"I shut my eyes.

"'How could you think I would put you in jeopardy?' he was saying, 'You must trust me, my love, trust me...'

"I moved as silently as I could toward the door. The last thing I heard as I escaped the courtyard was Jael's voice, soft and still naïve: 'I do trust you, Lucifer,' she was saying. 'I do.'

∽

"I FELT DISTURBED THE NEXT DAY, and avoided the prince, staying in my chambers, trying to focus on the maps that were spread out all over my tables and floors. Late in the afternoon, there was knocking at my door, which I ignored. It came again, and in my agitation I cried, 'Leave me be!'

"There was a moment of silence and then I heard the door pushed slowly open. I leapt to my feet in frustration, rushing toward it. 'I told you to let me be!' I shouted, then stopped abruptly. There in the door stood Jael, her cloak pulled tight around her, so that she seemed startlingly small. She was almost entirely hidden in its hood. 'Jael,' I started, my voice dropping in surprise. She did not move.

"'I'm sorry to intrude,' she said quietly. 'I didn't mean to upset you, Adrian.'"

"'No, no,' I assured her. 'It's only that I'm consumed with the work! Excuse my manners, come in.' She hesitated still in the doorway, glancing about my apartment. It was a rather large chamber, with high ceilings and a verandah that looked down at the sweeping miles of city below. But I had not furnished it lavishly, content, from years of military life, with only the necessities: a large wooden table for my work, several chairs, comfortable enough, a couch by the hearth. She smiled as she took in the scene.

"'It's just as I expected it. You're a straightforward man; Adrian the priest, the warrior, the commander.' Still she did not move. 'You're the kind of man who does what he says, one that others count on and come to. I've always admired that about you.'

"'Really,' I felt unnerved by her steady gaze, 'I've hardly thought that you admired *me*, Jael.'

"'But I have, Adrian,' she said earnestly. 'Always, ever since you saved me that day at the temple gates. I remember how safe I felt with you, how comfortable ...' She trailed off and we stood there awkwardly for a time. I couldn't think what to say. There was something about her that was different, reserved and remote. She wanted something from me, I could feel it in her, but she was confused and unsure.

"'Please,' I said finally, 'come in and sit down.' I turned to move toward the couch, but she reached out, taking hold of my arm.

"'No, Adrian, I shouldn't have come.' There was a desperate look in her eyes. 'It's just that I needed a friend, someone I could trust.'

"'What's the matter, Jael? What's wrong?'

"'I shouldn't say. I should go.'

"'No!' I almost yelled it, taking hold of her. 'No, I repeated more gently, 'I'm here for you, and you're right, you're safe with me.' She seemed uncertain, biting her lip, gripping my arm harder. 'What is it? Tell me. Maybe I can help.' My hands were soft on her shoulders, a delicate current passing through them. She looked up at me, her eyes wide, rimmed with tears.

"'I've done something,' she whispered. 'Something I can't take back or undo.' Her body trembled, and instinctively I pulled her to my chest.

"'It will be all right, Jael, I'm sure.'

"'No, it won't be, Adrian. I tell you, I have set something in motion that can't be stopped. I've gone against my family,' her voice choked, 'against my mother! And she will know it soon enough!' Then came the tears, quiet, tender offerings. I held her for a long time as her body shook against me. It was a miraculous comfort to have her in my arms, even in such pain.

"Somewhere in the distance the evening bells began to ring, the sound swelling up the hill to fill my rooms. She stiffened, pulling away from me, wiping at her cheeks. Pulling the hood farther over her head, she backed toward the door.

"'Don't go, Jael, it's all right. Let me help you.' I was almost pleading with her.

"'But she shook her head. 'No, Adrian, I shouldn't have come! I have to go now. I'm expected at the citadel and I'm late.' She held up a hand as I began to protest, her voice stronger now, 'No, I will be all right. The thing is already done and I shouldn't have come here.' She turned toward the door, then paused. I could feel a struggle within her. She turned back to me for a moment. 'Thank you,' she said quietly, looking into my eyes. She forced a smile. 'Thank you, Adrian.'

"I stood there, rigid and afraid as she left. All command and fortitude was lost to me as I struggled with what to say or do. I had been so foolish! I knew why she was upset and what she must have done. I should have said something, or done something to help her make it right. What had Lucifer been thinking to ask this of her? How could he have involved her like this? These thoughts rushed through my mind and took hold of my body until a stark anxiety began to build. I paced the room impatiently. Should I go to the prince? If I did, what could I possibly say? Then I realized I could never go to him, for I could not say that she had come to me, that I had held her, and had in that holding been overwhelmed by my love for her, frozen by the thought of that moment ending. He would know, surely, if I let down my mask, how utterly in love with her I was.

"I don't know how long I paced until, finally, I sank, helpless and alone, onto the cold stones of the verandah. My heart ached. I had held her in my arms, pressed her close to me, protecting her. The sensation still lingered, like a ghost, against my chest. Dusk came and went. I could see the first stars brilliant above me. Tepid gusts of wind pressed through the palms, so that the night seemed to bear down on me like a black wave. I thought I would drown in it, this ocean of feeling that I could not convey.

"Then, somewhere in the whisper of the wind in the trees, I began to hear a voice, low at first, so that I thought it only my broken thoughts. But it persisted, growing louder, until I got to my feet, looking over the balcony to see whom it might be. The voice was haunting, coming from nowhere, then everywhere, calling my name. Suddenly, it came clear: it was Jael, her tone unmistakable. Spinning round and round, I was shocked to find I was alone. Then it came again: 'Adrian,' it said, help me!' I grasped the marble railing, my heart beating fast, my head spinning. Taking a deep breath, I tried to quiet myself, to call my intuitive gifts to me. An image came to me then, a ghostly apparition:

she lay broken on the ground of the stadium, her arm twisted in an impossible position, her white tunic stained red. 'Adrian!' I heard her voice again. 'Help me!' And then there were hands on her, and people shouting, and the bull was charging again.

"I did not wait to see the rest of the vision. I ran to the courtyard and leapt upon a soldier's horse, tearing the reins from his hands. Kicking the steed hard in the sides, I raced to the citadel, but was blocked from entering by a mob. I turned the horse around, galloping to the back of the stadium, to the small hospital kept for the bull riders. It was strictly guarded, but as I pulled my horse in, I recognized a woman from the healer's temple rushing through the gate. Calling to her, I pressed past the guard as if I were her companion.

"'Adrian!' she cried as she recognized me. 'I'm glad you're here! We'll need you.' I followed her inside.

"'What's happened?' I demanded.

"She answered me roughly as she hurried down the corridor. 'The Moon Goddess has taken a fall. It's bad!' I cringed. She meant of course, Jael.

"'I had a bad feeling about her ride.' Her voice was bitter and shaken as we rushed forward. "'Before the opening ceremony, I could see she was distracted and emotional. I should have refused her ride; I had the power to do it!'

"We had reached the hospital door before I had time to react. People moved out of her way to let her in. I followed. Jael was laid out; her arm had been carefully set, but a slow, steady stream of blood ran from a wound in her chest. Several healers had their hands on her, but the surgeon was shaking her head.

"'I can't repair the rib cage, and her heart is too badly damaged for repair,' she was saying softly to Lucifer. 'There's nothing else we can do for her but ease the pain and take her gently to her death.'

"'Impossible!' shouted Lucifer. 'She will not die, not now, not like this!' He turned to the table and Jael, and as he did, he caught my eye. 'Adrian!' he cried out, reaching for me. 'Stay here with her, Adrian, keep her alive.' He grabbed me hard by the arm and pulled me to Jael, thrusting my hands on her chest. Then he turned wildly to the other people in the room. 'Get out!' he shouted. 'Get out now, leave us!' The doors flew open before anyone could move. 'Get out!' he roared. I felt a strange force move from him, and the bodies around me began to rise, as if lifted by an unseen hand, and were thrown from the room. There were cries and shouts and people running, and the doors came closed with a crushing sound. I stood transfixed. It seemed as if his image had grown taller somehow, his black hair tousled as if windblown. He stared at me fiercely.

"'Keep her alive, Adrian!' he commanded. 'I have a holy oil that will save her yet! But you *must* keep her *alive!*' I felt his hand on the back of my neck as he pulled my head close so that I could feel his breath, hot on my cheek. 'Keep her alive!' he hissed. Then he was gone.

"I was stunned by the sudden emptiness in the room. The only thing I could hear was Jael's labored breath. Looking down at my hands, I realized they were covered in her blood.

"'Jael,' I whispered. Her eyes did not open. 'Jael!' I was desperate. I tried to calm myself, to tell myself that I was a master healer, that I could do this thing. But then the healer's words rang hard in my head, 'she was distracted and emotional.' I began the chant to calm my mind, and then the breath of fire to ignite my hands. Yes, it was working; I could feel the heat moving from my body to her cold flesh. But it did not last long. Soon I could feel her spirit slipping away beneath my fingers, slipping out of the gaping hole in her chest. Shutting my eyes, I tried to contact her.

"'Jael!' I called out with my inner voice. 'Jael!' I heard her voice again, just as it came in my room.

"'It's too late, Adrian. You cannot help me.' It was a whisper from somewhere above me. Her mouth did not move.

"'No, there must be a way, Jael!' Suddenly I saw her image standing next to her body, her hand outstretched. She was smiling at me.

"'No!' I cried out, but it was indeed too late. Her heart stopped beating beneath my hands. Grabbing hold of her broken body, now an empty shell, I pulled her to my chest and cried. A cold hollowness engulfed me and I was lost.

"When Lucifer returned he was calm. He did not have the oil with him, or at least he did not say so. He did not look at me as I left the room, the doors slamming shut of their own volition behind me. He stayed three days in that room with her body. I was told they could hear him, hour after hour, chanting the ancient songs for her soul's enlightenment. They heard him sobbing through the night. And when finally he came from the chamber, they said her body had been anointed in the old way, with frankincense and myrrh, and carefully cleaned and wrapped with white linen strips. Then, her family came for the body. They were Lemurian priestesses, walking with a dignity and grace that spoke of celebration rather than mourning.

"All the while I shut myself in my chamber and, quietly, my faith in myself died."

Seven

ADRIAN GREW SILENT. There were tears in his eyes. I felt his pain in my own chest.

"And the prince, Lucifer, he forgave you?"

"He drew me closer to him after that, as if I would be his comfort. He turned us completely to the work at hand, giving us a reason to persist. You see, he was convinced that she would come again, reincarnate, and that we would find her. When I tried to point out the impossibility of such a thing, he only laughed and told me of his holy oil, something she had helped him procure. We would anoint ourselves with this oil and continue our work for the betterment of humanity, all the while watching and waiting for her return."

"So you followed him." He nodded his head sadly.

"For over a thousand years I have followed him, investing my heart and soul in his leadership as if I were a seed and he were the earth. I forgot that there could be another way. I forgot my past and my teachings and my master."

"The priest who stepped off the cliff today, he was Master Thoth?" I asked gently.

"Yes."

"He reached for you today; it was as if he wanted you to come with him," I ventured.

"Yes."

"But why, Adrian? Something else must have happened."

Adrian closed his eyes, leaning back into the pillows.

"IT WAS THE NIGHT WE LEFT ATLANTIS, before the ocean claimed the continent. I had wanted Thoth to leave with us. I did not believe that he could ascend. The prince had already anointed himself; I had witnessed his transformation, and so I had naturally thought it the best way! I knew of the occult arts of astral projection and lucid dreaming, everyone did, but to raise one's vibration beyond the physical plane as Thoth expected to do? To move beyond the state of life without experiencing a physical death... well, I could not imagine how it would be done. And I loved him, so, I went back to the temple that night, through the storm, to reason with him. I wanted him to come with us, and serve as we would serve.

I raced through the great empty halls, eerie in their ghost-like presence. I knew I would find him in the inner chamber, for that is where his power was greatest. As I rushed down the long corridor to the inner sanctum, I could hear the thunder and rain pounding on the tiles above me. My footsteps echoed in the hall. The corridors were dimly lit, and I found myself alarmed by the shadows cast by the carved pillars and statues that lined the halls. But then I was in sight of the inner sanctum and a warm orange glow drew me in. I passed through the door and found Thoth standing, dignified, in the center of the circular room, a goblet in his hand.

"'Adrian!' he called across the room, beckoning me to him. 'Come here, my son, come here. I have something yet to give you.' I came to him at once, prepared to begin my persuasion, but he did not give me time.

"'The elixir,' he began, 'nectar of the goddess from the temple of Mu, this is what I have here.' His eyes dazzled me as I approached. 'The scent ripe and full and rich, like the women who made it.' Closing his eyes, he passed the goblet beneath his nose and inhaled. 'Sweet mango juice warm on my lips. Yes, Adrian, sumptuous is the life that makes me a vehicle for joy and pain. Oh, resplendent is the depth of my soul, and I tell you, Adrian,' he leaned close so that I could smell the juice on his breath, 'you are ready to join me here. I will not take you all the way, my son, it's not your time. Just a sip, Adrian, and you shall see it all from the beginning to the beginning again. Let the cold ardor of fear drop from your heart, and drink!'

"He was intoxicated from the drink in his hand. I could smell its tropical flavor. My own mouth began to water. My eyes focused on the goblet, its gold rim stained where the juice would slide from its belly into my mouth. I thought, *I cannot drink this!* Thoth laughed as if I had spoken aloud.

"'Courage, Adrian!' he thundered. 'Courage, child, the night is young and there is yet time for you. Come here and drink.' He reached out a hand, his skin glowing with an angelic light, and stepped toward me. 'Come,' he whispered, and I could smell his breath, sweet as wine, luring me. I backed away, stumbled, bowed.

"'My lord,' I began, but he was on me in a moment, his big hand warm on the back of my neck, his fierce gaze on my lips. 'You must drink, my son.' His voice was a cello taking me somewhere far away.

"I felt fear. Sweat broke on my brow and I struggled in his grip. What was I to do? Whom was I to follow? Had I not already made my choice? I fought just to breathe. Then his voice came again, laying a web of calm upon me, so that I steadied and, slowly, met his eyes with mine.

"'All the wisdom of this golden age will fall, my son, but you will remain.' I heard his voice like a song, breathed in his languid scent, and I relaxed, soft, floating on a sea of gold.

"'Yes, Adrian, drink, for you have been chosen to come with me for a short time. I must show you your divine roots to carry forth the seed of this golden age. Your soul is already with me; you are safe, my beloved, gentle, child.' The goblet was pressed to my lips, and I drank.

"Sweetness then. Throughout my body, bursts of sensation beat into my cells and pushed me forward as if I would fall into Master Thoth. My flesh tingled, and a piercing note rushed through me. Then I was light. I was the wind and the sky, and then the stars, and then the very sun itself. Glorious, beloved light! I was crying—no, laughing—at the transformation I had accomplished. I was a child, a man, and then a woman—then all three at once. And he was there, somehow, holding me, leading me through the cosmos.

"'Yes, Adrian, look and remember, for you shall see how it all began. You must remember these things, my son, for humanity will need you. One day, you will tell your story, so remember all that I show you now.'

"Suddenly, a scene lay before me. It was the city of Atlantis, and the waves outside the city wall had risen and were crashing over the towers and gates. People were running in chaos. Confusion drove them to hysteria, and they became a mob that trampled even the children into the ground. The water rose higher until the walls tumbled in on themselves, and a wave, larger than the sea itself, rushed into the beloved city and up over the land for miles and miles, until all that was in its wake was covered by the sea. People were gone. Buildings and farms inundated. And I watched in cold horror.

"'Our people? Our children? Our land?'

"I heard Thoth's voice answer, 'All will be lost.'

"The scene began to shift. I saw the rise and fall of many different civilizations, temples turning to dust and new ones built upon them. Populations grew and were lost again, and again, and again.

"'With every golden age on this planet, it has happened that when humanity has come close to realizing its true potential, they have fallen from grace and destroyed themselves,' Thoth said. I heard his voice, deep inside me, an ancient rhythm speaking into my very bones. He gave me a chant, sewed it into my body just as he would carve it into the stones of Egypt a thousand years later. I hear the words now, as if he were speaking them again.

To know the Divine, one has only to know oneself.
The universe is a source of wonder to be revered.
It is the great creation.

In times to come, people will stop pursuing the Divine
with purity in their hearts.

201

Those with grudging and ungenerous hearts
will try to prevent humanity from discovering
the priceless gift of immortality.
Spirituality will become confused, making it hard to comprehend.
It will be corrupted by deceitful speculation.

I foresee that in times to come, clever intellectuals
will mislead the minds of humanity,
turning them away from pure spirituality.
It will be taught that our sacred devotion was ineffectual,
and the heartfelt piety and assiduous service
with which we honor creation itself was a waste without reward.

The Earth is an image of the heavens,
and the whole cosmos dwells here.
But in times to come, humanity will desert the beloved Earth,
abandoning this land
that was once the home of spirituality.

Humanity will progress in its sciences and wars
until they exceed all other times in cruelty.
The dead will far outnumber the living,
and the survivors will continue on the path of death.
Nothing will remain of Atlantis and this golden age,
nothing but an empty tale.

People will weary of life,
and will cease seeing the universe
as worthy of reverent wonder.
Spirituality, the greatest of all blessings,
will be threatened with extinction,
and believed a burden to be scorned.
The world will no longer be loved

as an incomparable work of the Divine,
a glorious monument to the Divine feminine,
an instrument of the Divine Will
to evoke veneration and praise in the beholder.

Although other great civilizations will rise,
one by one they will be widowed.
Every sacred voice will be silenced.
Fear will be preferred to love.
No eyes will raise to heaven.
The pure will be thought insane,
and the impure will be honored as wise.
The madman will be thought brave,
and the wicked esteemed as good.
Knowledge of the immortal soul
will be laughed at and denied.
No reverent words worthy of heaven will be heard or believed.

So, I, Thoth of Atlantis,
he who knows the truth,
inscribe our story in you, Adrian,
that someday a future world may be reminded
that immortality is their birthright.

Nothing is more visible than Divinity!
All things are created so that you can find the creator in them.
Tell them, Adrian, to love each other deeply,
for it is in communion that they will find what they seek.
Tell them to drink in the beauty of the Earth,
to take each step as though it were on holy ground,
for there is nowhere that the Creator does not live.
There is no place that is not sacred,
no person who is not Divine!

"These are the words that he beat into my chest, hidden sometimes even from myself. How I loved him then, his mighty form holding me, rocking me through the cosmos. It must have been hours that I listened and watched as the cosmos revealed itself to me. Then it all began to fade and grow dark. I felt his presence but could not see his form.

"'This will not be the last Golden Age, Adrian, remember what I say now.' Grief seized my heart, and I felt tears pushing up from my breast. I was weeping as he turned me toward the Earth, his immortality embracing me. 'Adrian,' he leaned close and whispered, 'listen and remember what I say. *Everyone matters. Every moment is precious. No one is ever alone; the Creator lives within them all.* Remember who you really are and what you may aspire to become again, Adrian, my son, *remember . . . .*' His voice faded and I felt his grip loosen. I began to fall through the dark night.

"A searing pain shot through my head. Longing for him, his light, the warmth of his presence, and the sound of his voice, I lay in this state between the worlds for a long time. Thoth did not come back to me, nor did I call to him. Floating alone in the cold and the dark, I cried until I became aware of being lifted and flung, like an empty sack, over someone's shoulders. I tried to call out, to struggle against it, but it was no use. My body would not respond to my commands. I heard a familiar voice as I was carried through the corridors of the temple and outside. The sound of people screaming surrounded us, but we did not stop. I could hear the ocean crashing about us — it must have risen above the wall, as Thoth had showed me. Again I struggled to take control of my body, but I was incapable, stuck in some kind of dream. But then there was that familiar voice again. It was not Thoth, but it was warm and steady.

"'Be calm, Adrian. You will be safe, I have you.' It was the prince. I strained to take control of my limbs and speak, but I heard him say, 'Be still, the elixir has your body and you are better for it. Atlantis is lost to the sea, as I have said it would be. I have you, Adrian, you are with me now.'

Eight

ADRIAN WEPT. I MOVED CLOSE TO HIM, pulling his head to my breast. He did not resist me, but rather, surrendered to my touch. Feeling the tears on my own cheeks, I was tender with him, and melted into my longing to touch him. I kissed him gently on the forehead, and with delicate hands brushed the tears from his cheeks.

"I am here now," I whispered, the candlelight only a dim orange glow. "You are with *me* now, Adrian." I felt his hands tighten around my waist. As the candle hissed and sputtered, leaving us shrouded in the dark, he whispered back.

"I love you, Justine. You are the soul that I loved in Atlantis. You are the spirit that I couldn't save. I failed you."

His hands moved over my breasts and I felt his lips brush my neck and chin. He was a ghost that moved over me in the dark, found my mouth, which opened for his kiss.

"Beloved . . . " he said again, and I let the words melt into my body.

I loved him that night. Communion is what he taught me. I opened my heart and my body to love with a fierceness that had died with my mother. I let Adrian carve his love for me into my bones, the way that Thoth had sewn the universe into him. In return, I breathed the breath and the depth of my love, its glory and its grief, into this man who took all of me. And in the quiet just before dawn, when we lay soft and open in each other's arms, just as sleep began to pull me away, I heard Adrian's voice for the last time.

"My beloved."

∞

WHEN FINALLY I SLEPT, I FELL INTO A DEEP DREAM.

There was a warm light, and an old man at the edge of a cliff, and Adrian was there...and then suddenly I knew it wasn't a dream at all, and I struggled to wake up. Then there were warm hands on my shoulders, shaking me hard.

"Justine, wake up." Dread. The voice pulled me back into my body, "Sweet princess, your lover needs you." I opened my eyes, alert and afraid. It was the prince, pulling me to my feet. "Come quickly," he said, chivalrously holding out a robe. "We must go to Adrian, he needs us now." I leapt out of the bed and snatched the robe, quickly covering myself. I was shaking. The dim light of dawn filled the tent, and I could hear servants stirring.

"Where is he? What have you done to him?" I boldly accused. But the prince only looked hurt, his hands opened on his chest, tapping his heart in an exaggerated gesture.

"What have I done to him? *I*, Justine?" He glanced at the bed and my discarded clothes.

"Really, my darling, do you think I would hurt Adrian?" A long pause in which I did not answer, a cold, sick fear still pounding in my chest.

"*I* came to *him*," I said. My voice shook despite my greatest effort.

He smiled at me. "Of course you did." Reaching out his hand, he stepped closer and brushed the loose curls from my cheek. "I didn't come to hurt Adrian, my dearest. Only to save him again, if I can." The knot in my chest tightened.

"Save him?" I began, but the prince put a finger to my lips.

"We don't have time. He is, as we speak, at the point of death. We *must* hurry."

He took my hand and led me from the tent. Barefoot, I ran behind him as he strode briskly through the camp and up the hill toward the empty buildings. As we reached the first steps, the sun filled the sky with bright orange streaks.

"Quickly now!" he said, pulling me up the long flight of stone stairs toward the temple.

When we reached the plateau, I saw them—Adrian and the master—standing on the cliff, just as the tribe had stood the day before. They turned as we saw them, a brilliant golden light shrouding them as if the sun were reflected in their bodies. I gasped at the beauty of the scene.

"Adrian!" His name flew from my lips. "Adrian, no!" I screamed, instantly aware of what they meant to do. I began to move toward him, but the prince took firm hold of my arm.

"No," his voice commanded, deep and slow. "No, Justine, call him here. Let him come to us." At the sound of my voice, Adrian had turned from the light and the master who held him. He stepped away from the edge and then hesitated. "Call him, Justine." The prince released my arm and stepped back behind me.

"Adrian," I said again, but it came out as a whisper. My heart was pounding and tears slipped down my cheeks. Breaking the horizon, the sun flooded us in a rich orange blaze that illuminated the master's face as he stood at Adrian's side. He was remarkable. Brilliant and glorious as he smiled, his eyes falling on mine in a moment of sublime awe.

"Call him!" The prince's voice was stern and urgent.

I did something then that was as remarkable as anything I had ever done. In that moment, I let my love for Adrian be greater than my need of him. I remembered his story, his neglect of himself. He had wanted this. He had forsaken it, and now he had another chance.

Taking a slow, deep breath, I called out to him, "Go, my love."

I felt the prince at my back, his voice enraged.

"What are you saying, *Justine?*"

Shrugging him off, I reached out my hand, pointing to the Master Thoth. Looking my beloved in the eye, I whispered again, "Go."

Smiling, the master laid his hand on Adrian's shoulder. The two of them turned to the edge of the cliff and stepped off into the morning light.

Epilogue

BELOVED,

The sun is rising as my chronicle comes to a close. I sit now, watching the sky paint itself with pink flames, wondering if you will think this tale a wild fantasy, or realize the truth on this page.

It has been more than a hundred years since you stepped off the cliff with the master. After you did it, the prince raged, pulling me to him sharply, his grip vicious. I thought he would strike me, but he hesitated, his face full of anguish.

"Why, Justine? He would have come for you!" I stood still and quiet in his grasp. "You could have saved him!" he shouted.

"I did save him," my voice came out in a sob, a bleak, ashen sound that surprised him. He loosened his grip and was silent as I wept, standing still beside me for a long time. The sun rose. The wind died down. Finally, as my tears abated, he let me go.

From that time on, I have been certain that you would take another body and that I would find you. I honed my powers of perception, my meditations and metaphysical senses, so that I would perceive your soul's return, yet always it seemed an overwhelming task, for how could I find one note among so many melodies?

As for the prince, I have not often seen him since. I traveled through the years alone, more an observer of life than a participant. I did not seek a companion, old or new, for I would not open my heart in that way again. The Guardians came to me at times, enticing me to return to them, to be a part of the prince's great work, but I would never go back.

Then, on a cold winter's day early in the twentieth century, I awoke to find the prince sitting at my bedside. I had settled myself in the New

World and was ensconced in a small flat in New York City, trying to find you in the mass of humanity.

I was startled to see him there, legs crossed casually, fingers resting upon each other in that familiar steeple, as if this were perfectly normal, and he had been there every morning when I awoke.

"Good morning, Justine," he said, smiling warmly. I bolted up in the bed, holding my breath.

"Lucifer..." I was disoriented for a moment, his voice so familiar even after so many years, his scent intoxicating. "My lord," I began, but he put up a hand.

"We are in a new age, Justine, and such outdated titles are not necessary, but perhaps you haven't noticed the change of century since removing yourself so completely from life?" He stood then, bringing his chair closer to my bed. I drew back, pulling the thick blankets tight about me. He smiled at this. "You must forgive my intrusion in such an intimate setting, but I thought, considering our past..." He seemed to think this charming as he resumed his graceful posture in the chair.

"What do you want?" I asked quietly.

"I want to give you something, Justine. I want to help you."

"I don't need your help," I answered flatly.

He looked around the cold, sparsely decorated room, his eyes falling, finally, on my simple dress, laid out over the tattered changing screen.

"You lived in castles once, and wore the robes of queens."

"There is nothing I can't do for myself, nothing I can't have, no place I can't live!" The words flooded out of me before I could think, and I was surprised by my bitter tone. The prince only nodded gravely.

"I see," he said. "So, you are learning the hard truth of immortal life. You can have anything and go anywhere, and if you choose, you could have almost anyone." I shuddered as he said it, so matter-of-fact. "Yet, it's not enough, is it? Look at you, cooped up in this miserable cage!" He shook his head with authority. "No, Justine, you have lost the most precious thing of all, and that is your heart. You have no will to live."

209

I could not speak. The bleakness I had come to call my life bore down on me with an unbearable weight.

"Yes," I said, "it's true. The years are long and I'm lonely, but that doesn't mean I want anything from you!"

He shook his head, looking hurt.

"Come, Justine, lay down your sword now. Have I interfered since Adrian left us? Have I troubled you in some way, or forced you to serve my cause? I could have, you know." This last he said softly and without authority, so that I looked him in the eye, shaking my head.

"No, you haven't done any of that."

"Well, then, temper your defense and listen to what I have to say now. I have a gift for you. I have found Adrian."

IT WAS A YEAR BEFORE I found you at that little house in Hana, on the island of Maui, standing in your garden, long black hair loose in the wind. I recognized the soul of my beloved in that beautiful female body. You were striking, tall and proud, brown skin gleaming in the sun. It was as if you had sprung from the Earth herself. And your eyes... when I approached you, I knew! How precious you were then, with this crazy white woman crying in your garden. Was it instinct that made you reach out to me? Did you sense the familiar in me? I cannot help wondering how so many people pass their beloved in the street without so much as a nod of recognition. But that was not so with us. You invited me in, and I stayed.

We had a wonderful life together. I told you my story and you took it in, every word, never doubting. The concepts I presented seemed common to you, part of your Hawaiian heritage. Once, when I asked you why your soul would incarnate here, this way, in this isolated place, you told me you must have wanted a whole life to do nothing but love me. Can you imagine? Could the purpose of an entire life be to love another person?

Perhaps.

When you died in my arms, I felt your spirit leave. It was indescribably big. I remember feeling as though I could reach out above your body and touch you. How I wanted to go with you! I beat on my immortal flesh and cried out to a spirit that lived in me only when I was with you. It was 1966 when you left me, and I have lived here alone since then, a white Hawaiian, loving this land that I buried your flesh in.

For forty years I have waited, until only a week ago, when I was planting in your garden, the prince came to me once more. He told me he had found you again: your soul had incarnated immediately, in America; you were in San Francisco as we spoke!

For the first time in centuries, I went with the prince. He accompanied me back into the world, introducing me to the modern day. His private jet was a shocking experience, and then the reality of San Francisco, with its skyscrapers and bridges, the limousine and lavish hotel suites. I struggled to adjust. Walking the streets, I was struck by the conglomeration of history and culture that mixed in this new millennium. The music banging loudly from the box on a boy's shoulder as he strolled down the street went unnoticed by the crowd on the steps of the opera house, their tuxedos and gowns accentuated by sparkling jewels. Art was filled with symbols and shapes that came from the walls of tombs and crypts. I found restaurants on every corner, offering food from every culture. All this diversity was set against the backdrop of colonial buildings with Roman arches … it seemed I was in many eras at once. I had been isolated for too long! It took me several days to adjust to all that was new. I stayed close to the prince's side. He was again my teacher and protector, and I soon came to find he was yours as well.

He took me to the Palace of Fine Arts at the edge of the bay, leading me beneath the sculpted arches of a building that reminded me of Rome. You were waiting there for us. Your eyes sparkled when you met me, and how you smiled! Again, there was recognition, a warmth as you reached for my hand, but this time I was frightened. Fear sucked

211

at my heart. How could I let myself love you again when your loss was inevitable?

It struck me suddenly that this was how it would always be; I would live through eternity seeking your soul, dependent on the prince to find you.

He left us alone to speak. You took my hand, leading me to a bench in the rose garden, overlooking the water. You did it as if it were the most natural thing, as if you had always behaved so. As we talked I began to relax, for you were so familiar, even in your new form.

Images appeared before my eyes as you spoke — soft, fuzzy outlines of times past. There was the city of Atlantis as you had once described it, and then my time in Wales, a sword at your side; then Italy and Spain and the New World. I saw you then as the warrior, the healer, the priest, until all the images became one and I saw only you, sitting next to me, your eyes ablaze. Yes, my love, I recognized you. All that you had been was here, and something more. I saw it in the way you gestured, the tone of your voice, and this energy, magnetic and pure, that seemed to move out from your chest and touch me. This was no ordinary life for you. No, there would be no quiet gardens and solitary love. You were bound to something more, something of the world and for the world.

The hours passed quickly. I told you what I could of myself, not sure how to share the rest, all that I have written here. Then it was time to part, but you reached for my hand again, and with the most charming of smiles you asked me to meet you tomorrow. Yes, I told you, tomorrow I would meet you here again. Yes, I had enjoyed myself immensely. Yes, I felt that I had known you before, as well.

I could hardly bear to walk away from you; my hand lingered in yours too long. It had been too many years since I had been touched, since I had felt you close. You hesitated as I began to pull my hand away, gripping my palm and then lifting it to your lips. It was a surprising thing to do, but as your lips brushed my skin, I knew that loving you in your mortal state would always be a torment. Pulling away, I climbed into the black limousine the prince had sent for me, my hand burning where you had kissed it. Running my fingers over my flesh, I knew there was only one thing to do.

I ordered the driver back to Lucifer's offices. He owned a building downtown overlooking the City and the Bay Bridge. The offices of Prince International occupied the entire top three floors. It was a modern-day castle from which he could look down on his people just as he had centuries before. When I opened the door to his suite, he was standing by the glass wall that looked down on the City.

"And how is it to be with your beloved again?" His voice was warm and genuine, but he did not turn around to face me. I moved to the window and stood beside him; the cars and people below looked like colorful marbles spilling down the avenues.

"It's not the same, Lucifer," I said coolly. "I can't love again, not like this. I can't bear it." He turned then, brow furrowed. He had not expected this.

"But I thought this was what you wanted! To have your beloved in a body again, and with such ambition and purpose ... I had imagined this would bring you out into the world again."

I did not look at him, only stared blankly at the little streetlights, like toys, changing from green to red.

"What is it, Justine, that would stop you from loving even Adrian?"

"I can't lose my love again, Lucifer. I won't do it. I can't." I reached for him, something I had not done in centuries. I touched his skin and squeezed his hand.

"I know what happened in Atlantis. I know that you lost me then, that you grieved for me, and that you waited a thousand years for me to return." Looking into his eyes, I saw them soften. "Then you lost me again, in Jerusalem. I pulled my love away from you. You could have done anything to me, banished me, hurt me, frightened me, but instead you gave me a gift. You knew I loved Adrian!"

The words stunned me as I said them, but I knew they were true. "You knew Adrian had loved me. You knew that if you sent us together

213

we would succumb to that love. You knew you would lose me to him, yet you did it anyway!" I was shaken as the understanding dawned on me. The prince squeezed my hand gently.

"Yes," he said. "I knew."

"But you did it because you loved me?"

"Yes. I owed you at least that much, Justine. There are things that happened in Atlantis, things you helped me to accomplish, that cost you too much, and I have never been able to repay you. And always I've known that Adrian would never have asked of you what I did. You deserve to be loved by him." He dropped his hand from mine, turning back to the window. "Adrian will always recognize you and love you, and so he is the gift I will give you, again and again."

"But it's not enough for me, Lucifer. I don't want to lose him again. I want more."

Silence. He stood straight, the crisp lines of his suit accentuating his taut, angular frame. He was distressed. Finally, he spoke. "You want the oil?"

"Yes."

"You would bring the soul that you love back to us, turn that flesh into a permanent prison from which it could not escape?"

He did not say this accusingly. His expression was dispassionate. I felt a wall of tears rising in my throat. "I cannot bear to lose him again!"

"Justine, I know what it's like to lose a beloved. I know what it's like to want to bring the one you love into immortality. I know what you're asking; I just don't think that you do." He tapped on the window. "Look out there, at the masses of humanity driving home from work, single file, day in and day out, spending more time in cars and in cubicles than they do with one another. Look into their unhappy hearts, restless and afraid. They think that life is what they can grasp with their hands, and that all things invisible don't really exist. They turn away from the rich, fulfilling invisibility of which they are all a part. They turn from their potential for greatness in love and beauty, and waste their lives on mediocrity, instead. And they know it, too. They watch the impending approach of their planet's destruction as if it were a television show rather than a reality. As quantum physicists prove that all life is made up of energy, and that all energy is intricately linked, humanity shies away from their obvious interconnectedness. Though scientists prove to them that what is invisible really exists, they still turn away from the simple reality of their immortal souls!" He laughed at this, pressing his forehead against the cool glass.

"How magnificent is the immortal soul, whether it clothes itself as female or male, black, white, young, old, gay, straight, fat, or thin. It doesn't matter how it looks, does it? Not when you can see the soul itself. That changes everything."

He shut his eyes.

"It's been my downfall, I think, seeing souls instead of flesh, because nothing divides souls, nothing raises one above another! I always believed that humanity would remember this, that they would see that perfection and brilliance were so close at hand, only a choice away! I could not imagine that they would struggle so hard and long against it, that the great majority would choose hatred over love, selfishness over service."

Opening his eyes, he looked at me sadly.

"But I will tell you, Justine, that every one of them is luckier than you or I, for we are trapped in our bodies! But mortals, there is no such thing as death for them!"

Listening to him, something in my heart softened. I realized that I did not hate him. As he had revealed himself, his eyes so human, his heart at last exposed, I saw that his life was ripe with seasons of pain. I saw that he was no different than I. How many times had his heart been broken? How many times had his dreams come crashing down? I looked at the way he was staring down at them, humanity, buzzing through the city below. Oh, I saw it, then, and it was so obvious—he loved them, all of them! His whole purpose was tied to them, right or wrong. He had thrown everything into his scheme of redemption, his vision of righteousness. Indeed, he was being as true to his oath as Guardian as he knew how to be.

So this is love, I thought. How easy it had been to love you, Adrian, as man or woman, how simple to adore my mother, or Miriam, or my dearest brother Nicholas. But the prince, with his dreadful plan, his intention to perpetuate evil and injustice, I had hated him for it. Now, able to see that he was driven by his pain, compassion washed over me. I did not like what he did, and I would never agree with his method, but suddenly I could see more than those. I suppose you could say that, finally, I had glimpsed more than the flesh before me; I had beheld his soul, and it was as beautiful as any I had ever seen.

"It's all right," I said softly. "I know why you can't give me the oil. I understand now."

"Thank you," he said.

MY DEAREST, FORGIVE ME. I was going to come back to you then. I had meant to do it, to be bigger than my fear of losing you. I imagine how you must have felt when you sat on that bench and the hours passed and I did not appear, but when I left the building without the oil, I could not face you.

I fled home to the island, to the wet, tropical garden of the past. Here, I thought I would be safe, sheltered from loving or hating, for both, it seemed to me, demanded a price of my heart that I could not pay!

It was dusk when I arrived at the cottage. I stood outside, letting the solitude of the land seep into me. The wind brushed the banana leaves. Waves crashed on the jagged boulders below the bluff. Looking out on the endless miles of blue sea, I pulled off my shoes, skirt, and blouse, and stood naked in the rose-and-orange twilight. It began to drizzle, a light mist of heaven's tears falling on my skin. I dropped to my knees in the grass, the wet green scent pulling me down. I was broken; I could feel the crack in my chest, a dark hollowness expanding inside me.

Needing to hold on to something real, I dug my fingers into the soil, now growing wet and soft. *How had it come to this—a closed heart and a broken life?* I began to cry, to sob, hysterical and uncontrolled, naked on the ground, weeping, weeping. The drizzle turned to rain, warm Hawaiian rain, banging hard on my body as I lay on the earth.

Rain beat on the old tin roof as if it were an ancient drum. I cried until I could not tell the difference between my crying and the rain, my wailing and the torrent pounding on the tin. At some point I became aware of a hand brushing my forehead. How long had it been there? And then I felt the body, a soft female form, lie down behind me, pressing itself against me. Arms enfolded me. Gentle, familiar arms. It was Miriam.

Miriam.

All those long years and no word from her, but now she was here, just as she said she would be. She lay with me a long time, holding me close. When the rain began to calm, she lifted me from the earth as if I were a child, light in her arms, and walked me to the porch. Pulling back my wet hair, she wrapped me in your white chenille bedspread, setting me down in the rocker. Then she pulled up a chair. She was all grace, and I noticed that she was completely dry, not a wrinkle in her gown, nor mud, nor wet grass clinging to her. She was perfect in every way.

She did not speak right away. We sat listening to the birds sing their lullabies. It grew dark. With a wave of her hand, the candles in their big glass shells leapt to flame.

"You are not well," she said, finally. I sat, watching her, my eyes burning with fresh tears. She leaned toward me; putting her slender hands on my face, brushing the tears from my cheeks. Then she pressed her lips to my forehead and gently stroked my hair.

"Listen to me," she whispered, her lips by my ear so that I could feel her breath. "You may think you are broken from having loved, Justine, but this is not so. Loving has been your greatest teacher, your gift. Perhaps you thought it could come without pain, as if it were a safe harbor amid life's storms, but this is not so. Loving is the storm itself.

217

"Nothing must be left unwashed by the tidal wave of love. Each time the wave comes you will be broken open a little further, until one day you will love fearlessly, and each person you meet will wear the face of your beloved. Do you understand what I am saying?" She stared intently into my eyes and I felt a strange sensation in my head. I tried to nod.

"I have lived a long, long time," she said, "I am Miriam, the Magdalene, keeper of the Holy Grail. Perhaps I should have come to you sooner and taken you into my service, but how could I ever teach what you will learn from this pain? How could I bring you to the path of compassion any better than your own life has?" The wind rose as she spoke, making the palms outside beat against each other in a menacing cadence.

"The Magdalene?" I stammered, trying to speak, but it was difficult. A strange, dull sensation seemed to hold me suspended, as if a mist were rising between us.

"Yes," she said, "Magdalene is my title. It means "watchtower of the flock," and that is the duty to which I am pledged. I follow the path of the Holy Grail, the path of service, Justine. It is the path I would have you follow as well, but I have come to see that only through surrender to the wave of love and all the disorder it wreaks — the joy and the pain — do people come to have compassion and kindness and a genuine desire to serve."

She leaned forward, pressing her lips to my forehead. A wave of heat shot through my body. I was startled, shaken from my daze of emotion.

"You must never give up, Justine!" She was reaching for something at her throat — the alabaster jar I had seen so long ago. Leaning back, she stared into my eyes again. She was so beautiful, so soft, yet there was a command in her gaze that kept me entranced. I was dimly aware of her raising the jar above my head, and the sound of it cracking in two. The oil spilled down on the top of my head before I could understand what was happening. I swooned. Pain streaked across my chest, pulling me down into my body, into my blood and my bones. Then there was light everywhere, a river of light, and then ecstasy. I heard Miriam's voice.

"This is my gift to you, Justine. I give you back your mortal flesh. I give you back your immortal soul."

My body shuddered in delight, my mind a blaze of joy. The image of my mother appeared before me, and she was smiling. And then, those spirits from long ago, those women who had come to me at the temple in the blue hills appeared.

"Now she can grow," said one.

"Now she can give back to the people," another added.

"Now she is free."

Acknowledgments

I AM DEEPLY GRATEFUL TO MY SPECIAL GROUP OF ANGELS, friends and family who have stood by my side through the most challenging times. You encouraged me and cheered me on, and I hold each of you in my heart. I could not have written this book without the love and feeling of community you taught me. To my dedicated first manuscript readers: Ann, Barbara, Victoria, Gala, Mom, and Allee...I love you big! Renata, my dear friend, and dedicated editing angel...thank you for giving your love, support, and heartfelt commitment, so fully, to me and this project. You gave me the courage to see it through.

I WOULD LIKE TO ACKNOWLEDGE MY GRANDMOTHER, Roz, for being a living example of true compassion; Francesca, thank you for nurturing me through the beginnings of this book, and sharing your brave journey and your heart with me; Jane, thank you for teaching me about dedication to truth, and for tirelessly guiding me in my search for my Self. Martin... I could not have done this without your belief in me, and your support. You are my champion, my teacher, my cherished love. Thank you.

TO ALL WHO HAVE MADE ME WHO I AM, I bow to the divinity within you.

About the Author

FROM EARLY CHILDHOOD, Julien has been captivated by mysticism and the eternal journey of the soul. Raised on an island, she was strongly influenced by earth-based spiritual traditions and the healing properties of nature. Julien holds a B.A. in psychology and an M.A. in Humanities and Leadership, with an emphasis on Creation Spirituality. When a life-changing injury forced her to leave the life she had known, she turned within, practicing the traditions she had studied, and meditating on inner treasures. This novel is a synthesis of her passage into the heart of pain, and the transformation that took place there.